BLOWBACK

Other Books by E. R. Paskey

The Guardians:
Bad Faith
Portal Woes
Treason's Edge
Freedom's Children

Ink Realm Duology
Lady Ink

Finder Series
Head Case
Magna
Old Wounds
Overload

Stand-Alone Novels
The Other Side of the Horizon
Galaxy's Way
In Plain Sight

E.R. PASKEY

BLOWBACK

FINDER SERIES BOOK 5

E Minor Press

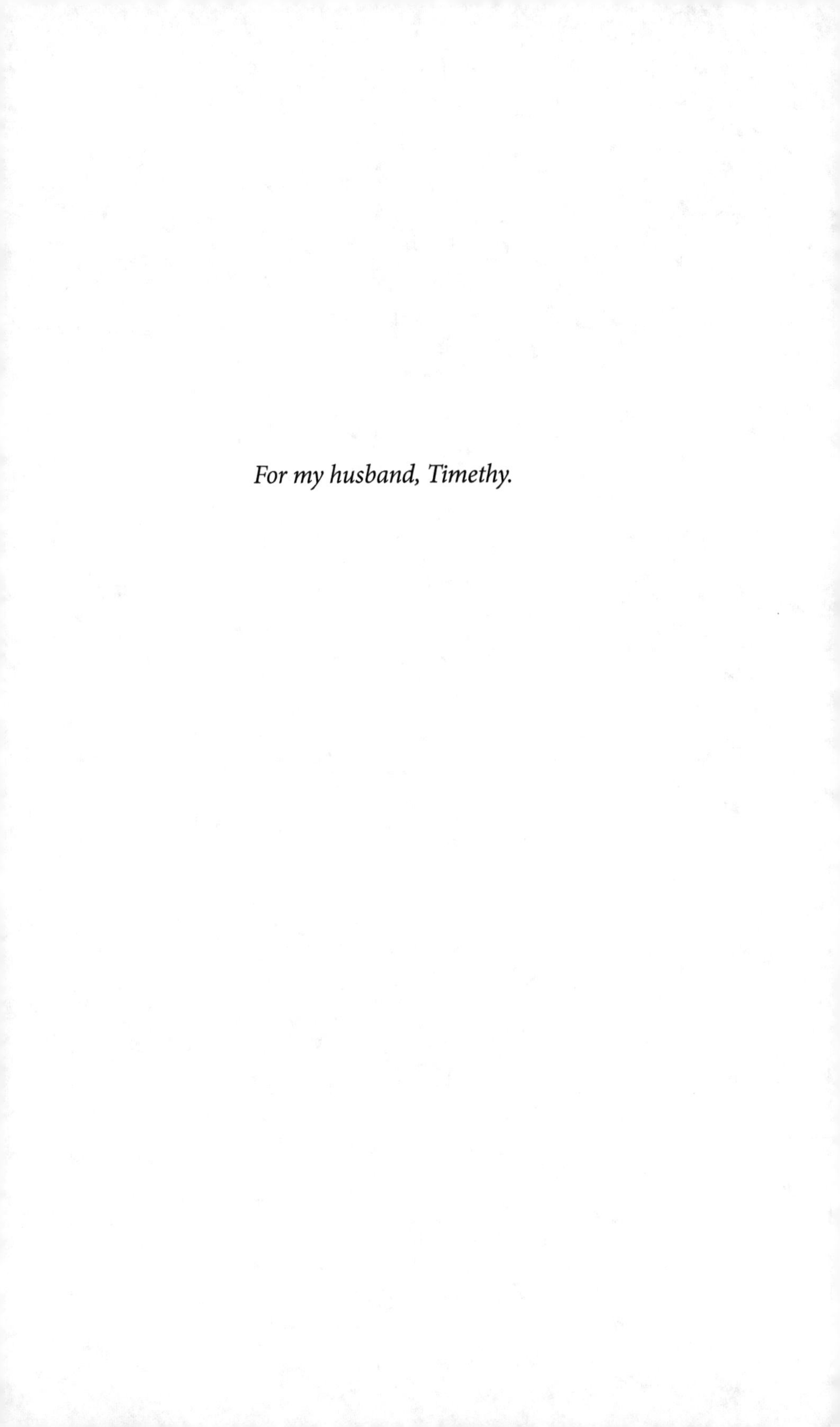

For my husband, Timethy.

CHAPTER 1

The lights died in Finder Vince Grable's small office right in the middle of a conversation he was having with an increasingly hysterical middle-aged woman about a missing family heirloom. Conversations like this weren't unusual. Vince's job was to find missing people and things and he was pretty good at it.

The power cutting out on Zyga Space Station, on the other hand? *That* was unusual.

Seated in his comfortable desk chair behind his jade green desk, Vince froze, wide-eyed, in the sudden blackness. His personal office airscrubber died mid-cycle, leaving an awful silence in its wake.

His client, Mrs. Kawana, cut herself off mid-sentence.

At her desk two meters away, Vince's dark-haired assistant Bella Escovedo also froze, but unlike Vince, Bella could see in the dark. Being a human mind stuck in an android body had its upsides.

For one heart-stopping moment, Vince felt gravity lose its hold on him. He was weightless; his slightly stocky, average-height body no longer confined to his chair. He swallowed. The sound seemed too loud in his suddenly tomb-like office.

The dark silence was complete, pressing in around him like some giant living being attempting to swallow him whole. The only difference was that the crushing vacuum of open space hadn't killed him.

Vince took a breath that still smelled faintly of Bella's floral perfume and strained his ears, trying to determine if even the ever-present thrum of the space station's engines had ceased. In the more than ten years he'd lived aboard Zyga Space Station, he had never ever experienced a power disruption.

Just then, the Station's emergency backup system kicked in and gravity reasserted its hold. Vince's rear end thumped back into his chair. The furniture in his office made muffled thuds as everything fell a centimeter or two to the floor. Something ceramic made an awful cracking sound and the scene of fresh aloe vera filled the office.

At the same time, tiny red emergency lights flared to life along the edges of the beige carpet covering the deck. They cast an eerie red glow over everything, lending a perspective to his office Vince could honestly say he'd never seen before. At the same time, the two massive holoscreens he'd hung on opposite walls to keep his small office from seeming claustrophobic switched back on, displaying an emergency message Vince had never seen before.

He glanced to his right at the large glass window that separated his office from the enclosed boulevard outside. Lines of red lights appeared along either side of the boulevard. Dark shadows made the lights blip in and out as the pedestrians who had been traveling along the boulevard scattered in a panic. It looked like the power had gone out in most—if not all—of Level 7.

Still clutching his comlink to his ear, the Finder then glanced over at Bella. His assistant stared back at him, her almond-shaped eyes wide with shock. Half of her ivory, heart-shaped face was splashed red, and the other half lay in shadow. It was an odd effect; it looked like half of her black hair and blunt-cut bangs had disappeared.

In her dark eyes, however, he saw reflected the same question running through his mind: what in the galaxy had happened?

Vince planted his feet flat on the deck and prepared to launch himself to his feet, but at that moment his client got over her shock and started shrieking hysterically into his ear. Wincing, Vince yanked his comlink away from his ear and held it out in front of him. The red glow from the emergency lights looked strange against the darkness of his skin. Dimly, he wondered if the red light made his black goatee and curly, close-shorn black hair look as strange as Bella's.

He didn't have time to think about that now, though. He finally stood up, unconsciously holding onto the edge of his desk as though he expected the grav generator to go on the fritz again.

Although, really, he thought in bemusement, *the desk isn't likely to help me much. It's not like it's bolted to the deck.*

His shock passed, and Vince started processing everything. Mrs. Kawana was still shrieking hysterically. She lived on Level 8 in Zone 2, so this power outage, whatever it was, was affecting at least two of Zyga Space Station's five spoke-like Zones.

That…was not good. Particularly since Zone 2 housed the Station's agricultural department.

"Mrs. Kawana, please." Vince kept his deep voice as calming as he could. "Breathe. Just breathe. It's going to be okay."

It took a moment before the woman could speak coherently—and not in an ear-shattering pitch. "What is going on? Why is the power out?"

"Are the emergency lights on where you are?"

Instead of reassuring his client, this only set her off again. "Of *course* the emergency lights are on! They're *supposed* to be on when something like this happens! But why is this happening? What is going on?" She barely seemed to be even drawing breath.

A soft snicker drew Vince's attention sideways, just in time to see Bella clap a hand over her mouth. Her long fingernails glinted reddish-silver in the emergency lights. She raised expressive eyebrows at Vince as though to say, *Is she for real?*

Vince rolled his eyes. Mrs. Kawana's stream of borderline hysterical comments and questions continued. He opened his mouth, preparing to find a good spot to cut in and take control of the conversation again, but at that moment the glow panels in the overhead flickered back to life.

Blinking in the sudden wash of warm golden light, Vince focused his attention on the deck beneath his feet. Even through the beige carpet, he thought he felt the faint vibration that signaled the Station's engines were functioning properly.

It could have been his imagination. He wasn't completely sure you could even *feel* that vibration out in the Zones, away from the Core, the center of the space station.

Mrs. Kawana drew in a sharp, sudden breath—and Vince knew the power was back on in Zone 2 as well. Crisis averted.

At least temporarily.

"The power—it's back!" she cried exuberantly. "I—"

"Mrs. Kawana," Vince cut across her. "I'm glad you're all right. Thank you for all the information you've given me. I will keep you posted on my investigation. Now, if you'll excuse me, I have other clients to attend to."

The Finder barely gave her time to stutter some sort of acquiescence before he ended the transmission. He then dropped his comlink on the jade green surface of his desk and turned to his assistant.

Bella sat at her desk, one hand still flattened on its matching green surface as though she thought she could somehow hold it down by sheer force. She looked as unnerved as Vince felt.

If she'd still been human, he was sure she'd be breathing heavily, one hand pressed to her chest. But Bella wasn't strictly human anymore, and so little things like unconscious physiological responses no longer applied to her.

"What was that?" she asked, her voice higher-pitched than usual.

Vince suppressed a wince. Okay, make that *most* unconscious physiological responses. He'd once seen Bella literally shatter glass with her voice; they didn't need a repeat.

Bella shook her head, the movement making her long, shiny black hair glint under the light from the glowpanel. "I've lived here my entire life and I've never seen the Station lose power before."

"Never?" Vince stared at her, his mind working furiously. He'd only been here a little over a decade. "Ever?"

"No." Bella shook her head again, a little too enthusiastically. For somebody who'd been transported into an android shell against her will, she had handled the transition fairly well, but there were still moments when her lack of full control showed. "Not in my lifetime."

Well, that was interesting. Vince blew out a considering breath, his client and her missing heirloom temporarily forgotten. "Then you know the media will be all over this."

He kept abreast of Zyga Station News, but he didn't often watch the news feed. The official narrative was helpful, but there were many times he needed information from people in parts of Zyga Space Station the media would never cover.

Rubbing his goatee, which was bristling, Vince wondered what category this power outage would fall under. He turned to one of the holoscreens mounted on the wall to his left.

Only one way to find out.

CHAPTER 2

V INCE USUALLY SET BOTH OF HIS HOLOSCREENS to cycle through stunning planetary or space holos when he wasn't watching anything or using them as giant secondary screens. The one on the wall to his right currently displayed a gorgeous view of sunlight glinting off a lake at sunset with blue-gray mountains in the distance, while the other displayed an incredible shot of a pink, purple, and blue nebula from somewhere on the other side of the galaxy.

Swiping his palm over the right-hand corner of his jade green desk, Vince triggered a pop-up holographic panel and touched a translucent silvery button. The nebula on the holoscreen to his left dissolved into the round, dark-skinned face of one of the Station's most popular newscasters.

"…reporting live from Zone 5, we have Zach Melawi." Marissa Nedo's melodic voice and stunning smile were famous all over Zyga Station, but the newscaster wasn't smiling now. She looked somber.

The screen split to show Nedo on one side and a young man with light tan skin and stylish dark hair on the other, standing in front of a string of shops and eateries Vince recognized as being somewhere around Level 6. Not the ritzy upper-class Levels 1 and 2, but definitely above the lower levels.

Melawi nodded solemnly to the cam. "I'm here in Level 6, where celebration of a local bakery's twenty-fifth year in operation was interrupted by a power outage that lasted approximately four and a half minutes."

Four and a half minutes? Vince made a soft sound in the back of his throat as he rested a hip against the edge of his desk. It had felt like much longer.

Maybe that was because he knew too much about what would happen to people aboard Zyga Space Station if the power died permanently. He'd grown up on a planet; you didn't have to worry about losing oxygen on most worlds. Depending on where you were, you could maybe freeze to death, but outside of drowning or being in a fire, lack of breathable air wasn't typically a problem.

"Is everyone all right?" Need asked, looking concerned.

Melawi nodded again. "Some residents are pretty shaken up, but as far as we can tell, everybody is okay." He motioned to the shops and eateries behind him. "As you can see, the power is back on." He did a good job of keeping his expression only pleasantly concerned, but he couldn't quite hide the fear in his brown eyes.

On a space station orbiting a gas giant, one of the last things anybody wanted was a power outage.

"That's a good thing," Nedo said.

Vince snorted, before exchanging a disbelieving look with Bella. "That has to be the understatement of the decade."

His assistant nodded silently from her chair behind her desk.

"Today's celebration will continue," Melawi continued earnestly, "but residents of Zone 5 want answers. Why did this happen? And, more importantly, how can we keep this from happening again?"

Nedo smiled slightly. "I think I speak for everyone on Zyga Space Station when I say we would all like those answers. Thank you, Zach."

Melawi nodded solemnly, and then his feed vanished.

Nedo then faced the cam. "In addition to Zone 5," she said briskly, "Zone 2 also temporarily lost power. We have footage from the captain of the *Elantris*, a freighter en route to dock in Zone 2."

Her face disappeared, to be replaced by a vid feed from the approaching freighter. As seen from space, Zyga Space Station resembled a giant wheel, with five spokes connected to a large outer ring and a smaller ring just outside a spherical center known as the Core. The outer ring, known as the Rim, held the ritziest, most expensive living quarters on the Station, while the inner ring, called the Hub, provided the best Zone-to-Zone access. The Core held the Station's massive engine and life support complex, along with what had become living quarters for the Station's detritus.

Two of those spoke-like Zones were black splotches against the deeper blackness of space, while the rest of the Station remained aglow with golden light.

It was the eeriest footage Vince had ever seen—the more so because he knew he'd been right in the middle of one of those black splotches.

"…Zyga Station's Council Chairman issued a brief statement assuring everyone there is nothing to worry about and that the Council and Station Authority are looking into the power loss." Nedo smiled reassuringly at the cam. "In the meantime, Station Authority urges everyone to stay calm and continue as normal. We will continue to keep you updated on this breaking story as it—"

Vince tapped the holographic button on the corner of his desk, shutting the holoscreen off. He hadn't expected much in the way of real information, but he couldn't help the ever-present hope of that possibility. Not today, apparently.

"'Nothing to worry about,'" Bella echoed, her tone sarcastic. "Of course not. We're only talking about a power outage on a space station in the middle of, you know, *space*."

Vince shook his head. "I wouldn't want to be on the Council or in Station Authority right now."

"I wonder what happened." Frowning, Bella tapped her full red lips with one finger. She leaned back in her ergonomic desk chair, which matched Vince's, even though she didn't have to ever worry about things like carpal tunnel or neck strain again. "Do you think it'll happen again?"

Vince glanced at her. He was sure that same thought was currently running through *everyone's* mind. "No telling."

His pulse had settled back into something approaching normal now that the Station was functioning like it was supposed to. "The real question is whether or not Station Authority will actually *tell* the rest of us what actually happened."

Bella bolted upright in her chair, her dark eyes wide again. "I know there's a lot of corruption aboard Zyga Station and all, but surely they wouldn't actually try to keep us in the dark about this?" She made a slightly exaggerated face at her accidental pun.

"Depends on what 'this' is." Vince lifted one shoulder in a shrug. "And what's at stake."

He'd lost any illusions he might have had about the people in power here doing the right thing simply because it was the right thing a long time ago. But, in that, they weren't any different from the people in power anywhere else he'd ever been.

And Vince liked living aboard Zyga Space Station. Even with its problems, he'd rather live here than anywhere else in the galaxy.

The implications of a recurring power outage, however…

The Finder gave himself a mental shake. *No point worrying about that now.* Zyga Station had better minds than his to put to work on that particular problem.

Setting the mystery of what had caused the power outage aside, Vince turned to survey the damage in his office. Since the Station's inertia dampener and grav generator had only quit working for a few seconds before the emergency backup system kicked in, his furniture hadn't had much chance to migrate. His desk and the two brown armchairs in front of it had only moved a few centimeters.

The matching brown couch on the wall perpendicular to the front door had fared about the same, as had Bella's desk and the jade green credenza on the back wall facing the front door. The drink-maker on top of it had, surprisingly, landed without tipping over, but Vince's basket of different teas had fallen over, spilling teabags across the surface of the credenza.

The scent of aloe vera permeating the office told Vince that his potted plant on a tiny glass stand between the couch and the concealed door that led up to his apartment above the office had not fared as well. He glanced at it and frowned. The pot had drifted just enough in those few seconds that only part of it had caught the shelf when gravity returned. The plant had crashed to the floor, the source of the loud crack they'd heard.

Still frowning, Vince crossed to the glass stand and straightened it before he picked up his plant and gave it a critical once-over. Several of its broad dark green leaves were bent and broken, but apart from that it seemed to be all right. The glossy red pot was intact, despite the horrible sound it had made. Shaking his head in small amazement, Vince set the plant back on the glass stand.

He liked having a plant in his office, and this one had the added benefit of occasionally being useful beyond producing oxygen. Zyga Station encouraged its citizens to buy plants and take care of them, but only certain kinds of decorative plants were allowed. Just about anything that required pollination was not allowed to leave the Restricted Agricultural area of Zone 2. Responsibility for the potted trees, bushes, and other plants spread throughout the Station fell to Maintenance.

Just before Vince turned back to Bella, his eyes caught on the door leading up to his apartment. Only then did it occur to him that there might be a be a few things out of place up there as well. He gave a mental shrug. He could deal with the mess later. It wouldn't be anything major.

At that moment, his comlink vibrated with an incoming call.

Hope this isn't Mrs. Kawana again, Vince thought as he strode back across the small office and swiped his comlink off his desk. He didn't recognize the comm number, but then, most of the calls he received on a regular basis were from complete strangers looking to hire someone to Find people or things for them.

He'd barely said hello before a familiar gruff voice said, "Grable, this is Detective Ron Commosky. We need to talk."

CHAPTER 3

Vince went very still, his dark eyes narrowing. There were only a couple of reasons that he could think of why this particular detective from Zone 3's Station Authority Precinct 1 would be calling him—and none of them were good.

"Commosky." He risked a quick glance at his comlink display. "Looks like you're not calling from an official comlink, so talk away."

"Not now. Later."

Vince inhaled through his nose, barely registering the smell of aloe vera still filling the office. He took exception to the peremptory way Commosky treated people sometimes. "Detective, you're not the only one around here who—"

"It's important, Grable." Commosky hesitated, then said grudgingly, "It's in regards to our last case."

A sharp jolt of adrenaline spiked in Vince. He perked up, instantly alert. The last case they'd both worked had involved murder—something Vince didn't often handle, as he preferred less violent cases.

It had also involved a classified investigation Commosky had been leading for months.

Out of the corner of his eye, he saw Bella straighten in her seat behind her desk, looking interested. Her hearing was spectacular.

"Oh, really?" Vince narrowed his eyes to slits, staring at his old brown couch without really seeing it. He chose his next words carefully—if Commosky was being cagey, there was probably a good reason. "I was under the impression that particular case had been closed."

"You'd think so," Commosky said cryptically. "Tonight, Grable. I'll send you the time and location."

The detective ended the transmission before the Finder could respond.

Two seconds later, Vince's comlink vibrated with an encrypted text. Commosky wanted to him to show up at a little fish and chip shop in Zone 3 on Level 8 at 8:30pm—and he wanted Vince to make sure he wasn't followed.

Vince was not surprised that Commosky wanted him to come all the way to Zone 3 instead of coming to Zone 5 himself, or even meeting him halfway.

He was also not surprised at all when the text self-destructed.

"He's not paranoid at all," he said wryly, holding the comlink up for Bella to see.

For her part, Bella looked confused. She canted her head to one side. "Didn't your last case together involve finding out who killed Dent Antwerp?"

"Yes."

"And wasn't our client innocent?"

"Yes."

She spread her hands. "So what does he want?"

"Not sure." Vince slid his comlink into his pocket and returned to the other side of the room to straighten the basket of tea that had fallen over on the credenza. "I have an idea, though."

A few heartbeats of silence filled the office, and then Bella said flatly, "The Ruby Gauntlet."

If it wasn't such a sobering thought, Vince would have smiled with pride. She really was an excellent assistant.

He set about brewing himself a cup of green tea, but nodded grimly over his shoulder. "That's what I'm thinking."

Dead silence flooded the office again as Bella absorbed this.

The Ruby Gauntlet was a nightclub inside the virtual world of *Everheart*, one of the most popular multiplayer games aboard Zyga Space Station—a nightclub with an elite, illegal gambling club hidden inside. Gambling was illegal on Zyga Station unless it took place at one of the few casinos and online venues authorized to operate aboard the Station.

Technically, everybody paid a cut to Station Authority and Zyga Station's governing body for the privilege of being open. The two Families that controlled the Core each owned—or at the very least owned a vested interest in—one of the physical casinos. Given that their influence stretched throughout the entire Station like dark, poisonous vines, they probably also had ties to several of the online operations, though one of *those* was owned by a wealthy playboy who lived on the Rim and had nothing else to do with his life.

The Ruby Gauntlet, however, had neatly bypassed Station Authority and kept all the profit for themselves. They'd gotten away with it for more than a year, until they grew too popular to stay under the radar any longer. Starlit and Lumen, the nightclub's mysterious owners, had been buying up property all over the Station from people who'd gotten in too deep.

And then they'd branched into murder.

Usually, gambling sharks kept their victims alive, so they could squeeze every last drop of blood out of them, but the Ruby Gauntlet's owners took things to a new level. If they believed someone truly couldn't pay…they killed that person and then went after family and friends for the rest of the money they were owed. It was a truly insidious operation.

Dent Antwerp had been one of those people. He'd also been one of Detective Commosky's best informants on what happened in the club. When he was murdered, the detective had thought he had his chance to pin the Ruby Gauntlet's owners to the bulkhead.

Things hadn't quite worked out that way, but at least the real murderer had been caught.

Vince had helped with that investigation, because the alternative was that his client, Corwin Antwerp, ended up convicted of murdering his brother.

And, in the process, Vince had given Commosky more leads and evidence and wished him luck in hunting the owners down.

Those leads had apparently had hit a dead end of some kind, given that Commosky, with all of his Station Authority resources, was turning to Vince for help again.

"Things got a little hairy at the end of that case," Bella said wryly. "I hope this doesn't end up with us getting stuffed into shipping containers again."

A memory of waking up in darkness and realizing he was trapped in a narrow box returned to Vince in a flash. He banished the memory, a fine shudder working its way down his spine. "You and me both. That is not an adventure I'd like to repeat any time soon."

Blowing on his fragrant tea to cool it, the Finder carried his mug back to his desk and resumed his seat. The desk, he realized suddenly, was a little more off-kilter than he'd thought, but he didn't feel like righting it this moment. His mind flooded with thoughts of the Ruby Gauntlet.

Starlit and Lumen might not have been responsible for Dent's murder, but they *were* probably responsible for other deaths. Vince and Bella had turned up a trail of bodies during the course of their investigation, and Commosky was digging into them.

"Do you think he's stuck?" Bella leaned forward to prop her elbows on her desk. "Or do you think he's found something new and he needs your help to investigate it?"

"My gut says he's stuck." Vince glanced down at his mug, watching steam rise in swirls. "He wants something, though. That's for sure."

"Well, that's obvious." Bella waved a hand. "You'd think he'd have the decency to pick something in Zone 5 though, instead of making you trek all the way to him."

She'd picked up on that too. Vince nodded slowly, considering. Commosky was a good detective, and as far as Station Authority officers went, someone he, Vince, trusted. Mostly. But the man had a hard shell, and he had that proud streak Vince had encountered in other Station Authority officers that was often hard to work around.

A human being simply couldn't be right all the time. It wasn't possible, mathematically speaking or otherwise.

"I do have to admire his tenacity." Vince shook his head. "He knows there's a deeper mystery—a bigger crime involved—and he's not about to let a few setbacks stop him."

Bella huffed. "Well, I'm in as long as we don't get kidnapped and almost shipped off-station again."

It was easier to smile about that now than it had been a few weeks earlier, even if the memories weren't great. Taking another sip of his tea, Vince tried to shift his mind back to his own caseload. Now that the excitement of the power outage was over, he needed to start investigating Mrs. Kawana's missing sculpture.

Commosky and the Ruby Gauntlet would have to wait until later.

His goatee bristled, but Vince ignored it—or tried to. He had work to do. Paying work.

He swiveled his chair to face his computer terminal on one side of the desk. No point in letting his mind get all wrapped up in a case that wouldn't earn him a single credit.

Liar, whispered a small voice in the back of his mind. *You didn't get into the Finding business because of money. You did it because you like unraveling mysteries and solving puzzles.*

And without a doubt, the Ruby Gauntlet was both of those things.

Vince suppressed sigh, irritated with himself and with Commosky. His gaze strayed to the cool blue numbers floating in the corner of his computer display. It was going to be a long day.

8:30 pm couldn't come soon enough.

CHAPTER 4

At a quarter to eight, Vince pulled a little green plastic tub from a desk drawer. A strong smell of eucalyptus and a jumbo of other earthy scents wafted up to greet him as he opened it and dipped a fingertip into the pale cream inside. He dabbed a bit behind his ears and under his nose, and then replaced the little tub of magic salve in his desk drawer.

He wrinkled his nose, resisting the urge to sneeze. From past experience, he knew in a few minutes he wouldn't even notice the eucalyptus any more. The important thing was that for the next eight hours, the salve would banish that ever-present tickle in the back of his throat he always experienced any time he left his extra-scrubbed air.

Vince shook his head. He'd lived aboard Zyga Space Station for more than a decade, and he had yet to figure out what exactly in the filtered air irritated his throat. Magic salve indeed.

From her desk, Bella offered him an encouraging smile. "I'm glad that stuff works for you, Boss."

The salve had been a gift from her during the Antwerp case, and while Vince had initially been leery, he'd soon wholeheartedly embraced it.

"Me too." He rose to his feet and headed for the front door. Time to go.

He paused with his hand on the door panel. "I'd tell you not to wait up, but I have a feeling it'll fall on deaf ears."

"Completely." Bella schooled her features into solemnity. "I'll just shut my hearing off." She tilted her head to one side. "I think I can do that."

Vince just shook his head. "You need a life outside of work, Bella."

"Hey." She spread her hands. "I told you I'm working on that. I just really want to know what Commosky wants."

Their gazes met and held for a moment, and then Vince shook his head again. "If you weren't the best assistant I've ever had…"

"Aren't I the *only* assistant you've ever had?" Bella asked cheerfully. She smiled at him, before waving her hands in a shooing gesture. "This ought to be good, Boss. Can't wait to hear all about it."

Seconds later, Vince found himself standing outside his office, blinking in bemusement. He had the distinct sense that he'd been managed, somehow, but he couldn't quite work out how Bella had done it. Ah, well.

He gave a mental shrug. They could work on that later. For now…well, he really did want to know what Commosky wanted.

The faint scent of eucalyptus gradually faded away as the Finder traded the confines of his office for the large, enclosed boulevard beyond. In the upper part of the Zones, the boulevards were big enough that it was easy to forget that they were completely enclosed. Shops, eateries, and offices mingled with apartment complexes. They reminded Vince of city streets back on the planet he'd once called home, but with a completely different flair.

In the overhead, the glowpanels had dimmed to their night-cycle settings. Though still plenty of light to see by, they provided an illusion of a distinct difference between day and night in a place that could otherwise look the same all twenty-four hours. The architects behind Zyga Station's construction had taken human beings' circadian rhythms into account and had tried to create a system that was friendlier than a space station that never slept.

Even though Zyga Space Station never did truly sleep. Vince half-smiled to himself, despite the edgy anticipation curling through him. Someone was always awake somewhere doing something.

He took a deep breath of recycled air, smelling half a dozen different kinds of foods from the various eateries along this section of the boulevard. The Station's airscrubbers worked hard, but at busy times like this, it took them a little longer to remove all traces of cooking food from the air.

Vince set off toward the center of Level 7, blending in with the pedestrian traffic flowing up and down the gray metal sidewalk. As usual, he kept his expression pleasantly neutral, the sort of expression people registered as a non-threat and then promptly forgot. It was better that way; the last thing a Finder needed was to be memorable when he didn't *want* to be memorable.

The momentary terror and panic of the morning's power loss seemed to have been forgotten. Vince passed families on their way home from a late dinner, couples out on dates, and maintenance and manufacturing workers either returning home from their shifts or just heading out. Zyga Space Station's industrial and manufacturing efforts were all located in Zone 4, but not all of the workers lived in Zone 4.

Egg-shaped silver pods belonging to the Station's transportation system zipped up and down the center of the boulevard. Some headed straight, while others turned right or left when they reached the boulevards and corridors that intersected this one. In every Zone, each Level was laid out in blocks to facilitate movement and keep any one corridor or boulevard from becoming a bottleneck at certain times of the day.

When he reached the end of this particular block, Vince raised a hand. One of the silver transport pods headed down the boulevard broke from the flow of traffic and glided to a halt in front of him. The door on the side closest to him popped open and he climbed inside.

Some of Zyga Transport's pods were cleaner than others. This was one of the less than fresh pods; Vince wrinkled his nose at the almost overpowering scent of air freshener overlaying stale sweat. The pod could comfortably seat four, but he was currently the only passenger. He preferred it that way.

Leaning back against the dark green cushion, he told the pod's onboard AI, "Elevator bank."

The transporter pod obligingly slipped back into traffic. Vince sent a cautious glance over his shoulder through the rear window, but nothing pinged his trained senses. So far, he didn't think anyone was tailing him or otherwise seeming to take more interest in him than was warranted.

Not that he was worried about being followed just yet.

In fact, normally he wouldn't worry about being followed at all when meeting with Commosky, but the detective's message had been a good deal more furtive and cloak-and-dagger than usual. Something was going on, something big enough to put the generally un-flappable Commosky on edge. Vince had already decided he would use caution in approaching the restaurant

To that end, Vince pulled up a mental map of Zone 3 inside his head while his transporter pod carried him through Level 7 to the main elevator bank. He might not have been to Zone 3 in a couple of weeks, but he'd spent enough time roaming Zyga Space Station in his capacity as a Finder to have a good working map inside his head. Being familiar with many of the shortcuts and access tunnels and the little out-of-the-way nooks and crannies that existed on this space station came in handy when it came to locating people who had disappeared.

Or for clandestine meetings with informants or Station Authority officers.

CHAPTER 5

B Y THE TIME THE TRANSPORT POD STOPPED at the elevator bank in the heart of Level 7, Vince had worked out a couple of different routes to take to the restaurant once he entered Zone 3, depending on circumstances. Returning his thoughts to the here and now, he pulled a prepaid credit chip not connected to his name from his pocket (his standard procedure for something like this) and swiped it through the chip reader mounted beside the door inside the transport pod. Then he exited onto the sidewalk beside the shiny silver turnstiles blocking access to the elevator bank.

Vince looked up, his gaze catching as always on the massive, gleaming synthglass elevator bank, which stretched up to disappear beyond Level 7's overhead. Translucent cabs floated up and down along its length; even at this hour, the Station was busy. Vince was sure the elevator banks in each of the Station's other four Zones were equally busy. Each elevator bank connected every level in a Zone, from the bottom all the way up to every ritzy Level 1.

Stepping up to a turnstile, he swiped his credit chip again and passed through to join a queue waiting to head down to Zone 5's lower levels. Casual chatter and the occasional burst of laughter punctuated the air. He scanned his waiting fellow citizens as he waited, seeing a few faces he recognized, though none of them noticed him.

That was fine; he didn't have time for chitchat right now.

The queue moved quickly. In no time, Vince stepped into an elevator cab and obligingly moved aside to make room for a family of six—two parents and four elementary age children—who joined him. He listened with half an ear as the children gleefully—and loudly—recapped their evening to each other and their parents.

The children were still laughing and chattering excitedly when the elevator cab stopped on Level 22 and Vince exited. Once he'd made it past the turnstile and out onto the main sidewalk, he flagged another transport pod.

This one was a little cleaner than his last ride. Vince leaned back against the cushion, feeling marginally more comfortable, and told the pod's AI, "The Hub."

Technically speaking, a transport pod could carry you anywhere on Zyga Station. Vince just preferred to make the trek from Zone to Zone through the Hub on foot. It satisfied the part of his brain that constantly assessed whether or not he was being tailed, or whether or not somebody was paying more attention to him than was warranted.

Ten minutes later, the pod deposited him at his destination. Vince paid, mentally adding the fare to a running list he'd started for this evening, and exited the pod.

He looked around at the Hub, his breath catching a little. No matter how many times he visited, he still found himself blown away by its beauty.

Both the Rim and the Hub were circular rings that connected each of Zyga Station's five Zones, but the Hub was much smaller, since it was so close to the Core at the heart of the space station. Both rings had been designed with an eye to beauty, however. The Hub's outer bulkhead was translucent, providing a jaw-dropping view of star-studded space and the distant glitter of the Rim beyond the edges of the Zones vanishing toward it. On the other side of the Hub, Vince knew, the swirling pink and orange mass of the gas giant Cartha was visible as well.

He set off to the right, along a walkway covered in a colorful mosaic comprised of swirling patterns of blue, red, green, and gold. The walkway was wide enough for both pedestrian and transport pod traffic, and it was always busy, regardless of the time of day or night. Glossy silver benches had been set at regular intervals along the translucent bulkhead to allow people to spacewatch, and a few of them were occupied.

The Hub might not be big enough to provide ritzy living quarters for the wealthy and well-connected like the Rim was, but it had two vital features the Rim lacked. One, it was the only way to get to the Core. Two, it provided the fastest Zone-to-Zone travel—the fact that it was so close to the Core meant that its synthglass and metal walkways were shorter.

As Vince strode along the curved walkway that would eventually lead him to the entrance to Zone 3, he glanced to his left. From the Hub, the last fifty meters of Zone 5 narrowed into a giant utilitarian Gate that provided access to the Core. The Gate was open—in all the years Vince had lived here, he'd never seen one closed, even though access to the Core from each of the Zones could be regulated via giant emergency hatches.

The Finder kept walking, feeling a weight lift that he hadn't realized he was carrying. If he was honest with himself, part of him was glad he didn't have to deal with the Core today. He didn't feel like navigating tricky Family politics right now.

The Bok Family and the Oswari Family shared control of the Core, though Station Authority ostensibly ruled the Station by way of the Council. In reality, however, the Families' influence traveled out from the Core to infect the rest of Zyga Station like sticky tendrils of some poisonous vine. Vince had lost count of the number of cases he'd worked as a Finder aboard Zyga Station that had involved one of the Families, however slight the connection.

After a few minutes' brisk walking, he reached the entrance to Zone 3, where he flagged a third transport pod to take him to the main elevator bank. He then rode the elevator up to Level 8 and joined a trickle of pedestrians leaving the elevator bank there.

Each of Zyga Space Station's Zones had a few unique peculiarities that set them apart from each other. Whether the Station's architects had intended things to be this way or not, the Zones had developed decorative themes that ran through most, if not all, of their Levels. Some places aboard the Station were more utilitarian than others—this was especially true when it came to the living quarters in the Core—but most of the Station's inhabitants tried to inject a little color and individuality into their home Zones.

Nowhere was this more evident than in Zone 3, which handled all incoming and outgoing cargo space traffic (personal and business travel was all routed through Zone 1). To offset the otherwise gray and greasy docks, the rest of the Zone exhibited an exotic, colorful air that paid homage to its proximity to people from all over the galaxy. Flags, silhouettes of ships, and all sorts of mosaics and paintings that resembled colorful fabrics adorned the bulkheads throughout Zone 3's corridors and compartments.

Vince had always thought this was particularly fitting.

Once he reached the gray metal sidewalk, the Finder strode leisurely along for a couple of blocks. He soaked in his surroundings, even as he kept an eye out for anyone following him. Bright flags and banners in every color imaginable lined both sides of the main boulevard here. More stretched across it from side to side, catching the light from the glowpanels in the overhead and creating colored patches on the deck.

Despite the Station's hardworking airscrubbers, a faint undertone of engine exhaust and lubricant always seemed to hang in the air throughout much of Zone 3. At the moment, however, it was overwhelmed by the smell of various kinds of foods—pepper, garlic, and the delicious scent of baking bread. Vince inhaled deeply, enjoying the fact that he could do so without having to cough.

Smiling a little, he strolled onward. Strains of music from little restaurants dotting the boulevard and the occasional apartment lilted through the air, mixing with the chatter and shuffle of the people streaming up and down the metal sidewalks. Here too, silver transport pods glided back and forth in the center of the boulevard, the faint whooshing sound of their passage all but inaudible beneath the space station's usual bustling noise.

A sudden loud metallic clank carried across the boulevard. Vince wasn't the only one who glanced sharply sideways to see what had made that sound. A couple of Station Maintenance in navy blue uniforms (working overtime, apparently) were carrying a length of pipe out of a shadowy narrow access tunnel that jutted off to the left between a small computer repair shop and a tea shop. They looked harassed.

Vince wondered briefly if that pipe had anything to do with the power outage earlier, before he remembered that the power outage hadn't affected Zone 3. *That was only Zones 2 and 5*, he chided himself.

He used the loud noise as a distraction, however, and cut across the boulevard to the other side. Turning down the next block, he hailed yet another transport pod and directed it to take him two blocks from the restaurant where he was supposed to meet Commosky. But when the pod discharged him on the sidewalk, he proceeded to head in the direct opposite of where the detective sat waiting for him.

After cutting down a corridor that lay between two sections of apartment complexes, Vince gradually wove his way back around through the narrower side corridors of Level 8 until he finally approached Wendall's Fish 'n Chips from the opposite side. He still had no reason to believe he was being followed, but he wasn't taking any chances.

Not if Commosky wanted to talk to him about their last case.

CHAPTER 6

As Vince neared Wendall's Fish 'n Chips, the tantalizing smell of fried whitefish and potato chips—all grown on-Station in Zone 2—floated down the sidewalk to greet him. The aroma grew stronger with every step he took, making his mouth water and his stomach start growling. He was ready for dinner—he'd deliberately held off until now.

He didn't eat fish often—like beef or chicken, it was expensive to raise and even more expensive to ship in from elsewhere in the galaxy. But on occasion, it was worth paying for.

Hence the reason a place like this was still in business on a space station. People still had to eat and they wanted good food. There was something about frying fish in batter and oil that was strangely appealing, though Vince himself couldn't eat it more than every couple of months.

Bright neon letters strung along a large window next to the electric blue front door advertised fresh fish, hot chips, and cold beer. Vince could personally attest that the fish and chips held up to their advertising, but he had no idea about the beer. He refused to touch the stuff, cold or otherwise.

The second the Finder stepped through the door, he noticed a marked difference in the temperature. The air in here was a few degrees warmer than out in the rest of Level 8, no doubt due to the kitchen. Vince didn't relax—he was far too on edge for that—but he approved of the warmth. He might even, depending on how he felt when he got to a table, actually take his brown leather jacket off.

The restaurant was lit by a utilitarian series of strips of glow-panels in the ceiling. The brightness had been turned down a little, but it was still brighter than the street-like corridor outside.

Vince's eyes adjusted quickly to the brighter lighting and he nodded courteously to a young man standing at a short counter next to the doors to the kitchen. He then sent a quick, sweeping look around the large room in search of Commosky.

Regardless of it being late evening, the restaurant was over a third full. It was separated into the usual mix of booths and tables, both to facilitate socializing and privacy for those who wanted a little space to themselves. He spotted the short, stocky detective two booths from the back left corner and one corner of his mouth lifted in a smile.

Commosky was leaning back against the navy blue booth cushion, staring at a holographic menu floating above the electric blue table in front of him as though he was internally debating whether or not it was telling him the truth about the day's specials. Feeling Vince's gaze on him, he glanced sideways and their eyes met.

The expression on Commosky's clean-shaven, square-jawed, swarthy face did not change, but Vince had the distinct sense that the black-haired detective was relieved to see him. Strange, that.

Keeping one eye on handful of other patrons seated at the tables and booths that stood between them, Vince casually strolled toward Commosky's table. He didn't pause to greet the Station Authority officer, but wordlessly slid into the booth seat on the other side of the table.

"Finder," Commosky said over his holographic menu. He was dressed in casual clothes, but even without his usual crimson and gray uniform, he still had an air about him that said he was either military or a Station Authority officer.

"Detective."

Again, nothing changed in the other man's face, but Vince felt sure he had relaxed a little. Only a little.

Vince doubted Commosky ever fully relaxed.

Commosky was shorter than Vince, and stocky, with powerful shoulders and keen black eyes. He looked hard—and he was hard in his dealings—but he was also fair. Vince didn't care for the man's personality or the way he handled people sometimes, but he respected him.

That was more than the Finder could say about most Station Authority officials he'd met over the years. (Sergeant Anita Rychek not included.)

"Ever been here before?" Commosky motioned to his menu. "Usually get the fish sandwich, myself, but I've been trying to cut back on carbs lately. Too much desk work." He drummed his fingers on the table's glossy, if a little weathered surface, looking momentarily restless.

"I come here every once in a while." Vince tapped a small, hourglass-shaped insignia in the center of the table and a holographic menu popped up in front of him as well. He read it quickly, before concluding that he wasn't interested in any of the specials. He dismissed the menu with a flick of his fingers. "Don't much care for their bread."

"More of a fried potato man?"

Vince lifted one shoulder in a shrug. "If I'm going to spend the money to eat fish, I'm not paying for crummy bread too."

"No pun intended." A ghost of a smile crossed Commosky's swarthy face, before it vanished. He tipped his chin toward the hourglass insignia. "Order whenever you're ready. I'm buying."

Something tightened in Vince's chest. So this *was* official. Or, at the very least, officially off the record.

He inclined his head in a wordless show of thanks and placed an order for chips, three pieces of fried fish, and lime seltzer water. Places like this didn't serve tea. He then leaned back against his own booth seat and studied Commosky while the detective placed his own order.

That done, Commosky leaned forward to prop his forearms on the table. "How's the Finder business these days?"

"Can't complain." Vince shrugged again. "Right now I don't lack for work." He smiled wryly. "In this business, it's either feast or famine."

"Your last couple of cases haven't hurt your publicity, I'm sure." Commosky's voice was dry, but he seemed genuinely interested.

"It won't last forever. It's tapered off a little already, and honestly, I don't mind."

"Business picks up like that again, you'll have to hire more help."

Vince shook his head. "I'd scale back first. Don't have time to train anybody else right now."

"And you're not sure you would even if you did." Commosky gave Vince a knowing look. "I still can't believe you hired Miss Escovedo."

Well, well. Vince narrowed his eyes slightly. Maybe the detective knew him a little better than he realized.

Movement from the side drew both of their attention to a plump, middle-aged woman with light cocoa skin in a bright magenta dress sailing up to them with a tray of drinks.

"Here you go," she said with a pleasant smile, setting the drinks before them. Commosky had ordered what passed for cola on Zyga Space Station. Both men's drinks fizzed and sparkled in their glasses. "Your food'll be out shortly."

They thanked her and she sailed back toward the counter.

Once she was gone, Commosky eyed Vince's seltzer water. "Never understood the appeal of that stuff."

"It's an acquired taste." Vince picked up his glass, which was cold, and took an appreciative sip. "Flavor and carbonation without sugar."

"It's disgusting," Commosky said flatly.

"So's alcohol." Vince eyed him over the rim of his glass. "Talk about an acquired taste, and yet people drink it."

Commosky waved that aside, as though he'd reached the limit of his tolerance for small talk, but before he could say anything further, their waitress was back with another tray, this one loaded with plates.

In a jiffy, she had set Vince's fish and chips in front of him, and Commosky's matching fish and chips in front of him. Then, with a motherly smile and an admonition to let her know if they needed anything else, she left them to eat in peace.

The delectable smell rising off from Vince's golden chips and steaming, golden-fried fish made his mouth start watering again. He salted his chips and then picked one up and took a bite. It was almost too hot to eat, but oh, so delicious.

After he swallowed, the Finder jerked his chin toward Commosky. "Why am I here?"

Another ghost of a smile crossed the detective's swarthy face, but it vanished even faster than the first one. "That's one of your finer points, Grable. You don't beat around the docks."

Vince pointed a particularly long chip across the table. "Didn't think you did either."

"It's sensitive." Commosky's gaze flicked around the room, assessing things again. "Waitress won't bother us now." He picked up his sandwich, but did not take a bite. "How are the Antwerps?"

Vince's goatee began to prickle. Now they were getting to it. He shrugged easily. "Fine, far as I know. Corwin's set to graduate as an electrical engineer in a couple of months."

"And they're raising Dent's kid?" Commosky asked, before biting into his sandwich.

"That's right." Despite the foreboding he felt curling in the pit of his stomach—a separate and distinct entity from the way his stomach was still growling—Vince had to smile. "Cute little thing." He reached into his breast pocket and withdrew his comlink. Pulling up a holo still he then pushed the device across the table for Commosky to see.

Mrs. Antwerp had sent him a holo still of the little girl a few weeks back. Maribel had lost the pinched look she'd had when Vince had helped Corwin and his mother first get custody of her. She had two pearly teeth and a gooey smile, and a few tiny blue beads adorned her curly black hair.

Commosky studied the picture for a moment, before pushing the comlink back across the table. His expression turned the tiniest bit pensive. "I'd say it's a shame she has to grow up without her dad, but with Dent Antwerp's track record, the odds were only ever going to be fifty-fifty that he'd be part of her life."

"Guess we'll never know now." Vince tucked the comlink back into his jacket and picked up a piece of fish. As he took a bite of the hot, flaky meat, he appraised Commosky across the table.

This was fascinating. He wanted to ask questions, wanted to do what he did best and prod at Commosky until the detective started talking, but he refrained. Commosky had called him here to talk, but he was clearly having trouble getting to the point.

That was…extremely unusual for the detective.

Commosky seemed to realize the same thing. Dropping his sandwich with a little moue of irritation, he leaned forward in his seat to rest his forearms on the table. "I don't know how else to say this, Grable, so I'm just going to say it."

His dark eyes bored into Vince. "I want you to help me take down the pieces of flotsam that own the Ruby Gauntlet."

CHAPTER 7

Vince stared back at Commosky, his own face impassive. The detective's words hung between them for a moment, full of somber weight. Vince felt that weight, but he couldn't say he was surprised. Not even the slightest.

He let one corner of his mouth tilt up in a wry smile. "What, the combined might of Station Authority isn't enough to accomplish that?"

Commosky's face puckered as if he'd tasted something sour. "No. Unfortunately." He picked up his sandwich. "Starlit and Lumen are operating illegally and making thousands, if not more, in unreported income." He took a bite, chewed savagely, and then swallowed, his expression darkening. "Not to mention the fact that there's a trail of physical holdings here on the Station with evidence of extortion. And a trail of bodies."

Vince nodded, reaching for his seltzer water. He and Bella had made that connection, while they were working to clear Corwin's name. He couldn't help feeling, though, that there was something Commosky hadn't told him yet. Something…else.

He cleared his throat. "Were you ever able to connect the user-names of people who lost big in the Diamond Gem Room with their real-world identities?"

He, Bella, and his favorite information broker, a man who went by the name of Brill, hadn't been able to legally trace people who'd lost everything in the Ruby Gauntlet's infamous Diamond Gem Room, but Vince had been sure that Commosky would have been able to get a warrant for that kind of information.

Instead of looking pleased, the detective's face darkened further. "Yes, I did. For all the good it did me."

Vince raised an eyebrow. *That* was cryptic. "I would have thought you'd have Starlit and Lumen identified and arrested by now."

"So did I." Grimacing, Commosky waved the hand that held what was left of his sandwich. "It's all more complicated than it should have been."

Vince picked up another piece of fish. "I'm listening."

After sending another quick, discreet glance around at the restaurant's interior again, Commosky leaned forward and lowered his voice. "I took what you gave me and got a judge to make the gaming company that owns *Everheart* hand over the personal information of those players on the loser list. Started running them down one by one. Most of them have Nasard Mutual in common. I was this—" he held up his thumb and forefinger with barely a space between them "—close to cracking Starlit and Lumen's identities when everything came crashing down."

Vince frowned. "What do you mean, everything came crashing down?"

"I mean everything crashed." Commosky sat back in his seat, folding his arms across his chest. A sardonic smile curved his thin lips. "I'm done. Finite. Case dropped."

"What?" Vince's fish fell from his fingers to plop on his plate. Genuinely astonished, he stared at the detective. Apart from Rychek, Commosky was probably the last person on Zyga Space Station he would have expected to abandon a case he'd worked on with such energy and passion.

"Not by my choice, you understand." Commosky's dark eyes glittered with resentment. "Seems somebody went over Detective Inspector Romulus's head and talked to the Council." He waved a hand. "All of a sudden, my investigation isn't 'worth Station Authority resources' anymore."

"What could they possibly have used to get you off the case?" Vince shook his head, still gobsmacked. "I could see money being a factor, but wouldn't it take an awful lot to cover up an illegal gambling casino with homicides connected to it if somebody like you is already running it down?"

"Oh, it would." Commosky picked up his glass of cola, but did not drink it. "And money *is* a factor, there's no doubt about it. It would have been more than the Ruby Gauntlet's owners I brought down, and that was making people nervous. But, no." His fingers tightened on the glass, his knuckles turning white. "That's not the reason."

Vince wracked his brain. If it wasn't bribery, that left only a few other options. His eyes narrowed. What was the crew behind the Ruby Gauntlet famous for, after all?

Extortion, with a side helping of blackmail.

He stared at Commosky. "They've got something major on somebody important."

It wasn't a question.

Commosky raised his glass in a silent toast of acknowledgement. He smiled, but his eyes were ice cold. "Worse than that, actually."

Vince raised a hand to his goatee, which was prickling fiercely. "How can it be worse?"

Instead of answering, Commosky hesitated. He visibly swallowed, his eyes darting around the restaurant again, before he shook his head. Unfolding his arms, he pushed his plate to one side and leaned forward over the table.

He met Vince's gaze frankly. "I shouldn't be reading you into this." He lowered his voice still further. "It's classified, and you don't have clearance."

"But you're going to tell me anyway." Vince matched his tone, one corner of his mouth lifting in the barest hint of a smile.

This time, the detective didn't hesitate. "Yes, I am. Because this has gotten bigger than just an illegal gambling casino and a handful of murders, and we both know that you're the best Finder on Zyga Station."

Vince barely even had time to acknowledge the compliment—Commosky must really be desperate—before the detective's next words left him cold.

"You know that power outage in Zones 2 and 5 this morning?" Commosky didn't wait for Vince to answer. "That was a warning from Starlit and Lumen. Either I drop the case, or they shut the power off again. And this time, more of the Station goes dark."

CHAPTER 8

"What?" Vince's jaw dropped. He stared at Commosky in horror and renewed astonishment, a small part of him hoping the shorter man would laugh and say it had all been a joke. But Commosky didn't have a sense of humor—or if he did, it was buried somewhere deep in the pit of his soul.

Inhaling sharply, Vince sat back in his booth, his appetite suddenly gone. "Who *are* these people?" He managed to keep his voice quiet by sheer dint of effort. "The owners of a virtual nightclub, inside a game they don't own, no less, with the power to shut of power to certain parts of Zyga Space Station?"

"See what I mean?" Commosky's mouth twisted grimly. "They've got the Council spooked enough to overlook ongoing homicide investigations in order to keep something like this from happening again."

"And they honestly think that will work?" Vince snorted, half-disgusted, half-amazed. "I thought Station Authority didn't negotiate with terrorists." Reaching for his seltzer water, he tipped the glass toward the detective sitting across the table from him. "That's what whoever is behind this is, strictly speaking."

"You don't have to tell me." A muscle twitched in Commosky's jaw. "I know."

Vince swirled his seltzer water around in his glass while he considered this. The carbonated water sparkled in the piped sunlight from the glowpanels in the overhead. "Are they that afraid? Your bosses, I mean." He fixed Commosky with a questioning look.

"They're terrified." Commosky smiled, but there was no mirth or joy in his expression. "Imagine the panic that would ensue if parts of the Station suddenly lost power for a couple of hours, or a day, or who knows how long."

"I like to think I have a fairly good imagination. That's not something I want to contemplate."

"Nobody does."

Vince considered for a moment, his gaze fixed on a glossy drop of water on the electric blue tabletop while his mind worked through various explanations and scenarios. Commosky fell quiet to give him space to think, slowly sipping his cola and occasionally glancing around at the rest of the restaurant.

The buzz of conversation and the clink of silverware against dishes all faded to the background. In his mind's eye, Vince studied the blueprints of Zyga Station he'd memorized over the years. There were a few people who knew the Station better than he did, the Engineers who kept everything running, for starters, but he had a better working knowledge than most of his fellow citizens.

After a moment, the Finder returned his gaze to Commosky. "Correct me if I'm wrong, but outside of Authorized-Access-Only engineering levels in the Core, there are only a couple of places somebody could access the Station's power grid, right?"

"That's right."

Vince considered again. The precision involved with something like this…somebody had to be well connected.

He shook his head. "Surely Station Authority and the Council have already launched an investigation into how anybody was able to pull this off."

Commosky's expression soured again. "They've opened an official investigation because they have to, in order to keep the general public from knowing there's a larger problem." He snorted in disgust, spreading his hands. "Don't know how far they'll get with it, though, because of the blackmail. For all I know, Starlit and Lumen included a caveat about investigations into the power grid, too."

"That would be difficult to pull off." Vince looked askance at the detective. "Unless their inside man is positioned at a very high level, how would they even know Station Authority is investigating?"

"They'd have to assume we are, though they wouldn't know the particulars." Commosky's shrug was as curt as his tone. "That's not the problem, though. The problem is that the Council doesn't know how much power the Ruby Gauntlet really has. They don't *know* if Starlit and Lumen can follow through on their threat, but at the same time, they can't take the risk." He pointed a cocked finger at Vince like a gun. "*That* is what has them terrified."

"Understandably." Vince twitched a shoulder in a shrug of his own. When you lived on an essentially a man-made ball of metal in open space, maintaining a stable power grid to keep little things like life-support going tended to be a priority.

He eyed Commosky. "What do you want me to do?"

"That's the million-credit question." Commosky let out a harsh laugh as he shifted in his seat. His gaze slid sideways again to take in the rest of the restaurant and make sure nobody was paying them any attention before he leaned forward to address Vince once more.

"I can't pay you, Grable." The detective quirked a shaggy black eyebrow, smiling wryly. "But you probably already figured that, given that I'm officially off the case."

"I did." Vince inclined his head in a nod. Didn't take a genius to see that coming.

"That said, if we track these soul-sucking leeches down and bring them in, there will be a reward of some kind." Commosky waved a hand. "Don't know how much. But I will personally guarantee you get a cut of whatever it is." He let out a snort. "Hell, I'll comb through Station Authority's official bylaws and fill out whatever paperwork is necessary to ensure you're fully reimbursed for your time and energy."

Vince offered him a wry smile in return. "I already knew you were serious."

"I am. Dead serious." Commosky's dark eyes bored into his face. "This *is* serious." Frustration leaked into his voice. "The Council may have launched an investigation, but even though they've got all my records and notes, it'll take them days to catch up on everything. *Days.* They don't know this case as well as I do."

He set his jaw. "They don't know the Ruby Gauntlet like I do."

"Will you be able to access your records and notes?"

A cagey smile played across Commosky's swarthy face. "Not officially. As of this morning, I can't technically access any of it."

"But?" Vince prompted. There had to be a 'but'.

"But…" Commosky shrugged. "I've, ah, been taking work home with me lately. I have copies of all of the most important things."

Vince considered him across the table. That didn't surprise him at all. Commosky was a hard man, but he was thorough. When he latched onto something, he didn't let go without a very compelling reason.

The Finder cocked his head to one side. "No chance you'll overhear anything about the investigation at the Precinct the next couple of days?"

"I might if I was going to be there." Commosky's smile was razor sharp. "Detective Inspector Romulus saw fit to give me the next three days off. 'To clear my head', he said. Supposedly I'm in this case too deep." He huffed. "Like having three days off with nothing to do but think is going to make things better."

"I see."

Commosky drained the last of his cola. "I'd have just come straight to your office and saved you a trip, but I was concerned about being tailed. Figured I'd best stay in Zone 3 for the moment." He gave Vince that razor sharp smile again. "Jury's out as to whether or not it would be somebody from the Ruby Gauntlet or my own people."

"Were you? Tailed, that is?"

"Yes." Commosky shook his head in mild disgust. "Couple of undercover officers. I don't know 'em personally. They're good, but not good enough. Haven't seen anybody else."

The two men shared a knowing look. When you were as well trained as they were, it took somebody really exceptional to follow them without them being aware of it.

"Far as they know, I'm in a restaurant six blocks over." Commosky glanced at the comm band on his wrist. "Have to head back soon." He pinned Vince with a hard look. "Anybody on your tail?"

"No. I took precautions, but didn't spot anything." Vince half-smiled. "Doubt they were expecting you to call me."

"Yeah, well, somebody's got to do something." Commosky looked decidedly disgruntled. "Can't believe the Council is taking orders from these people." He leaned sideways, reaching under the table with one hand as though to scratch an itch on his ankle. When he straightened, he discreetly pushed a black datachip across the table.

Keeping his expression from showing the surprise he felt, Vince easily palmed the datachip. He hadn't expected the detective to turn information loose so quickly.

"Let me remind you," Commosky lowered his voice again, "that everything on that is classified. You shouldn't be reading it." He smiled sardonically. "I shouldn't be giving it to you. But, desperate times and all that." He flicked his fingers dismissively.

Vince narrowed his eyes at the detective, appraising him in a new light. "Better to ask forgiveness than permission, eh?"

"In this case? Absolutely." Commosky's dark eyes glittered like tiny pinpricks of stars in the vast blackness of space. "Even Internal Affairs won't care much once we nail these leaches to the bulkhead." He tipped his head toward Vince. "Read all of that and I'll be in touch. I have some ideas."

But you don't want to discuss them here. Vince heard his unspoken words loud and clear. He nodded.

Commosky inclined his head in response and then slid out of the booth. A moment later, he'd stopped by the counter to pay their bill, exited the restaurant, and was gone.

CHAPTER 9

KNOWING IT WAS BETTER IF HE AND Commosky weren't both seen exiting the restaurant together, Vince finished the last of his dinner. Even though at this point he still didn't have much of an appetite for it. Once he'd forced the last bite of fish down, he sent Bella a brief text to let her know he was on his way back.

Over the past few months, he'd come to the conclusion that it was a good thing to have an assistant who could do things like call Station Authority if he turned up missing. Besides, he knew she was still at the office. Even if she'd been a normal human instead of a human mind trapped inside an android shell, he suspected he'd still find her waiting up for him, anxious to hear to all the details. She was curious and inquisitive and reliable and really an excellent fit for this Finder business.

Vince was sure she'd been an excellent cleaning lady, in her past life as Bella Martínez, but clearly she was capable of so much more.

Sliding out from the booth, the Finder tapped the button in the center of the table, added a tip to the amount Commosky had left for their meal, and ran his prepaid credit chip. He then departed, nodding amiably to the waitress who'd served them on his way out.

It was just as well he had to travel all the way back to Zone 5. Gave him time to think. What Commosky was asking was dangerous and borderline illegal.

Vince snorted softly to himself. No, not borderline illegal. It *was* illegal.

If it was anybody else, Vince would have told them to shoot themselves out of the nearest airlock. Wasn't worth the risk of him losing his Finder's license.

But…it was Commosky. The detective knew full well what he was getting into—and what he was asking of Vince.

Commosky could get arrested and drummed out of Station Authority for insubordination. Vince could *also* get arrested and lose his Finder's license.

Normally, he would have bet that he'd be more likely to get arrested than Commosky, but in this particular situation, it seemed their odds were about even. People who were used to holding all the power in any given situation didn't handle being fearful and being powerless very well. The fact that Commosky, of all people, believed the situation was dire enough to risk bucking the system said a lot.

If Vince helped him, he'd be risking his neck too. Maybe even Bella's, since Station Authority could probably arrest her as an accessory if everything went up in flames.

Something twinged in the pit of Vince's stomach. *That* would be an unmitigated mess. He needed to keep Bella as far away from any situation in which somebody might find out she had an android body as possible.

The datachip, which he'd tucked into in the special flap inside the breast pocket of his brown leather jacket, seemed to burn a hole against his chest.

At the same time, given what he knew, how could he say no? Even without taking whatever information Commosky was giving him into account?

The people behind the Ruby Gauntlet had gone from threatening individuals for profit to putting the entire space station in danger.

This was bigger than him, bigger than Commosky, bigger than Bella.

Starlit and Lumen had to be stopped.

Vince narrowed his eyes, resolve swirling through his veins, filling him with strength. Somehow, the three of them were going to do it.

Vince took a circuitous route back to Level 8's main elevator bank. Along the way, he remained on the alert for anyone tailing him, but once again it seemed he was in the clear. The flow of pedestrian traffic was lighter now, and he blended right in with the people dressed in casual clothes heading home from late evening meals or trudging off to the late shift somewhere.

Apart from the fact that his fish and chips had decided to start churning uneasily in his gut, the journey from the main elevator bank down to Level 22 passed without incident as well. Once there, he flagged another silvery transport pod to take him back to the Hub.

Settling back against the green cushioned seat, Vince stared through the small viewport on the door nearest him. A series of living quarter doors and entrances to shops and offices flashed past on both sides of the transport pod, but he didn't see them.

His mind was fixed on the puzzle Commosky had presented him, melding the new information he'd received with what he already knew about the Ruby Gauntlet. The datachip hidden in his jacket pocket continued to burn, teasing him with its promise of the unknown.

His goatee bristled; Vince absently raised a hand to stroke it. The Ruby Gauntlet *was* a puzzle. A virtual gambling club with tentacles that stretched into the real world to kill people and steal their property.

But why? Were Starlit and Lumen making so much money that they'd run to of things to spend it on? Had something in their virtual world tipped the scale inside their minds that regulated the balance between right and wrong?

People died all the time in games. If you died, you simply respawned. Death wasn't permanent.

But out here in the real world…game over meant the end of everything. No second chances, no do-overs. Die outside a game, and you were gone forever.

There had to be a reason for those four murders. Vince drew his lips into a thin line. Outside of Starlit and Lumen being a couple of psychotic sociopaths, that is. If *that* was the case, he and Commosky were in trouble.

Hard to follow the money when the people you were following weren't in it for any of the normal reasons.

Vince's goatee bristled again. He had a gut sense, however, that Starlit and Lumen weren't psychotic. Cold, calculating murderers, yes, but not crazy.

The transport pod finally slowed to a stop in the Hub just outside of the entrance to Zone 3, breaking Vince from his thoughts. He made a mental note to review the locations of the apartments that had belonged to each of the four murder victims. Maybe there was a connection he and Bella had missed the first time.

After paying his fare, Vince disembarked. His silver transport pod immediately glided away, falling in line with several other pods headed back into Level 22. Vince then set off along the colorful curved mosaic walkway in the direction of Zone 5.

Even though he'd been though here less than two hours earlier, the view beyond the transparent bulkheads drew Vince's attention yet again. Looking out at those glittering stars always gave him perspective on his own place in the galaxy. That hit him especially hard tonight.

Human beings were nothing more than specks in the black vastness that was space. Zyga Space Station itself, huge as it might be, was nothing more than a pinprick compared to some of those stars. The Station hung suspended in space a safe distance beyond the Cartha's gravitational pull, but even against that gas giant it was little more than a small moon.

Vince mentally shook his head. If the worst happened and Zyga Space Station died—and everyone on board along with it—would the wider galaxy even notice?

The answer to that, of course, was no.

A few places in the outside galaxy might notice a disruption of the ore and other minerals that the Zyga Mining Corp provided from the Cartha system, but somebody else would eventually step up to take their place.

Life for the outside galaxy would go on.

Vince studied the stars out of the corner of his eye as he passed the entrance to Zone 4. On a grand scale, did human beings' lives matter in the universe? Maybe not. But here, on this scale, on this space station, a single person's life did matter.

It mattered to him.

It mattered to Commosky, curmudgeonly though the Station Authority homicide detective could be.

And so, they would—

The glow panels in the overhead abruptly died, plunging the Hub into total darkness.

CHAPTER 10

Vince froze, spots dancing before his eyes. The darkness was so thick it felt like a heavy, smothering blanket had been dropped over his head. He had a split-second to brace himself for the impending loss of gravity before he felt his feet leave the deck.

His stomach lurched alarmingly at being weightless again.

Frightened screams echoed around him throughout the Hub. Nobody else liked the darkness and weightlessness and strange, resounding silence either.

For a handful of seconds, the only things Vince or anyone else in this part of the Hub could see were the stars through the translucent bulkheads. Their serene, glittering pinpricks of light were unchanged by the instantaneous chaos that had just been created by Zyga Station's loss of power.

It seemed to take an eternity for the emergency backup system to come online. In reality, it was only a handful of seconds before lines of tiny red glowpanels flared to life along both edges of the walkway. Several things then happened in quick succession.

Beyond the Hub's outer bulkheads, lights blinked to life, illuminating the long, spoke-like expanse of Zone 3 stretching out into the distance toward the Rim. At the same time, every glowpanel in the Hub's overhead snapped back on, blinding everyone.

Gravity returned a split-second later, reasserting control with invisible, greedy fingers.

Vince hadn't had much momentum, and so he had not drifted very far. He was prepared when heaviness returned to his body. Eyes blinking in the sudden brightness, he fell a handful of centimeters to land on the deck in a slight crouch.

Others throughout the Hub were not so fortunate. More than one painful-sounding thud echoed through the air, followed by cries of pain.

The buzz of conversation filling the air grew exponentially louder as people turned to each other to demand what had happened, or frantically call friends and loved ones in other parts of the Station to make sure they were all right. Or, in the case of several men and women within earshot, to call Station Authority and start demanding answers in angry, strident voices.

Vince did none of those things.

Adrenaline pumping through his veins, he set off at a lope along the mosaic walkway toward the intersection where Zone 5 joined the Hub. He had to get back to his office. Unless Starlit and Lumen were just toying with the Council and Station Authority, something major had happened.

Why else would they have killed power to part of the Station again?

His comlink vibrated in his pocket. Vince pulled it out to see a text from Commosky.

::Wasn't me.::

Vince scowled. His first thought was to wonder how the homicide detective could possibly be sure of that. His next thought was a little kinder. Commosky was sure he hadn't been followed—and while talking to a licensed Finder was certainly suspicious, surely Vince didn't rate high enough on the danger scale to warrant Starlit and Lumen killing the power again.

No, Commosky was right. Something else was going on.

His comlink vibrated again. Bella, this time, calling him.

"Boss!" she said frantically, as soon as he answered. "The power died again!"

"I know," Vince said curtly. "It went off in the Hub too."

"I think it went off *everywhere* this time. The media is going crazy."

"Everywhere?" Vince blinked. He hadn't expected that level of escalation. Not yet.

"Yes! What is going on?"

"Don't know." Vince lifted a hand to flag a silver transport pod. "What's the media saying?"

"They don't know what to say. Nobody knows what's happening. They're trying to caution people to conserve power, since we're running on emergency—"

Overhead, the lights flickered, but stayed on. Vince darted a glance to the deck along the edge of the walkway in time to see the red emergency lights wink out.

"Did you see that?" Bella demanded. "Did that happen to you too?"

"Main power's back on." Vince glanced around the walkway. Ahead of him, a flood of panicked citizens streamed toward the entrance to Zone 5.

Apart from that, he didn't see anything out of the ordinary. But then, there wouldn't be much to see here.

The problem was elsewhere in Zyga Station.

Probably the Core, if Vince had to hazard a guess.

"Boss—"

A transport pod glided to a halt in front of Vince. "Hold tight, Bella." He opened the door and climbed in. "I'm on my way back."

CHAPTER 11

From a distance, Vince's office appeared dark and empty. His security protocols automatically turned his front window opaque from the outside every evening, regardless of whether or not the lights were on inside. As the Finder approached at a quick march, his thoughts churning madly inside his head, the front door opened.

Bella appeared in the doorway, backlit by a wash of warm golden light that spilled out onto the gray metal sidewalk. The light was welcoming, the more so because of what Vince just experienced in the Hub. He quickened his steps.

She'd been watching for him.

On another occasion, he might have chided her for opening the door before he'd officially reached the doorstep. Tonight, he just wanted to get inside.

"Boss!" Bella stepped aside to let him in. "I'm glad you're back."

"Me too."

Though perhaps not for the reasons his assistant meant.

Vince crossed the doorway, feeling for a second like some strange, shadowy thing had been following him, and hit the lockpanel. When the door slid shut, he felt a profound sense of relief. The rest of the Station might be losing their collective minds, but this office was his oasis, the eye in the figurative storm.

The Ruby Gauntlet's owners had upped the ante.

The real question now was *why*—

—and he intended to find out.

After running through his security protocols, Vince turned to Bella. "You all right?"

Office hours were more than over; he doubted any new business would have come in during his absence.

"I'm fine." Bella gave him a reassuring smile.

She did look remarkably calm, given the circumstances. She'd gained a lot of control over this android body of hers over the past few months, especially when it came to fine control of her expressions. Every once in a while an expression or movement was overly exaggerated, but, really, she'd greatly improved.

"Good."

Without further ado, Vince strode across his office to the jade green credenza to brew himself a cup of tea. He took a deep breath of clean, filtered air, tinged with the faint scent of either Bella's perfume or her detergent. (Did she wash clothes, he wondered, when she didn't have things like sweat or body odor anymore? He supposed she must—if nothing else, she'd have outside contaminates. It occurred to him he'd never asked, but this was hardly the time.)

"What is going on?" Bella asked from behind him. "Is the Station in trouble?"

Vince turned in time to see her sweep a hand toward the large holoprojectors on either side of the office, which were both set to the Station's two largest news stations. She'd muted the sound, but words ran along the ticker tapes at the bottom.

Station Authority investigating today's troubling power loss. Zyga Council issues statement: "Do not panic. Everything is under control."

Vince doubted that.

Bella's next words mirrored his thoughts. "They keep telling people not to worry, even while they're saying no official cause has been announced." She shook her head, her glossy black hair swaying back and forth. "What's that old saying, never believe anything until it's been officially denied?"

"They know what the problem is." Vince blew on the surface of his tea to cool it, his fingers tightening on the warm mug. "If Commosky is to be believed, that is."

"Commosky?" Bella's face was a mask of confusion. She stared at Vince, her brow furrowed. "What does he have to do with this? I thought he wanted to talk about the Ruby Gauntlet."

"He did." Vince carried his mug over to his desk, waiting for Bella to work it out.

It didn't take long.

Two seconds later, she gasped dramatically. "You can't be serious. He thinks the Ruby Gauntlet's *owners* are shutting the power off?" She threw her hands into the air. "How is that even possible?"

"That's a good question." Setting his mug down on his jade green desk, Vince sank into his comfortable, ergonomic chair and fished in his brown leather jacket for the datachip Commosky had passed him.

Bella moved to stand on the other side of his desk. She looked concerned now, the calm she'd projected earlier gone. "Boss, Zyga Station is supposed to have strict security protocols to keep people out of the Authorized-Entry-Only levels in the Core." She shook her head. "Otherwise, one of the Families probably would have taken over years ago."

Vince looked at her sharply. "That's an excellent point."

If his assistant could think of that angle, you'd think the Council and Station Authority, with all their combined brainpower and resources, could think of that. The Finder had learned years ago, however, that bureaucracy sometimes had a habit of getting in its own way and overlooking the obvious.

In a few brief words, Vince outlined his conversation with Commosky while he opened one of his desk drawers and pulled out a backup tablet. Easier to replace a backup that was a contained system, in case there was something on this datachip beyond what the detective had indicated.

Trust, but verify. It was a practice that had stood him in good stead throughout much of his life, let alone his career as a Finder.

"Sounds like Commosky is spitting hull bolts at being taken off the case," Bella said when he finished. She shook her head again. "I've only met him once and I know he…" she paused, as though searching for the right words, "…takes his work very seriously."

"That's a tactful way to put it."

"And they expect him to just walk away?"

"They're assuming he's not personally involved."

Bella snorted, a little indelicately. "Too late for that."

"It's not just that, Bella. Commosky has a sense of justice, which is more than I can say for other Station Authority officials I've encountered over the years."

"Except for Sergeant Rychek, you mean." One corner of Bella's pretty red mouth tilted in a teasing smile.

Vince just shot her a dry look. "Apart from her, yes."

Bringing the tablet to life, he inserted the datachip and then tapped on the folder that popped up. He braced himself for…something…he didn't know what, but the folder opened as usual. It held a mix of document files and folders containing holo stills, videos, and still more documents.

"What's on there?" Bella came around the desk to stand at his side, and together they stared down at the tablet.

Vince just shook his head. When he finally spoke, his voice held a grudging measure of awe. "When Commosky told me he sometimes took his work home with him, he meant it." He jabbed his forefinger toward the tablet's bright screen. "Won't know for sure until we drill down into it all, but offhand? I'd say this is everything Station Authority has got on the Ruby Gauntlet."

"Everything?"

"*Everything.*"

Absolute silence fell over the office as Finder and assistant stared at the Pandora's box they were about to delve into. Even the airscrubber had shut off, as though sensing their tension and anticipation.

His expression serious, Vince looked up at Bella standing beside him. "This is classified information. If we do this, and this whole thing goes sideways, we could be in some serious trouble." He let out a mirthless laugh. "Hell, even if everything goes perfectly and we manage to take Starlit and Lumen down, we could *still* be in some serious trouble."

"Are you telling me to walk away?" Bella arched a perfect, dark eyebrow at him.

"I'm telling you this is risky business and there's a chance we could both end up arrested." Vince took a breath. "We both know that there's more at stake here for you."

Silence fell over the office again.

Bella didn't draw a breath, but she did incline her head in a quick, sure nod. "Well, then, Boss, let's help catch these two cretins and not get caught ourselves."

Vince leaned back in his chair, a fierce, proud smile lighting his face. He shook his head in admiration. "I'm telling you, Bella, your talents were wasted as a janitor."

"You do what you have to do. Cleaning is important too." Bella shrugged as she strode around Vince's desk to snag her own chair, but he saw she looked pleased.

He glanced down at the information Commosky had given him, all organized into neat groups. His goatee bristled; he rubbed it briskly and set to work.

Surely, *surely*, they would find something here.

Because if they didn't? Well, Vince didn't even want to contemplate that alternative.

57

CHAPTER 12

Time fell away as Vince and Bella dug into Commosky's classified Station Authority case information. There was a plethora of information here. Under different circumstances, with a different homicide detective, it might have been more difficult to determine where to begin. But Ron Commosky was a logical man, and he made logical choices when it came to organizing information.

Vince found himself profoundly grateful for that. Even if Zyga Station hadn't lost power twice already in the same twenty-four hours, he had a gut feeling time was of the essence here.

He was halfway through his second cup of tea—mint tea with a dollop of honey from Zone 2's agricultural zone—when a strange buzzing sound broke the relative late night quiet filling his office.

"What is that?" Bella, with her enhanced hearing, whipped her head around to stare at Vince's computer terminal. She frowned, her eyebrows bunching almost comically. "I don't remember ever hearing that sound before."

Vince turned to stare at his computer terminal as well. He and Bella had been using both of his holoprojectors to view the contents of the datachip. He'd pulled out another cheap tablet for her to use, copied the datachip's information to it, and then used a direct connection to hook both devices up to the holoprojectors.

"That sound," he said slowly, "would be a notification that someone wants to video chat with me over an encrypted channel."

Bella's frown deepened. "I've worked for you for how many months now? and I've never heard that sound before."

"I don't use it often." Vince swiveled his chair toward his computer terminal. "Video and audio calls on regularly encrypted comlinks usually work fine for most of my clients."

In fact… Vince darted a sideways glance at Bella, his mind working furiously to narrow down the list of possible suspects. Well, 'suspects' was the wrong word, but it was the first that came to mind as he hit the 'accept' button.

He wasn't expecting the pale, pudgy face and round shoulders that filled his screen.

Vince blinked. "Brill?"

"Evening, Finder." The information broker smiled; the expression almost reached his dark, narrow eyes.

"To what do I owe this honor?" Vince leaned back in his chair, his mind spinning. He quieted his thoughts, however, and focused on the information broker's pale face, framed in curly black hair. Brill had turned the lights on in his swanky office for this call, illuminating the silvery green sweater he wore.

"Ah, is this your lovely assistant?" Brill's eyes fixed on Bella. Even through the computer screen, his gaze was intense. "Lovely to finally meet you face to face, Ms. Escovedo." He half-smiled, but there was a grim cast to it. "So to speak."

Bella lifted her chin, even as she self-consciously tucked a lock of glossy black hair behind one ear. "And you as well."

Brill waved a hand. "I'm sure your boss has told you all about me."

"He has," Bella said.

"Brill, it's late." Vince rubbed his chin; his goatee had begun to bristle again. "Not to be rude, but we're in the middle of something with a deadline."

"Whatever it is, it can wait. Trust me, Finder." Brill's tone was light, but his round face was unusually strained. He lifted one shoulder in a terse shrug. "This is more important."

Vince indicated the screen. "I can guess that much. You never call this way."

"Yeah, well…" Brill's gaze darted from Vince to Bella and back, and then he shook his head, an odd glint passing through his eyes. "It was this or show up at your office." He snorted. "This is more convenient."

Vince's goatee bristled again. He had the oddest sense that he knew where Brill was going with this, but…

Surely not. A coincidence, that's all. He looked at Brill, taking in the strained intensity in his expression, and knew he was lying to himself.

Neither one of them believed in coincidences.

Aloud, he said, "Well, go on. Don't leave us in suspense."

Licking his lips, Brill plunged right in. "I think today's power outages are connected to that gambling club you had me investigate a while back. The Ruby Gauntlet." His voice was low, his words a little more rushed than usual.

Despite the odd sense he'd had, a measure of shock still flooded Vince. He arched a questioning eyebrow, but otherwise kept his facial features under tight control. He didn't look at Bella. "What makes you think that?"

Instead of answering, Brill shifted in his seat—the chairs in his office were divinely comfortable, Vince knew from past experience—and scrutinized Vince through the computer screen. The intensity in his gaze gave the Finder pause…and he realized something else.

Brill was scared.

Vince eyed the information broker, taking in the details he hadn't noticed at first glance. The fine beads of sweat clinging to the other man's dark hairline, though he'd clearly wiped his forehead before he called. His breathing, which was more shallow than usual.

No, make that *terrified*.

"Power outages on a space station," Brill said at last, "are never a good thing. They happen sometimes, but they're rare. Two in one day?" He twitched a shoulder in a shrug. "Something is seriously wrong."

Beside Vince, Bella sat motionless. A stray corner of the Finder's mind hoped Brill wouldn't notice she wasn't breathing. He stared back at Brill, waiting for the other man to continue.

Brill had a flare for the dramatic sometimes that could be quite annoying. Particularly when you were paying him an hourly rate for his time. Since he wasn't paying Brill this time, Vince could afford to exercise a little more patience.

The information drew in a shallow breath. "They didn't make a big fuss about it, but I heard Station Authority over in Zone 3 has taken Detective Commosky off the Ruby Gauntlet case. Someone seems to think he's mined everything to be gained from that particular vein of ore." Brill paused for effect, eyes glinting. "I *also* heard that the Council's being threatened by one Starlit and Lumen, owners of said Ruby Gauntlet."

"That certainly wasn't on the news." Vince raised an eyebrow—he hadn't expected Brill to know that much—but Brill just shot him a wry look.

"You can drop the pretense, Grable. If Detective Commosky hasn't already contacted you, I'll eat my keyboard."

Vince allowed himself to crack a small smile at the mental image this provided, but the expression held no warmth. "What do you want, Brill?"

The information broker drilled him with a hard, assessing look, despite the stress he was clearly under. "Whatever you two are doing, I want in."

This time, Vince's surprised look was genuine. "Brill—"

"They went too far, Finder." A note of steel slid into the information broker's voice. His terror faded, to be replaced with anger. "People pay me for information and I provide it. I don't judge, and I don't usually take sides."

His voice grew even colder. "But threatening the Council, shutting the power off to the entirety of Zyga Station? Putting everyone on board this Station in danger?"

"They went too far," Bella said quietly, from her seat beside Vince facing the computer terminal.

"They've indirectly threatened *me*." Brill jabbed a pale, plump finger into his own chest, his dark eyes narrowing to slits. "Not to mention the entire population of Zyga Station, but that's beside the point." He brushed that away with a flick of his fingers. "Not even Bok Chul and Amal Oswari themselves have the stones—or sheer stupidity—to do something like this. They know better."

Vince agreed with *that* wholeheartedly. The sole benefit to there being *two* crime Families on Zyga Station was the fact that they were seldom—if ever—united in anything. In their own twisted way, they each provided balance to the other.

"And, so, Finder," Brill continued coldly, "whatever you and Detective Commosky are planning, I want in." He held one hand palm up. "It's not like I won't bring resources to the table. I *do* deal in information, after all."

The two men locked eyes, and Vince weighed his options. On the one hand, Commosky hadn't sworn Vince to secrecy. He also hadn't told him he could tell anybody else, but that was beside the point.

It was Vince's turn to narrow his eyes. Who better to help them solve this puzzle and finally take down the masterminds behind the Ruby Gauntlet than someone who was already familiar with the case?

"I have something else to offer, by the way," Brill added.

Something about the way the other man's tone changed put Vince on guard. He canted his head to one side. "And that would be?"

For the first time, Brill smiled. It was a smug smile, full of satisfaction and pride. The sort of smile that said he'd done something big, something he'd been dying to share with someone else.

Leaning back in his office chair, the information broker laced his fingers behind his head. "I cracked the Ruby Gauntlet's communications."

CHAPTER 13

"**Y**OU DID *WHAT?*" VINCE STARED AT him, certain he must have misheard.

"I cracked the Ruby Gauntlet's communications." On the computer display, Brill's satisfied smile deepened. "I know what Starlit and Lumen are telling their minions—and what their minions are reporting back to them."

"That is..." Vince searched for words, but they'd temporarily failed him. He could only gape at the information broker, truly caught off-guard for the first time in...well...a *long* time.

"...illegal," Bella said promptly, leaning forward in her chair to study Brill with wide eyes. "That's *really* illegal. If they catch you—"

"They won't," Brill said confidently.

Vince found his voice at last. "You don't know that." Depending on how a Station Authority judge sliced it...

"Oh, yes, I think I do." One corner of Brill's mouth lifted in a smirk.

Stars. This got complicated quickly. Vince drew in a deep breath, and then reached for his tea.

He took a healthy swig of the mint and honey concoction before setting his mug down and addressing Brill. "You're right—Commosky did contact me. He wants to continue his investigation, covertly, with my help. He gave me copies of his notes." Vince waved in the direction of his holoprojectors, which were out of Brill's line of sight. "That's risky enough without adding *hacking* private communications to the list."

"I'm prepared for that." Brill gave Vince a look, as if to say the Finder should know better than to assume the information broker didn't have failsafe contingency plans in place. "I might even be so inclined to help you, Commosky, and Bella, if it came to that."

"I don't—" Vince began, but Brill cut him off with another flick of his fingers.

"Worst-case scenario only, mind you. I doubt it will come to that. Point is, I can help and I want in."

Vince swiveled his chair around to face Bella. "What do you think?"

"Me?" She looked surprised that he'd ask, her red lips rounding in a startled 'O'.

"It's your neck on the line too, if this ends badly." Vince tipped his head toward Brill. "Think we should let him join the club?"

Bella's gaze automatically swung toward Brill. He looked back at her, a hint of impatience in the twist of his mouth. After a few seconds, she nodded slowly. "Yes, I think we should." She sent Vince a wry sideways smile. "I think we're going to need all the help we can get."

"All right, then, you're in." Vince gave Brill a casual nod.

"What," the information broker asked sarcastically, "you aren't going to run it by Commosky too?"

"Don't tempt me," Vince said, but then he leaned forward to stare at Brill through the computer display, all levity gone. "When did you crack their private communications?" He shook his head. "*How* did you manage that? I seem to remember you saying something about not being able to trace their money back when we were working the Antwerp case."

"I couldn't track their money, that's true." Brill shrugged, and then a sly grin played around his mouth. "But I've been working on their communications for a while. Took some time to crack, I'll tell you. They're paying for a good setup. Messages are in-game and routed through the same spoofing software that's hiding their money trail."

His smug tone implied he was better than whoever had set this up. Vince was inclined to agree with him.

"But even if I *had* cracked it back then, I wouldn't have been able to give it you." Brill shrugged. "We both know Station Authority would have ruled it illegal, and the last thing we wanted was for anybody to get off on a technicality."

His face darkened. "That's even more true now."

"What do you have?" Vince leaned farther forward, his tea forgotten on his desk. Even his fatigue at the late hour was gone, burned away by an electric jolt of adrenaline.

"Not much." Brill's expression turned thoughtful. "They're not chatty. Strictly business-only. Texts like 'payment due tom.'" He waved a hand. "Stuff like that."

"What about message history?" Vince stroked his goatee, his thoughts churning with possibilities. "Can you access any of that?"

"Yes and no." Brill shook his head again. "It's damned tricky, both getting *into* something like that and *then* poking around without tripping the security measures they've got set up."

Bella raised a hand. "Sorry if this is a stupid question, but didn't you just say we still can't give this to Station Authority?" She shook her head. "If that's true, how is it going to help us?"

Brill looked at Bella for a long moment. Vince could practically see the wheels in his head turning. The Finder knew instinctively that the information broker didn't have a concrete answer for that yet, but he was doing his best to come up with one.

"Haven't quite figured that part out," Brill said at last, his expression just a little chagrined. "But I will." His gaze flicked to Vince.

"Maybe Commosky will have some ideas on that front." He brushed that aside with a sweep of his hand. "At any rate, right now, they're domestic terrorists, Starlit and Lumen are, and I'm not too concerned with the legality of spying on them when they're threatening the lives of every single person aboard this space station."

"You should be." Vince drilled the information broker with a stern look. He understood the sentiment, but at the same time… "We don't get to just set the law aside whenever we want to." His stern look deepened. "That's how the Families operate. By their own rules. Look where that's got us."

"Yeah, well," Brill bristled, looking decidedly disgruntled, but also a little shamefaced. Some of the smugness had bled from his expression. "Would it help if I told you *how* I broke into their communications?"

Vince exchanged a glance with Bella, who looked wary. "Will it make that much of a difference?"

"It might."

"Well, if that's the case, then let's hear it."

Brill studied Vince thoughtfully for a second, and then all of a sudden, the expression on his pudgy face *changed*. Shame, smugness, and irritation all smoothed away, while his dark eyes sharpened and his shoulders straightened with the business-like air Vince usually associated with the man.

"I thought you'd react this way, Finder," he said briskly. "Good to know I can count on you to be consistent."

It was Vince's turn to narrow his eyes. He felt a bit like Brill had just purposefully yanked his chair out from underneath him. "Were you *testing* me?" His voice dropped an octave, almost into a growl.

"You understand, of course." Brill fluttered a hand. "Given today's events, it's hard to know who to trust anymore."

"Brill—"

The information broker's face grew larger in Vince's computer display as he leaned closer to his own computer display. "I found someone in their inner circle, Grable. One of their lieutenants. That's why I had to be sure."

Vince sucked in a sharp breath. That was…incredible. He could only imagine how Commosky would react. "You did? How?"

"Long story. Not currently relevant." Brill waved a hand again. "Point is, I now have an asset on the inside we can use."

The ramifications of *that* unfolded in Vince's mind like the petals of a beautiful flower opening beneath a sunlamp in one of the Agricultural Zone's greenhouses. He glanced sideways at Bella, who looked excited, before turning his attention back to Brill. "Tell me more."

It was early morning before Vince finally crawled into his bed in his little apartment above his office. Bella had opted to stay at the office instead of heading home, and Vince had let her. Even if she had needed mundane things like sleep anymore, sleeping on the office couch would have been a better option than her making the trek all the way home only to return a few hours later.

When they'd finally finished talking to Brill and Vince had left her to head up the stairs to his apartment, his assistant had been studying the data from Commosky. Vince would have loved to have kept going as well, but he, at least, required sleep.

And while time was of the essence, it was unlikely that anything dire would happen this early in the morning.

At least, that's what Vince told himself before he set his alarm for six hours later and let exhaustion pull him under.

CHAPTER 14

IT WAS MID-MORNING BEFORE THE GENTLE, BUT increasingly insistent tones of Vince's alarm roused him to consciousness. His alarm system also gradually turned his bedroom's sole window from opaque to translucent, allowing the day-cycle light of the boulevard outside to stream inside. Vince awoke all at once, and lay in his full-size bed staring up at the pale white overhead.

The events of the past twenty-four hours washed over him like the gentle breeze from the little fan on his black dresser, one after the other, but the thought that struggled to the surface, breaking past all the others, was a simple question. Why were Starlit and Lumen actively threatening the Council and Station Authority with power outages aboard Zyga Station?

Everything else—their identities, the murders, the question of who they'd been bribing—paled in comparison to this one glaring oddity in their overall game plan.

Throwing back his smooth gray sheets and matching comforter, Vince climbed out of bed. Apart from his ergonomic office setup, a nice bed large enough for him to be comfortable was probably his only concession to luxury. He figured since the average human being spent a third of his or her life sleeping, he might as well do it comfortably.

His bedroom was barely big enough for his bed, a black dresser, and a matching nightstand. A closet door stood at one end, opposite the door that led out into the tiny hall that connected his bedroom and hygiene unit to the small living area. He'd never bothered with curtains for his windows.

After padding into the hygiene unit clad only in his bright red boxers, Vince took a quick shower and then dressed for the day. Most of his wardrobe contained muted colors and patterns—articles of clothing that didn't stand out in people's minds. Being remembered when you didn't *want* to be remembered was a problem in his line of work. His concession to bright colors and patterns came in the form of his socks and boxers.

It didn't matter that nobody else knew they were there. *He* did, and that was enough.

He lived in this tiny apartment, but his office was his home. He spent more time there than he did here. There were times when Vince wondered if that was strictly healthy, but he loved what he did.

Most of the time, anyway. Some days and cases were easier than others.

While he fixed himself a quick breakfast in his tiny kitchenette— bland-but-filling reconstituted powdered eggs on toast—Vince checked the Station's news headlines. The power outages were still a major topic of concern, but nobody had any new information.

That's good, he thought. *Means Starlit and Lumen haven't done anything else yet.*

They had time to figure this out.

Vince carried his plate from the kitchenette to his little dining nook and sat down at the table. It had two chairs, and like most of the furniture he owned, was jade green. (His nightstand and dresser were an exception; he'd gotten a really good deal on them later.)

From here, he could see his small living area, which was just big enough for an end table, a couch, and a recliner. It wasn't a big apartment, but there were certainly smaller ones aboard Zyga Station. That was head-shaking, given that the space station had been constructed in, well, *space*, and money was the only limitation on its size.

Turned out, money was a big limitation. The Zyga Mining Corporation might be operating in space, but their attitude mirrored that of their colleagues elsewhere in the galaxy. Those who could afford to pay for extra space got it. Those who couldn't…well…the term 'close quarters' came to mind.

Vince was halfway through his breakfast—when his comlink trilled with an incoming text. He glanced at the display and shook his head.

Commosky. He wasn't surprised.

What *was* unusual was that the detective had sent only one word.

::*Well?*::

Vince swallowed a mouthful of eggs and huffed a laugh. Well, maybe not so unusual after all. He could almost imagine the expression on the taciturn detective's face.

He debated the best way to answer while he polished off the remainder of his toast. No doubt Commosky wanted to know what Vince thought about all of case files he'd given him, but the Finder couldn't comment on that yet. Nor could he straight up tell the detective what had delayed him.

Commosky might be using a burner comlink, but with the situation at hand, it was best to avoid taking chances if at all possible.

After a brief deliberation, Vince sent back a brief message.

::*Something's come up you should know about. My office.*::

He hesitated briefly, then added, ::*Come through the back. Apartment building entrance. Ring the doorbell.*::

His gaze flicked briefly to his seldom-used front door. With as much time as he spent in his office, and the fact that he had a set of stairs leading down to it, he hardly ever had a need to use his apartment's actual front entrance. Funny, that, when you thought about it.

Vince expected the detective to balk, or at least take some time to consider his options, but Commosky's response came almost immediately.

::*On my way.*::

Vince rubbed his chin thoughtfully; his goatee had started bristling. *He really doesn't like being off this case. Or off work, period.*

On that note, at least, Vince could sympathize with him. That stretch he'd had a while back without any cases had just about driven him up the bulkhead. He couldn't speak for women (though he suspected it was much the same for them), but in his experience, men weren't mean to sit around and do nothing. They needed something to occupy their time and attention, keep them from going stir-crazy.

There was only so long a man could putter around his apartment before boredom drove him to either insanity or trouble—and Vince suspected Commosky's boredom threshold was even lower than that.

Moments later, having cleared up the remains of his dishes, Vince headed downstairs to his office to make himself a cup of tea and confer with Bella. He didn't know how today would play out, but he had a gut feeling they would be busy.

CHAPTER 15

"**M**orning, Boss." Bella turned her head to offer him a chipper smile as Vince emerged through the hidden entrance. She sat at her desk, her elbows propped on its jade green surface. Her tablet lay before her.

"Still at it?" Vince raised his eyebrows, doing a mental calculation. How many hours had she been studying without him?

"Oh, I finished a while ago." Bella waved a hand, her silver fingernails catching the light from the broad window behind her desk. "Figured I'd go through it again in case I missed something."

Vince blinked. "That's…thorough." He started to turn toward the jade green credenza and his drink maker, but paused. "Bella, I didn't mean for you literally to work all night."

His assistant had changed clothes, at some point in the past few hours, exchanging what she'd been wearing before for a rose pink short-sleeved shirt over medium-wash blue jeans. Her black ankle high boots were the same. Vince didn't know if she kept a change of clothes—regardless of whether she really needed them or not—in her desk or if she'd pulled them from the over-large purse she was fond of carrying. She'd twisted her black hair up into a careless bun on the top of her head, held in place by a couple of silver decorative hair sticks.

Now Bella shrugged a slim shoulder. "I don't really sleep, Boss, remember? What else am I supposed to do?"

Her voice was light, her words spoken matter-of-factly, but something about them wrenched something deep inside Vince's chest. He busied himself with fixing a cup of black tea, discreetly clearing a lump in his throat.

"Well," he said gruffly, "I'll put it down as overtime pay."

He could feel Bella's eyes on his back, but she made no answer.

A moment later, steaming mug of tea in hand, Vince made his way to his desk. He set his tea on the jade green surface and settled into his comfortable chair. A few routine morning tasks to handle, and then they'd dive into Commosky and the Ruby Gauntlet mess.

He flicked a sideways glance at Bella. "Any calls this morning?"

"None. No emails either."

"Well, can't say that's a bad thing at the moment. The fewer things we have to handle on top of the Ruby Gauntlet, the better."

It was Bella's turn to glance sideways at him. "Mrs. Kawana will want an update at some point." Her lips twitched in a smile. "She made that pretty clear through all the hysterics yesterday."

Vince rolled his eyes. "She knows there isn't anything else I can do on that front yet. That'll sink in, if it hasn't already."

He took a careful sip of his tea. "Detective Commosky is on his way here."

That elicited a response from Bella. She reared up a little in her seat, her dark almond-shaped eyes going wide. "Boss, do you think that's a good idea?"

"No idea." Vince shrugged. "Don't see a better option, at the moment." He paused. "Might even be for the best, having a Station Authority homicide detective working on it with us. if we *do* run afoul of some legality, he's got a better chance of spotting it first."

Bella propped her chin in her hand, her expression thoughtful. "I hadn't looked at it that way."

"Me either, until this morning." Vince took another sip of tea, before waving a hand toward her tablet. "Anything interesting?"

"Oh, yeah." Bella brightened, straightening up in her chair with excitement. "Detective Commosky knew a *lot* more than he told us while we were helping Corwin a while back."

Vince's goatee bristled. "How do you know?"

"File creation dates." Bella nodded to her tablet. "Some of this info goes back months and months. Of course, it also looks like he took what you gave him and ran with it. He made a really extensive investigation into Nasard Mutual." She tapped her tablet with a fingertip. "Ran background checks on the employees and everything."

"Did he find anything?" Vince would pore over all this data himself, but it helped to get the highlights.

"Not on the employees themselves. He concluded they were actually handling real estate transactions."

Vince nodded. That made sense. If you were going to have a front, it had to function such that it didn't draw attention to itself. "Let me guess. The issue is where the properties were coming from and how they were obtained."

"Among other things, yes."

"I'll ask Commosky about those shortly." Vince brushed that subject aside. "What else?"

"Well…" Bella wrinkled her nose. "I've seen some crime scene holo stills that can't be unseen." She tapped the tablet again. "He's got everything in here—all of the deaths that we thought were connected to the Ruby Gauntlet."

Vince's goatee bristled again. He smoothed his fingers over his chin. "Any suspects?"

"A couple. Doesn't look like he found anything really concrete, or if he did, I don't know how to tell the difference."

"What about the most recent additions to his files?"

Bella hesitated. "That's what I was going over again." She shook her head. "I don't quite understand what he's got here. They're lists, but I can't make port or starboard of them."

"Let me see." Vince brought his own tablet to life and proceeded to poke around the most recently modified files. He skimmed past further case notes until he found the lists Bella had mentioned. Eagerly, he read through them.

Then he read through them again.

"Well?" Bella asked.

Smiling wryly, Vince looked up at her. "Don't feel badly. We'll need Commosky to explain all this." He indicated the tablet with a wave of his hand. "I can't tell if these are supposed to be case reference numbers or some sort of strange code Commosky's developed."

"That…would actually make a lot of sense, Boss." Bella frowned down at her own tablet. "Maybe it's just me, but I've been picking up a hint of…" she shrugged, a little helplessly, "…paranoia? while I've been reading through all these. Like Detective Commosky suspected somebody was coming along behind him and reading his case notes."

Interesting. Vince considered that for a moment. "He can't operate autonomously," he said at last, "but that's an interesting assessment. No, no," he held up a hand as Bella started to shrug and apologize. "You're probably right. Especially given what's going on right now."

They traded meaningful glances, and then Vince said, "Add that to the list of things to ask Commosky about."

A notification pinged on his security system; he glanced at the readout that popped up on his tablet. Someone was ringing his apartment doorbell. *Speak of the devil…*

"Commosky's here." Rising from his chair, Vince rounded his desk and strode to the hidden door that led back up to his apartment.

"Wow." Bella blinked a couple of times. "That was fast."

No kidding, Vince thought, as he opened the door and took the stairs two at a time. Commosky must have been 'in the area'.

Vince wasn't sure if that was a good thing or not.

CHAPTER 16

Detective Commosky barely waited for Vince to open his apartment door before he slid neatly through the doorway. Today he was dressed in civilian clothes again—dark jeans and a dark gray jacket over a green plaid button-up shirt—and he'd added a matching soft gray hat. He still had that Station Authority official look about him, but Vince had to admit Commosky had managed to tone it down at little.

Only once Vince had closed and locked the apartment door did the shorter man grace him with a curt nod. "Grable."

"Commosky."

The detective flicked his gaze around the interior of Vince's small apartment as he removed his hat and stuffed it into his jacket pocket. "Nice place." One corner of his mouth lifted in a smile, though it didn't meet his eyes. "Looks about like mine."

Meaning they both lived at the office and not at home. Vince shrugged and led the way to the staircase. "It works."

Commosky's smile turned genuine when he realized Vince's office was literally a set of stairs away. "I wondered." He trailed a hand along the wall as they descended. "I'd like this setup too."

"It does have its uses."

They emerged into the office and the detective paused to sweep a piercing look around and take everything in. Vince had no doubts he'd memorized it all and tucked it away for future reference.

Commosky's gaze landed on Bella, who was leaning back in her chair, surveying him. He stepped forward, hand outstretched, that small, genuine smile on his lips again. "Miss Escovedo."

"Detective." They shook hands over Bella's desk, and then she tilted her head to one side. "I'm surprised you remembered my name."

"Why?" Commosky snorted a laugh. "Apart from being his—" he jerked a thumb in Vince's direction, "—assistant, you're rather unforgettable in your own right." He shook his head. "I doubt a couple of my detectives will ever forget you marching into the Precinct in high dudgeon."

"Tea, Commosky?" Vince waved a hand to his drinkmaker. "I even happen to have some coffee on hand."

"Coffee would be appreciated. Thanks." Commosky stood in the center of Vince's office, his hands on his hips, as though he wasn't entirely sure what to do with himself.

Silence fell over the three of them, a rather awkward silence. Bella opted not to make awkward small talk, and so did Vince. He just fixed his guest a cup of coffee, waiting to see what the detective would do.

The airscrubber abruptly kicked on, and Commosky blinked. He turned to stare at Vince. "You have your own airscrubber?"

"Yes." Vince shrugged. "Allergies."

"On a space station?" One of Commosky's dark eyebrows lifted in surprise.

"I don't understand it either." Vince tipped his head toward the large window behind his desk, indicating Zyga Station at large. "But something in the air here bothers me."

"Never would have thought." Commosky removed his jacket and dropped it on one end of the couch.

"Here, Detective." Vince handed Commosky a steaming mug of coffee and motioned to the credenza. "Fixings are in that other basket. Help yourself."

"Thanks." Commosky stirred in a packet of sugar and then turned to take a chair opposite Vince's desk. He glanced from Vince to Bella. "So, what was so important that you couldn't finish reading my *classified* case information?" He stressed the word 'classified', as though to underscore how much of a risk he'd taken in sharing it.

Vince shared a look with Bella before allowing himself a small smile. "A conversation with somebody who's got access to something you'll appreciate."

The change in Commosky was almost instantaneous. He straightened, leaning forward with an alert, almost hungry air. "Who?"

In a few brief words, Vince explained about Brill without actually giving away the information broker's name. Commosky's hungry air sharpened into grim disapproval with every syllable.

By the time Vince finished, the detective was leaning back in his chair, a thunderous scowl etched across his craggy features. His grip on his coffee mug was so tight his knuckles were white.

"Finder," he growled, "you had *no* authority to—"

"To what?" Vince met Commosky's furious gaze head on. "Hand over classified Station Authority information?" He shook his head. "I haven't."

Yet, one corner of his mind whispered.

"Enlist help?" Vince shrugged. "This is a mutually beneficial agreement. He came to me. Just like you did, Detective. Further, at no point did you swear me to secrecy."

The two men locked gazes.

After a moment, Commosky subsided, albeit still seething. Setting his mug on Vince's desk, he folded his arms across his chest and regarded the Finder through narrowed eyes.

Clearly, Vince thought, reaching for his own tea, which had cooled considerably, *he has a problem with not being the person in control.*

That wasn't a surprise—he doubted somebody could reach the heights Commosky had achieved as a homicide detective if he didn't have a strong drive and some control issues—but it *would* make working closely together on this particular case a bigger giant pain in the neck than anticipated.

"Detective." This from Bella. Both men turned to look at her, but she fixed her gaze on Commosky. "Don't we all want the same thing? And don't you trust my boss?"

Commosky was forced to mutter a begrudging, "Yes," to both questions. Before Bella could continue, he held up a hand. "And next, you're going to ask me why we're wasting time on this, then." His thin lips twisted into something that was almost a rueful smile. "And then I'll have to admit that you are correct and that we should just get down to business"

"See?" Bella gave him a dazzling smile. "That wasn't so hard, was it?"

Commosky just grunted and reached for his coffee, but his black scowl lessened.

Vince caught Bella's eye across his desk and gave her an almost imperceptible nod of approval. *Good job.*

His assistant dropped him a wink and resumed her seat at her own desk with a quiet little rustle.

The Finder then glanced at the time. A few more minutes and Brill would be calling for his conference call. He mentally scanned through a list of possible topics he could discuss with Commosky that wouldn't need to be gone over again for Brill's benefit, but came up short.

No. That's not true. There is one question I can ask.

But first, he needed to let Brill know that Commosky would be joining them in person this morning. To that end, Vince discreetly sent a quick text.

It took the information broker a couple of minutes to respond.

Vince glanced at his comlink. ::*For the best, I think. Saves time.*::

The Finder agreed with that wholeheartedly. This was part of the reason he preferred to work alone (well, as 'alone' as one could with an assistant like Bella). He'd never liked doing anything by committee.

Now for Commosky.

Taking another sip of tea, Vince swallowed and addressed the detective. "Commosky, have you had any luck figuring out what Starlit and Lumen are after?" He lifted an eyebrow. "Other than getting you kicked off the case, that is."

The scowl etched onto Commosky's face deepened, but Vince had the sense it was directed more at the situation than anything else. "No. I've tried, but my sources are either not quite high enough—" his tone said he doubted this, "—or else they're too scared to talk." He twitched a shoulder in a restless shrug. "Not sure why."

They're thinking that if the people behind the Ruby Gauntlet can shut off the power to an entire space station, what else can they do? Vince thought, but he wisely kept this to himself. Commosky was smart enough to reach that conclusion on his own, if he cared enough to ponder the situation.

Vince's internal clock told him it was nearly time for Brill's call. He waited a few beats and then nodded to his computer terminal. "Fortunately for us, my friend should be able to answer that question."

He had a second to appreciate the startled look Commosky gave him before his computer terminal started buzzing with an encrypted incoming call.

With a brief—but fierce—swell of satisfaction, Vince tapped a button on his keyboard to allow the call. They had a space station to save.

But instead of Brill's familiar visage, a stranger's face appeared on his computer display.

CHAPTER 17

Vince blinked, taken aback as he stared at a man he'd never seen before in his life. The stranger was probably a decade older than Vince and Commosky both, with strong features. His skin, what could be seen of it behind a neatly-trimmed full golden-brown beard, was peach-colored, and he sported a full mane of wavy golden hair Vince knew at least one woman on Zyga Space Station would kill for.

Concern mixed with the tiniest smidge of panic flared to life inside the Finder's chest. Not many people could contact him via this particular method. Where was Brill? What was—

The man's light blue eyes studied each of them in turn before he tilted his head and said, "So you're Detective Commosky."

His voice was deep and scratchy—the product of a voice scrambler similar to the one Magna, another information broker Vince had worked with in the past, favored to conceal her real identity. That altered voice wasn't familiar…but the cadence was.

The knots of tension that sprung to life throughout Vince's muscles relaxed. He mentally shook his head. He should have known better than to think Brill would just show up and introduce himself. The information broker had used some sort of special security program to overlay his real features with somebody else's face.

Somebody Detective Commosky would never be able to track down aboard Zyga Station, should he ever be inclined to attempt it.

"I am." Commosky didn't move in his chair, but he suddenly seemed more alert, more…intense. "And you must be this mysterious Brill."

The bearded face in the computer display split into a cheeky grin. "That I am."

"You don't look at all like I'd imagined," Commosky said frankly.

Brill's grin widened. "We information brokers never do." He acknowledged Bella with a nod before fixing his attention on Vince. "Well?"

"Have a question for you first." Vince watched Commosky out of the corner of his eye. He wanted to see the other man's reaction. "Has your source told you what Starlit and Lumen are demanding from the Council?"

Commosky tensed, but Brill's borrowed face twisted with disgust. "Yes. For all their creativity, they really are just common criminals with big ambitions." He waved a hand—it, too, seemed to belong to a different man. "They want a casino license and immunity from any and all crimes that Station Authority might be investigating them for."

"Son of a black star," Commosky hissed through his teeth. A muscle jumped in his cheek. "They don't want much."

"Indeed," Brill said dryly.

Vince tapped his fingers thoughtfully on the jade green surface of his desk. That did seem a lot to ask. "And in return?"

"They will agree to pay Zyga Station the same percentage cut the other casinos pay, and they'll leave the Station's power grid alone."

"Ha." A harsh laugh erupted from Commosky. "That's all?"

"That's all." Brill smiled again, but this time it was all sharp edges. "From what I understand, the Council's none too pleased about it."

"I'd be shocked if they were." Commosky ground his teeth. "But they'll take it." He abruptly pushed back his chair and hurtled to his feet. He started pacing the confines of Vince's office, the expression on his craggy face thunderous.

Bella watched him, fascinated, her almond-shaped eyes wide.

Vince opened his mouth to ask another question, but Commosky suddenly stopped and whirled to point a finger at Brill's borrowed face on the computer display. "Has your source heard them discuss anything about the number of crimes Starlit and Lumen have committed? The number of people they've hurt?"

"You mean their *alleged* crimes?" Brill held Commosky's furious gaze for a few beats.

Vince hid a wince; he understood Brill's point, but this was hardly the time for a lesson in semantics. Particularly when the information broker himself was hot under the collar and neck-deep in this attempt to bring the Ruby Gauntlet's owners to justice. He mentally shook his head. It was strange hearing Brill's voice so distorted.

"Their *alleged* crimes," Commosky said through gritted teeth.

"Oh, well, in that case, I'm sure they discussed it. Right before they obviously decided to pull you from the case to keep the lights on." Brill indicated the Station around them.

Commosky clenched his hands into fists, a muscle in his jaw working again. He took a deep breath, and then he visibly relaxed and pulled himself together. One second his dark eyes were flashing and he was breathing heavily, the next he had morphed into the calm, controlled version of himself Vince was most familiar with.

The change was just a tad disturbing.

"The Council," Commosky said in a cold, level voice, "says they don't negotiate with terrorists, but in this case..." He smiled; there was nothing mirthful about the expression. "They clearly do."

"Interesting." Brill canted his head to one side again, eyes narrowed as he studied Commosky. "Nobody's made any mention of terrorists yet."

Commosky spread his hands in a mute gesture that said, *What else would you call them?*

Vince, meanwhile, considered—and then promptly rejected—the terrorist label. He stared down into the depths of his tea mug, his mind catching on the implications of Starlit and Lumen's demands and turning them around like they were a fascinating mineral specimen.

They all pointed to one thing: Starlit and Lumen wanted to *stay* aboard Zyga Station.

"They want to stay." Vince abruptly looked up from his mug to stare at Brill. "Why do they want to stay aboard this space station? Why not just..." he waved a hand, "...leave? Take their money and move their operation somewhere else?"

Brill opened his mouth to answer, but then he stopped, a strange expression on his borrowed face. He leaned forward a little, his face growing larger in Vince's computer display. "That, Finder, is an excellent question. I hadn't considered that angle."

"It's obvious." Commosky rolled his eyes, folding his arms across his chest as he leaned a hip up against the edge of Vince's jade green desk. "They have a good setup here. Why pack up and move everything if they can avoid it?"

It was a logical conclusion, but...something about it felt *wrong*. Vince's goatee bristled and he rubbed his chin thoughtfully, glancing from Commosky to Brill. No, complacency wasn't it.

A virtual empire like the Ruby Gauntlet could operate from anyplace in the galaxy that had a good ComNet connection and enough power connectors.

Vince drummed his fingers on the surface of his desk again. "It'd probably be safer for them to find another base of operations, so why—"

"It's the game itself." Bella interrupted him, her musical voice full of dawning realization. "It's all tied to *Everheart*."

All three men turned to look at Bella. She was leaning forward in her chair, her elbows propped on her desk. Her expression was hesitant, but with an underlying confidence that grew as she met Vince's gaze.

The game. Vince felt a shock of realization. *Of course.* They should have thought of that earlier. He smiled grimly at Bella, a thrill of fierce pride running through him. She was an *excellent* assistant.

Bella motioned to her tablet, shaking her head. "*Everheart* was developed here on Zyga Station, and all its servers are here. I don't know how easily they could just…move…the Ruby Gauntlet somewhere else. I think it's going to be a lot more complicated than that."

"Very astute, Ms. Escovedo." Brill offered Bella a congratulatory nod, and then his mouth quirked in chagrined smile that was half-hidden by his fake face's golden beard. "That should have occurred to me immediately." Commosky stirred and Brill held up a hand to forestall any comment the detective might have made. "I'm man enough to admit it didn't. But—"

Vince shot the information broker a knowing look. There was always a 'but'.

"I'd have thought of it eventually," Brill finished briskly, before addressing Bella again. "Any other insights you'd like to share?"

Even through the overlay he'd put on his features, Vince could see the interested gleam in Brill's eyes. He exhaled softly, his protective instinct flaring to life. He liked Brill, but that didn't mean he thought it was a good idea for Brill to show an interest in his assistant.

For her part, Bella straightened in her seat, looking excited. "Yes, actually. I've spent a lot of time going over all of the case notes and information we have on the Ruby Gauntlet." She waved to the tablet in front of her again, before looking at Commosky. "Detective, you determined that the Ruby Gauntlet had only been around for five or six years?"

"That's true." Commosky's dark eyes sharpened with keen interest. "The first reports of what I would call criminal activity—" he shot a dour look at Brill, "—don't start until about two years ago."

Vince nodded slowly. "They managed to stay under the radar for a long time."

"Yes, they did." Bella tapped a long silver fingernail on her tablet. "And per your information," she nodded to Brill, "the first whispers of the underground casino didn't start until the Ruby Gauntlet had been around for a while. So, clearly, they didn't start off breaking the law."

She tapped her tablet again. "That's why they built the Ruby Gauntlet inside *Everheart*. They didn't know they were going to end up being criminal masterminds."

"But now that they are," Commosky said slowly, giving Brill the side eye as though daring him to object, "they have a problem."

"A big problem." Vince set his now-empty mug of tea on his desk. "Their entire operation is tied to Zyga Space Station." He shook his head. "Not enough to do here with all that money."

"Except to buy real estate. Although…" Bella scrunched up her nose, "you'd think if they were making all this money in their illegal casino they wouldn't need to go to such drastic lengths to get a small handful people to pay up."

Vince's mind flashed back to the homicide reports he'd read and he shuddered, feeling as though he'd just been doused in icy cold water. No, given all the new information they had, this made perfect sense. His eyes met Commosky's, and he knew the detective was thinking the same thing.

"They have a reputation to protect, Bella." Vince swallowed, a bad taste in his mouth. "Pay up or face dire consequences."

"Just like the Families," Commosky said quietly.

Vince nodded. "Exactly like the Families." He leaned back in his chair, exhaling slowly as a number of pieces fell into place inside his head. "And now they've proved they've got the ability to hold the entire space station hostage."

He shook his head in wonder at the sheer audacity of it all. "Looks to me like they're making a play to become a third Family."

CHAPTER 18

FOR A FEW SECONDS, ABSOLUTE SILENCE FILLED Vince's office. Even the airscrubber had shut off. Commosky seemed to be holding his breath, and of course Bella didn't breathe. She just stared at Vince in horror.

As for Brill…

On Vince's computer display, the information broker's jaw visibly dropped. His mouth worked twice before he managed to find words. When he did, the deep, voice-scrambled tones of his voice sounded gobsmacked. "A *third* Family?"

"Or whatever you want to call it." Vince lifted one shoulder in a curt shrug. That part didn't matter. The important thing was that Starlit and Lumen—whoever they were—had much loftier ambitions than anybody on Zyga Station had realized.

It was his turn to shoot up from his chair and start pacing the beige carpet. His mind worked furiously, reviewing everything they knew—or thought they knew—through this new prism.

In his chair in front of Vince's desk, Commosky leaned back and stared up at the overhead. "That…makes a lot of sense." He scrubbed a frustrated hand through his short dark hair before pulling a com-link out of his pocket. "It's terrifying, but it makes sense. Why didn't I see that earlier?"

"Don't feel badly," Brill said dryly. "I don't think any of us saw that coming."

"We're not used to thinking about anybody competing with the Families." Bella tilted her head to one side. "At least, I'm not."

"Oh, you're not alone on that front." Commosky set his comlink aside to wave an impatient hand toward her. "You have all my data on that thing? Let me see it. Please," he tacked on as an afterthought. There was a tense urgency to his face, as though a maelstrom of information was swirling through his mind as well and he was reaching the same conclusions as Vince.

Bella's gaze flicked to her boss for an instant; Vince gave her a tight nod. Bella then scooped up her tablet, rose to her feet, and rounded the desk to hand it to Commosky.

The detective accepted the device with eager fingers. He'd barely set it down on Vince's desk before he was swiping through files, searching for something. Bella remained standing next to him, peering over his shoulder with great interest.

Vince finally stopped pacing to stand with his back to the jade green credenza and his drink-maker. "What are they doing with all the property they're buying up on Zyga Station?"

"That's what I'm wondering," Commosky said grimly. He huffed out a breath, giving his head a little shake of frustration. "Can't remember how many pieces of property we'd connected to them and Nasard Mutual."

"I doubt they'll keep most of it." Vince folded his arms across his chest, staring at the boulevard visible through his large window without really seeing it. "The places they *have* kept don't make much sense."

"We need to find their base of operations," Brill cut in, his scrambled voice tense. He was looking to the side, his attention on another computer display in his own office. "Even if they *weren't* looking to rival the Families—which it certainly looks like they *are*—they have to have a central location."

"Not necessarily." Commosky shrugged, a little bleakly. "The Ruby Gauntlet is online, remember? The members of their group could be anywhere—and the fact is, they're probably scattered all over Zyga Station."

"I don't think so," Bella said thoughtfully. "At least not as far as Starlit and Lumen are concerned." She motioned to her tablet in front of Commosky, but did not touch it. "From everything we've got, it looks like they're really close partners. And at this point, wouldn't it be safer for them to be able to communicate in person instead of over the ComNet?" She looked at Brill. "Even if they have really secure communications?"

"Not so secure now—" a shark's grin flashed across Brill's fake bearded face, "—but, yes, I see your point."

"Wait." Commosky perked up, like an engineering tech hearing the beep that signified life support was back online. He glared at Vince, before transferring that glare to Brill. "What do you mean?"

Brill considered the detective for a few seconds before he launched into a brief explanation of his source.

For the second time in the past hour, Commosky looked thunderstruck. "What?" He half-rose from his chair. "You have an actual source in Starlit and Lumen's inner circle?"

"It's taken time and careful cultivation, I assure you, but, yes."

"Son of a black star." Commosky sank back down in his chair, his usual jaded, no-nonsense air shaken. A hungry light came into his eyes, and then he threw back his head and laughed. "Looks like we might have a better shot than I expected."

Vince exchanged a knowing look with Brill, although it was still odd to look at the information broker and see somebody completely different looking back at him. "This is where we were hoping you could help us determine what is…legal…and what's not." He shook his head. "I'd hate to see Starlit and Lumen literally get away with murder because we went outside of protocol."

A muscle twitched in Commosky's jaw again. "That's why I haven't nailed them yet. Because I don't have enough evidence the court wouldn't promptly throw out." He glanced down at the tablet, but he'd clearly forgotten whatever he'd been looking for. A second later, he fixed Brill with a piercing look. "How in the galaxy did you cultivate a source in their inner circle?"

"Slowly," Brill said with a glib smile, but then he sobered. "As it turns out, this person has a conscience. The short version is that Starlit and Lumen went beyond what my source could live with, and he wants out."

"He?" Commosky narrowed his eyes.

"Or she." Brill grinned, but there was an edge to it. "We'll get to that part, Detective." He nodded to Vince's desk. "What were you looking for?"

"The list of properties they've bought—and the ones they've sold." Commosky looked back down at the tablet. "With all this money coming in, and the properties they're acquiring along the way, they have to actually be using some of it. Funneling it into buying property would be a good way to do that."

"And odds are good they've upgraded their living standard along the way," Vince said as he crossed his office to the drinkmaker. He needed another cup of tea. "It's a rare type of person that can come into a prolonged burst of extra income and not find a way to spend it."

"Exactly." Commosky scanned down the list of properties. "But they're good at staying under the radar, so it's unlikely to be anything too flashy."

"At least not them," Bella said from her spot beside Commosky. She folded her arms across her chest, frowning thoughtfully. "Their lieutenants, on the other hand? They might have problems with money."

"They've probably moved at some point in the last two years." Vince waved a hand without turning around to face the others as he brewed himself a cup of green tea. "Unless they really like their home or base of operations, or whatever you want to call it, that is. And probably somewhere a little nicer than they were before."

"And they probably went through Nasard Mutual to do it," Bella said.

"It's worked for them so far," Brill said. "Why fix something that isn't broken?"

Exactly, Vince thought. He stared down at the hot stream of pale liquid trickling into his mug and inhaled the light, steaming fragrance wafting off of it without fully appreciating its delicate notes. His thoughts circled from Starlit and Lumen's physical holdings on the Station back to Brill's mysterious source.

Something nagged at him. There was a connection here that they were missing…or at least, there *should* have been a connection.

"Brill." He looked over at Brill's face on his computer display. The information broker was watching Commosky, his borrowed face unreadable, but his attention snapped to Vince as soon as he said his name. "Does your source ever meet Starlit and Lumen in person, or is everything done online?"

CHAPTER 19

VINCE STIRRED A TINY DAB OF HONEY into his steaming hot tea while Brill considered this question. Anticipation filled the office as Bella and Commosky both looked expectantly at the information broker as well. It was a pivotal question.

"It's all online," Brill said at last. "Everything revolves around the Ruby Gauntlet." One corner of his bearded mouth lifted in a smirk. "Immersion gaming at its finest."

Commosky shook his head. "Never understood why somebody'd want to sit in a chair all day and pretend they were someplace else."

"Clearly, Detective, you must love your job," Brill said dryly.

Vince sucked in a breath involuntarily, a host of faces flashing through his mind, before he shot Commosky a chiding look. "Of course you can understand it, Commosky. Gaming is an escape."

He carried his tea back to his desk and sat down facing the detective, though he swiveled his chair slightly to keep Brill in view. "It's exciting, and, unlike drugs, it's not illegal."

"Most of it," Brill said sotto voce, giving Commosky a pointed look. "Sounds like Station Authority would like to make *all* of it illegal."

"Oh, no." Commosky held up both hands. "Not touching that subject. Not my department."

"Wait a minute." Bella tilted her head to one side, staring down at her tablet where it sat in front of Commosky. "I just had an idea." She motioned to the device. "May I?"

"It's yours." Commosky waved a hand.

"Thanks." Bella reached over, picked up the tablet, and swiped through a few things. "Is there any way of narrowing down where Starlit and Lumen might be?"

"We can fairly well guess where they *aren't*," Brill interjected. "If they did set up shop in the Core a few years ago, they have to be smart enough to have moved out once they started edging toward encroaching on Family territory."

Family territory. Vince froze with his mug halfway to his lips as another, more dire realization occurred to him. He swept his gaze around his office. "That's another thing. If the Families get wind that the Ruby Gauntlet is behind the power outages, they're going to be gunning for them too."

Brill laughed, but there was nothing mirthful about it. "Ah, but that's the brilliance of their little empire, Grable. The Families can't send goons after Starlit and Lumen if they can't physically track them down."

"But it still doesn't make it any easier for *us* to track them down," Commosky said in frustration. "At least not without doing all the identity tracing that I haven't been able to get a warrant to use." He paused, and Vince wondered if he was about to ask Brill if he could do it anyway.

"So they're probably not in the Core." Bella walked back around to her desk, holding the tablet. "They could possibly be in Zone 3 or Zone 4, but none of the properties that Nasard Mutual has handled in the past three years in either of those two Zones are more than pretty basic apartments."

"Basic would have worked for them in the beginning," Brill said, "but they can afford more creature comforts now, especially when they're not immersed in the Ruby Gauntlet." He shrugged, a very Brill-like expression even though he didn't look anything like himself. "I can relate to that."

"Well, then," Bella held up her tablet, "that leaves a handful of properties throughout Zones 1, 2, and 5."

Commosky shifted in his seat to look at her. "Anything on the Rim?" Some of the frustration had bled from his swarthy face, leaving behind the indomitable persistence he usually displayed.

"Surprisingly, no." Bella bit her lip. "Sorry."

"Knew it was a long shot." Commosky waved it aside. "That tells us something too—Starlit and Lumen aren't so full of themselves that they think they can run this from the Rim."

Vince had just taken a sip of hot tea. He set his mug back down on his desk and shook his head. "No, the Ruby Gauntlet is a solid operation. And there's no telling how long they've been planning this particular phase. Taking on Station Authority *and* both Families would be suicide, otherwise."

Leaning forward, he picked up his own tablet and pulled up a map of Zyga Station. He then set the tablet down in the center of his desk and tapped the screen once. Blue light blossomed out from the tablet as it rendered a three-dimensional holographic view of Zyga Station that stood half a meter high and covered most of the surface of his desk.

In miniature, the space station's resemblance to a spoked wheel was even stronger.

Vince pointed to Zone 1, Zone 2, and Zone 5 in turn. The blue hologram blurred slightly wherever he touched it. "Living on Level 1 or Level 2 of any of those three Zones would be almost as ritzy as living on the Rim itself, and draw less attention."

He glanced at Bella. "How many of those are—"

"On the top levels of each Zone?" She flashed him a cherry-red smile. "Already on it. Hang on."

"What are you thinking, Grable?"

Vince glanced sideways at Brill's strange, bearded face on his computer display. The information broker was studying him, as though attempting to read his mind. Vince shrugged, transferring his mug to his other hand. "I'm thinking there has to be a way for us to tie *Everheart* game players to physical locations on the Station."

"Oh, there is," Commosky said in disgust. "We just can't use it and have it stand up in court." Despite that grim pronouncement, the detective leaned forward to study the holographic map on Vince's desktop. "Same reason I can't ask the company to give me a list of their shareholders. Not enough evidence to get a warrant."

"There are five apartments total." Bella examined her tablet. "Two were 'acquired' from people who lost in the Diamond Room, and the other three were purchased."

"Is one of them in Zone 5?" Brill asked, his computer-scrambled voice deceptively mild despite its strange tones.

"Yes." Bella glanced up at him. "An apartment on Level 2. How did you—"

"I guessed." The information broker waved a hand on the other end of the screen. "I *have* gleaned that my source lives in Zone 5."

"You think they live on Level 2?" Commosky reached out a hand to touch Zone 5 on Vince's map and zoomed in. The rest of Zyga Space Station vanished as Zone 5 expanded across Vince's desk.

"I think it's a good bet." Brill's borrowed mouth stretched in another sharklike bearded grin. "No pun intended." His gaze transferred to Bella. "Ms. Escovedo, who bought that apartment?"

"Someone named Talia Romanoff." Bella looked up from the tablet. "Can you find out anything else about her financials?"

Commosky perked up at this, though there was a faint note of disapproval in his eyes. (No doubt the Station Authority officer in him coming out.) He tapped the tablet. "Let's look at the others."

In his pocket, Vince's comlink buzzed with an incoming call. He pulled it out to glance at the display—and felt a small electric shock go through him.

Sergeant Anita Rychek.

Her private comm, not her Station Authority frequency.

What was *this* about? Drawing his lips into a line, Vince moved toward the door that led up to his apartment. Both Bella and Commosky looked at him, but he only shook his head and brushed a hand through the air.

Universal code for: *nothing to worry about.*

Even though the way his stomach had tightened and his goatee was prickling said differently.

After all the years he'd spent as a Finder, Vince didn't believe in coincidences. When things like this happened, there was usually a reason. You just had to dig deep enough to find it.

He scrubbed a hand over his chin. Given that Rychek was calling him, he might not have to do that much digging this time. Maybe.

Either way, this didn't bode well.

CHAPTER 20

As Vince opened the door to the stairwell leading up to his apartment, a small round light in the overhead snapped on, flooding the narrow tan steps with soft golden light. The faint scent of aloe from the plant in his office mixed with the lingering smell of the eggs he'd eaten for breakfast not that long ago. Stepping inside, Vince shut the door behind him before clearing his throat and answering his comlink. "Grable."

"It's Rychek." Before Vince could respond, the sergeant barreled on. "Do you know a Detective Ron Commosky, works homicide in Zone 3?" Her voice was low, as though she was afraid she'd be overheard.

Vince narrowed his eyes, even as his stomach twisted again. That was definitely *not* a casual question. "Afternoon to you too, Rychek."

Any other day, she would have laughed, made some snappy comeback, and kept going. Today, the urgency in her voice didn't change. "I'm serious, Vince."

His eyebrows skyrocketed into his hairline. Anita Rychek didn't normally use his first name, either. "I've worked with him before, yes. The Antwerp case a while back. He was the lead investigator into the murder of my client's brother." He stared up at the closed door at the top of the stairs without seeing them. "Why? And why are you calling me on your personal comlink?"

"I'm on break," Rychek said grimly. "And this isn't an official call, it's a…" she hesitated, clearly searching for the right words. "Warning? Plea for information because what I'm hearing doesn't make any sense?"

Vince didn't answer. For one, he wasn't quite sure what to say. For another…Rychek wasn't the only one who needed more information. "What's going on?"

Rychek blew out a breath. Vince could imagine her frowning, the look in her dark eyes both serious and frustrated. "Station Authority just issued a quiet, Station-wide order to find Commosky and bring him in."

The bottom dropped out of Vince's stomach. Now *that* was a bold move.

"Ostensibly, it's for his protection, but they haven't specified *why*. And…" Rychek paused, clearly torn. "This is the part that doesn't make sense."

"I'm listening."

"If he doesn't cooperate, he's to be brought in by force."

Vince blinked, taken aback. "Sounds…a little unusual for Station Authority to handle one of your own. Does that happen often?"

"No. It doesn't."

It was his turn to hesitate, to calculate exactly how far he could push this without venturing into dangerous territory. "He's a homicide detective. Does Station Authority in Zone 3 not know where he is?"

"See…" Rychek dropped her voice even lower. "This is where things get really weird. Apparently, Commosky was put on leave yesterday. Official reason is that he has too many vacation days and needs a break."

"And unofficially?"

"Unofficially it sounds like he's in trouble, but nobody will say why. *That's* not normal. Anyway, in addition to putting him on paid leave, Station Authority posted officers to watch his apartment." Rychek paused, but Vince already knew what she was going to tell him. "This morning, it seems he gave them the slip and disappeared."

He leaned a shoulder against the smooth beige wall and propped a foot on one narrow step, thinking. "Can't say I'd want to stay in my apartment for days. Was he supposed to be confined to his home?"

"Not officially."

"So then what's the problem?" The words tasted like a lie in Vince's mouth; he thought he had a good idea of what the problem was.

"I don't know. That's why it's weird." She paused again. "But that's not even the strangest part."

Vince's eyebrows rose of their own accord again. "It gets worse?"

Instead of answering, Rychek said, "You remember the Roda case? Remember how I said I'd heard something was wrong?"

The Finder's mind flashed back to that night. Rychek had showed up at his office after hours, distraught because she'd learned both that an old friend's daughter had been kidnapped and that one of the officers she worked with had Family connections. "Yes."

"Well, my…friend…pulled me aside a little while ago. Told me a few more details about Commosky and hinted around that I needed to pass this information along to you."

Shock flooded Vince. "To *me*? Specifically?"

"Yes. The way he said it…" Rychek made a sound in the back of her throat. "He made it sound like Commosky's involved in something big and his life is in danger."

It was a good thing Vince was already leaning against the stairwell wall, because otherwise he might have fallen over in surprise. That didn't happen often—he was pretty good at rolling with the punches. But this…

He blew out a breath. "Are you saying *they're* concerned about Detective Commosky?" She'd refrained from mentioning the Families directly; he followed suit.

"That's exactly what I'm saying. Strangest damn thing I've heard in a long time. Frankly, I don't know what to make of it. Why would *they* be concerned about *him*?"

Vince bit his tongue. He had the sudden urge to tell her everything. Recruiting Rychek would make her a valuable ally.

It would also mean she didn't have plausible deniability for anything that happened after this point. She was a good Station Authority officer; he didn't want to do that unless he absolutely had to.

"Must be connected to one of his cases," he said at last.

Rychek huffed. "Doesn't take a genius to see that, Grable. But a case big enough that *they* or at least one of *them* is concerned about it? In a *good* way?"

"That *is* weird."

A pause. Then a suspicious, "You know something, don't you?"

Suppressing a sigh, Vince shifted his position to press his back against the wall and let his head fall backward. "Rychek…"

"I know, I know. You Finders and your angles. I won't ask. But…" she paused again. This time, the space that stretched between them seemed heavier, with grim undertones seeping into it.

"No," she said at last. "It's crazy."

Despite himself, a smiled curved Vince's lips. Rychek had fantastic instincts. And ethics. Part of the reason he admired her. She was one of the very few Station Authority officers he actually enjoyed working with.

He tried to keep the smile from his voice as he said, "Won't know until you ask. And you're running out of break time, aren't you?"

Rychek huffed again. "It *is* crazy. But…" She took an audible deep breath, and then lowered her voice even further. "Do you think there's a possibility this is connected to…you know…from yesterday?"

A swell of pride warmed Vince's chest. Oh, he liked this woman. "It's certainly odd timing, isn't it?"

A non-answer, but she was more than smart enough to read between the lines.

"Yes, it is."

Another pause fell between them, this time more contemplative. A silence between friends mulling over the same bizarre situation.

"Well…" Rychek roused herself, her voice brisk, though still low. "If for some strange reason you happen to run in Commosky somewhere, tell him his boss wants him to check in with his protective detail."

"Will do."

"Stay out of trouble, Finder."

It was her usual farewell.

"You too."

For a moment, after Rychek ended the transmission, Vince remained leaning against the stairwell wall. Rychek didn't know it—and he couldn't tell her—but she'd just illuminated a whole new range of possibilities he hadn't even considered yet.

CHAPTER 21

WHEN VINCE REENTERED HIS OFFICE, QUIETLY CLOSING the door to the stairs behind him, Bella looked over in his direction. Her face was oddly blank, but the way she tilted her head to the side a fraction told him she'd overheard at least part of his conversation. The Finder suppressed a resigned chuckle. Trust the overly acute hearing her android body provided her to kick in at that moment.

Rychek had no way of knowing her call had coincided with his airscrubber shutting itself off. Not that it was a big deal. Vince had learned over the past few months of working with her that Bella could be quite discreet.

Yet another reason Vince was glad he'd hired her.

His assistant raised both of her elegant black eyebrows in a silent question. She wouldn't flat out ask him who'd called in front of Commosky and Brill unless he wanted her to.

Vince shook his head imperceptibly. *No.* He wanted a few minutes to chew this new information over, to make sense of it in his own head before he shared it with the others.

Unfortunately, that wasn't in the cards.

Not when his partners in this investigation were a bulldog homicide detective and a nosy information broker. Both Brill and Commosky immediately gave him their full attention.

"Who—" Commosky began

"—was that?" Brill finished.

Vince huffed a laugh, running a hand over his close-shorn black hair. "Friend of mine in Station Authority here in Zone 5." He flicked his gaze toward Bella in time to see her dark eyes widen in realization. His assistant quickly schooled her features back into curiosity, before the other two could notice.

"Apparently, Station Authority has noticed you aren't home." Vince pinned Commosky with a half-amused, half-exasperated look before he returned to his desk and sank down into his chair. "They're not too happy about it."

Commosky's answering scowl was as black as his shaggy eyebrows.

In a few short sentences, Vince filled them in on the contents of his conversation with Rychek. By the time he finished, Commosky's scowl had deepened into something truly formidable.

"Good thing I left my work comlink at home," he said in disgust.

Brill, however, looked as though this was the best piece of news he'd heard all morning. He rubbed his hands together, his fingers twitching as though they couldn't wait to start dancing over his keyboard. "This is good. No, really, it is," he said, as Commosky shot him a withering look. "At least one of the Families has noticed something is wrong. And they've correctly assessed that you, Commosky, are important to fixing this problem."

"Eliminates any worries about them wanting you out of the way for some reason." Vince launched to his feet and began pacing his office. As comfortable as his chair was, he couldn't sit still now. He felt energized, as though his conversation with Rychek had been an electric shock delivered directly to his veins.

He whirled to face Commosky. "I think it also means that the answer to this is somewhere in your case file." He swept a dark hand toward his desk, indicating the information Commosky had given them. "You've got something that is key to unlocking all of this." He narrowed his eyes in satisfaction. "Otherwise, they wouldn't have gone to the trouble of shutting power off to parts of the Station to get you removed from the case."

A flash of something that could have been hope shone through a few cracks in Commosky's stony facade. "I don't know what I've got, then, clearly." His mouth turned down at the corners. "Otherwise I'd have nailed them to the bulkhead months ago."

"Only because your hands are legally tied." This from Brill, who seemed alight with the same electric energy Vince felt. The two men locked eyes through the computer display and Vince had the sudden sense that he and the information broker were on exactly the same wavelength.

Bella held up a hand. "This may be a dumb question—"

Vince shot her a look. "We've talked about this, Bella."

In the Finder business, there was no such thing as a dumb question. Sometimes, you couldn't see the asteroid field for the asteroids. So-called dumb questions had a way of bringing the obvious back into perspective.

"Okay, okay." This time, Bella held both hands. "Sorry, Boss. *Not a dumb question.*" She almost rolled her eyes at him, but restrained herself at the last second. "It's just—" She twitched both shoulders in a shrug. "If Starlit and Lumen are making a play to become a new Family, don't they need a bunch of minions?" She fluttered long, slender fingers. "Lots of people to do their bidding and support them and look up to them, blah blah blah?"

"That's usually how it works." Commosky straightened in his chair, a small measure of his disgusted attitude falling away.

"So where are their minions?" Bella spread her hands, looking around at all three men. "Surely they can't all be people online." She jerked a thumb over her shoulder. "*Somebody* is going around the Station terrorizing the families of people who've lost everything in the Diamond Room. *Somebody* murdered those people."

"Could have been Starlit or Lumen themselves," Vince said, nodding, "but I doubt it."

"No," Brill said thoughtfully. "I think they think they're above such things themselves now. Clearly, they have people for that. In fact—"

Without warning, the power cut out, plunging Vince's office into darkness. Brill's face disappeared from the computer display as both the power and a connection to the ComNet died.

In the darkness, Vince felt his feet leave the deck. Gravity had stopped working again. He looked across his desk, though he couldn't see anyone in the pitch blackness. "I could be wrong, Commosky, but I think Starlit and Lumen found out you're AWOL."

CHAPTER 22

THE POWER OUTAGE LASTED LONGER THIS TIME. Once again, Zyga Station's backup emergency system kicked on immediately, restoring lights, life-control, and gravity, but it took the Engineering techs in the Core a good fifteen minutes to restore the main power.

Bella switched both of Vince's large holoprojectors back to the media stations, but it was obvious within the first few seconds that the media was as clueless to what was happening as the general public.

Vince could only stomach watching them for a couple of minutes before he muted the sound. Those news anchors talked a lot, but there was nothing of substance in all those words.

"If this keeps up," he said irritably, picking up his poor aloe plant again, which had floated off its little stand and hit the beige carpet for the third time that day, "I'm going to need to rearrange my office."

Another of the plant's leaves had snapped off in the fall, filling his office with the smell of aloe again. Vince threw the broken leaf away, grimacing at the waste. As he turned around, he glanced over at Commosky, but the stocky man wasn't paying attention.

The detective had resumed pacing the small office, the set of his jaws and shoulder practically screaming tension. His gaze had turned inward, wrestling with something only he could see.

Vince returned to his desk and his gaze fell on his computer display. Brill hadn't called back yet. The Finder wasn't sure what to make of that.

He'd have expected Brill to immediately reconnect, not wanting to miss anything, but… Vince sat down in his desk chair, which, as always, immediately conformed to the contours of his body, and reached across his desk to pull his tablet in front of him.

It's probably nothing, he told himself. Brill had any number of clients, and something had probably come up that required his immediate attention.

"Boss!"

Vince's head snapped up. The tone of Bella's voice—sharp and shocked—sent a surge of adrenaline coursing through him.

Commosky, too, reacted. He stopped pacing, shifting toward Bella and automatically scanning for the source of the problem.

Vince's assistant wasn't looking at either of them, however. She stared, wide-eyed, at the still-muted holoprojector to her right.

Vince's gaze snapped to it as well. He drew in a short breath.

Commosky's face was staring back at them.

"Mute off," Vince said sharply.

Sound flooded the office. "…Authority officials in Zone 3 have issued a missing person's report for Detective Ron Commosky." The news anchor stared into the cam, his dark eyes full of manufactured concern. "The detective was last seen at his apartment in Zone 3. Station Authority is asking that anyone with any information about Detective Commosky's whereabouts please come forward."

"Ha!" A laugh exploded out of Commosky, but there was nothing mirthful about it. He sounded incredulous—and angry. "I'm missing now, am I?"

The news anchor listed a comm frequency where tipsters could send information and then briefly lauded Commosky's achievements in the homicide department. He then returned to the main news story at hand, and Commosky held up a hand. "Turn it off. I can't listen to any more of that."

Bella complied, her heart-shaped face thoughtful. She drummed her long silver fingernails on the surface of her desk, before shooting Vince a wry look. "Don't you have to be missing for at least twenty-four hours before somebody can file a missing person's report?"

"Usually." Commosky answered before Vince could speak. His thin lips twisted with a bitter smile. "It's brilliant, really." He threw his hands into the air. "A Station-wide Authority alert wasn't good enough? Now they have to recruit civilians? How am I supposed to get anything done if they've got the entire blasted Station looking for me?"

It *was* odd. Vince's goatee bristled; he stroked his chin thoughtfully. *You'd think making him stop and putting him under surveillance would have been good enough.*

The Finder studied Commosky, noting the unhappy slant to the other man's mouth, the frustrated set of his jaw. Then he looked down at his tablet—

—which was full of Commosky's case notes and other case information.

The answer slotted into place like a shiny new gear fitting into its home inside a newly-constructed piece of machinery.

"They're terrified."

"What?" Commosky almost laughed again, but the serious expression on Vince's face drew him up short. His anger faded, to be replaced with his usual keen intensity.

Oh, it made *perfect* sense. "They're not just afraid of you staying on this case, they're afraid of what you know." Vince leaned forward in his chair to stare directly at Commosky. "Think about it. They pulled this stunt—" he waved a hand to indicate the station at large, "—to get you off the case. Off their backs."

"There's clearly more to it than that," Commosky said dryly.

"Of course there is. But that?" Vince jabbed a finger in the direction of his holoprojector. "*That* tells me that you are a *serious* threat to them."

"The answer has to be somewhere in your case files." Bella bounced a little in her seat out of sheer excitement.

"I don't know." Commosky pressed his lips into a line, looking dubious. "I've been over them a hundred times." He waved a hand toward Vince and Bella. "You've been over them too, and all we've found today is a possible line on apartments."

"Don't discount that." Vince smiled sharply. "You of all people, Detective, should know that one of the best ways to solve a mystery is to follow the money."

"That's going to be a little difficult if I can't leave this office without somebody recognizing me." Commosky slumped back in his chair, and then chuffed a bitter laugh. "I hunt killers down for a living. Some of them walk around as bold as they can be. Others hole up and hope they can hide long enough to escape." He shook his head. "Never thought I'd be hiding out myself."

Bella shot him a sympathetic look. "It'll be temporary, Detective." She smiled reassuringly. "We'll get them."

Commosky didn't look convinced. He just frowned and slouched down in his chair a little more, his expression dark and brooding.

"Well." Bella pulled her large black purse out from the desk drawer where she usually kept it and rose to her feet. Slinging the straps over her shoulder, she looked at Vince. "Boss, I'm going to go pick up lunch."

Vince hadn't even realized how late it had gotten. He nodded and glanced at Commosky. "What—"

The detective beat him to it. "Thanks, but I'm not hungry." He held up a hand. "Plus, it's not a good idea for you two to deviate from your usual routine. Bringing back three meals will be suspicious."

Oh, if only you knew, Commosky, Vince thought

Bella put a hand on her hips. "You need to eat, Detective. And don't worry about me—I've got that part all figured out."

"Best just to say yes," Vince said in an undertone, tipping his head toward the other man. "Easier in the long run. She won't give up."

That was another of the qualities he'd come to admire in his assistant.

Commosky puffed up a little, like he intended to argue, but then his stomach audibly growled. He deflated, smiling ruefully. "All right, Ms. Escovedo." He held up a hand. "I surrender."

Bella bestowed him with a sunny smile. "Good." She proceeded to collect their lunch orders for one of Vince's favorite cafés down the street, but paused on her way out the door. "Let me know if anything exciting happens while I'm gone, Boss."

Vince inclined his head in a slight nod of acknowledgement. Once the door had shut behind Bella's slim form, he addressed Commosky. "As aggravating as this is for you, I think it's actually a good sign."

Folding his arms across his chest, Commosky blew out a breath. "I know," he said reluctantly. "If it was happening to anybody else in my department, I'd be rubbing my hands together in glee and telling them to sit tight while we double down on the investigation."

He snorted. "I suppose I should feel flattered that they consider me enough of a threat to actually shut the Station's power off. *That's* certainly never happened during an investigation before."

Vince lifted an eyebrow. Those words were tinged with a wry sense of humor. He hadn't thought Commosky *had* a sense of humor.

That thought was promptly followed by another—one that made him sit up straight, his goatee tingling. "How *did* they know how close you were getting?"

Commosky started to answer, but then stopped, cocking his head to one side as he considered the question. "They must have followed the Antwerp case. Particularly when I tried to get a warrant to find out *Everheart* players' real identities."

"And then they proceeded to keep an eye on you from there." Vince nodded thoughtfully. He pursed his lips, not wanting to say this next part, but at this point Commosky had to be thinking it. He fixed the detective with a piercing look. "You know they've probably got eyes and ears in your department."

"Among other places throughout Station Authority." Commosky looked like he'd just bitten into a rotten piece of fruit. "The sad thing is that until we take them down, I can't find out who they are."

"The answer to all of this is in your case information." Vince brought his tablet back to life. "We just have to find it and put it all together."

Commosky retrieved Bella's tablet. "Looks like I'll be hunkering down here for the time being." He shook his head. "I have a go bag stored in Zone 3 for emergencies, but…" He shrugged, a little prosaically.

Vince waved a hand in a wordless acknowledgement. Hard to retrieve a go bag when the Station's entire population was on the lookout for you because they thought you were in trouble.

"We're close. I can feel it."

Commosky drew his lips into a line. "I hope you're right."

CHAPTER 23

As the day wore on, Vince kept anticipating the buzzing sound that meant he had an incoming encrypted call from Brill. They'd been in the middle of something big, and at this point Brill was just as invested as the rest of them. Unfortunately, the information broker never called back.

Vince considered contacting him instead, but decided to hold off a little while longer. Brill *did* have other clients. Besides, if he was in the middle of something big involving the Ruby Gauntlet, there was a chance Commosky might need plausible deniability.

Bella had returned with lunch—minestrone soup and vegetable subs with a basil and oregano olive oil drizzle Vince loved—and both he and Commosky tucked in with gratitude. The food, combined with another cup of black tea, served to refresh Vince's brain. He turned back to Commosky's data with a sense of renewed purpose.

Currently, they were examining the four remaining apartments the Ruby Gauntlet owned on Levels 1 and 2 in Zones 1 and 2. Vince leaned forward in his chair behind his desk, trying to figure out which of the apartments was the ritziest.

"Nice places," Commosky noted, propping his hands on his hips as he surveyed the holographic map of Zone 1 and Zone 2 suspended above the jade green surface of Vince's desk.

"Really nice places." Bella leaned against the side of the desk, looking a little wistful. "I'd have loved to live there once."

Vince didn't think anything of that comment, but Commosky sent Bella a strange, sideways glance. "And you don't anymore because…?"

Completely unruffled, Bella waved a hand. "I've moved on. In another life, maybe." She twitched one shoulder in a shrug, before leaning over Vince's desk to tap on Zone 2. The map zoomed in and expanded to show a top-down view starting at Level 1.

She pointed to one apartment in particular, located between the elevator bank and the Rim, on the starboard side of the Level. "I think this is probably the nicest one. According to Nasard Mutual's records, a woman named Jasmine Nerhti bought it about six months ago."

"It would be nice, being on Level 1," Commosky said gruffly. He started to reach for his work comlink, before remembering he didn't have that one with him. He'd done that more than once since his arrival. His fingers clenched into a fist before he scowled and forcibly relaxed. "Not used to being on leave."

"Understandable. I'll get it." Vince swiveled his chair to his computer terminal and pulled up Zyga Station's information directory to verify that Nasard Mutual's sales record matched Zyga Station's data.

It did.

He then ran a quick search on the databases available to him as a Finder. Seconds later, he put everything he had up on his computer display.

"Wow." Bella blinked a couple of times. "She is not what I expected."

Commosky eyed the woman's date of birth. "Older that I expected." He shook his head. "I've thought for a while this was a younger crew."

Vince scrutinized the face staring back at them from his computer display. Jasmine Nerhti was not smiling in this official ident-card holo still (Zyga Station didn't let anybody smile), and the thin line she'd pressed her wide mouth into made her look grumpy and just this side of homely. Coppery bronze curls framed her round face.

If Vince had to guess, he suspected Jasmine probably considered her dark eyes to be her best feature. They were surprisingly large and stood out against her golden brown skin, making her look a few years younger. He scanned through the rest of her information—among other things, she was short, standing only 153 centimeters tall—and then glanced at the others.

"That's one thing I've learned over the years." He nodded to his computer display. "When gaming and the ComNet are involved, nothing is as it seems."

Commosky moved around Vince's desk to read over the Finder's shoulder. "No arrest record. Not married."

"Doesn't mean she's not in a relationship," Bella noted.

"No. Just means she's in control of all her finances." Commosky folded his arms across his chest, his dark eyes glittering with interest.

Vince absently rubbed his chin, staring at Jasmine's face while he fit all of this information into what he already knew. "If she's Starlit, then where is Lumen?" He gestured to the computer display. "They might not be a husband and wife team, but they're definitely working closely together."

"There's an apartment on Level 2 that could belong to Lumen." Bella touched the holographic map, drilling down to the next level. The holographic blue lines shimmered and then reformed into Level 2.

She indicated a spot not far from the heart of Level 2. "It's in an expensive apartment complex a couple of blocks from the main elevator bank. I'd say it's the second-nicest, next to Jasmine's."

Vince studied the apartment. "Who owns this?"

Bella consulted her notes. "Renji Kino. I've already looked him up." She swiped a finger on her tablet and sent the information to the holoprojector to her right.

Vince and Commosky both studied the man who appeared there. Renji Kino was over a decade younger than Jasmine, but judging by his vital stats, he had a good thirty centimeters on her and easily twenty kilograms. Even in his Station holo still, his blocky build was obvious. He bore a good resemblance to a human wall—if walls came with messy black hair, narrowed black eyes, and ivory skin.

Vince tipped his head toward the detective without taking his eyes off the holoprojector. "He's more what you were expecting."

He meant it in regards to Kino's age, but Commosky had fixated on something else.

"You can always tell the gamers." The detective made a sound in the back of his throat. "They spend too much time in chairs."

"Some of them, maybe." Vince thought back to all the people he'd Found over the course of his career. "Not all of them. They're like anybody who works a desk job." He lifted a shoulder in a shrug. "Depends on how much they take care of themselves."

"Yeah, well, this guy?" Commosky jabbed a finger toward the holoprojector. "This guy will not be easy to take down single-handed." He shook his head, frowning. "Not without a stunner or something. Too big."

Bella frowned at him before glancing sideways at Vince and raising her eyebrows in a question. The gesture was a little too exaggerated, but the Finder got her point.

He nodded in response. Yes, Commosky was anticipating them taking Starlit and Lumen down.

If, in fact, Jasmine Nerhti and Renji Kino were the owners of the Ruby Gauntlet.

CHAPTER 24

As afternoon bled into evening, Vince, Bella, and Commosky moved on to potential members of Starlit and Lumen's inner circle. Bella put up three more names and faces on Vince's holoprojectors. A twenty-something young woman from Zone 3, a man from Zone 2 who was around Jasmine's age, and a man from Zone 1 who was Vince's age.

The three of them worked their way through all five names. They started with Jasmine and Renji, before making their way down the rest of the list. Vince worked his way through several more cups of tea as well, and Commosky drank another cup of coffee. Bella pretended to drink water.

"You know," Vince said at last, standing up and rolling his shoulders to get the kinks out of them. "The remarkable thing about all five of these people is that there is nothing remarkable about them. At least not in person." He waved to the holoprojectors. "They keep to themselves, and none of them seems to have much of a social life."

"At least outside the ComNet," Bella said thoughtfully from where she'd ended up perched on the corner of Vince's desk, next to the holographic layout of Zone 1 still covering it. "They're probably pretty active online."

"Oh, no," Commosky said dryly. "Nothing remarkable about them at all except the fact that they're all living in relatively nice apartments and none of them seem to have jobs that pay enough for them to have purchased said relatively nice apartments."

"There is that." Vince picked up his mug and drained the rest of it. This last cup had been a light, refreshing white tea he sometimes forgot he had.

Commosky looked at Bella before motioning to the holographic map. "Take this back to Level 1, would you?"

"Sure."

Bella obliged and the blue holographic contours of Level 2 blurred and then shifted, blocky apartment complexes melting into the spacious open air lines of Level 1.

Commosky leaned in closer to the desk. "Can you magnify the area around Jasmine Nerhti's apartment?"

The holographic layout shifted again, providing a much better view of Jasmine's ritzy apartment. Like most living quarters on Level 1, it had wide windows that provided an excellent view of both the surrounding area, with its beautiful potted trees and careful landscaping, and the vast black expanse of space beyond the clear synthglass enclosing the top of Zone 1.

Vince eyed the apartment as well. "What are you thinking, Commosky?"

The detective did not answer for a moment. Then he looked up and met Vince's eyes. "I'm thinking we need to figure out a way to get in there and investigate." He jabbed a finger in the apartment's general direction. "It's possible that Lumen is the real brains of this operation, but I've always had a feeling Starlit is the one in charge. If Jasmine Nerhti is Starlit and Renji Kino is Lumen, I'd bet a week's pay they're living together and Kino only visits his own apartment occasionally."

Despite the gravity of the situation, Vince couldn't quite restrain a smile. "You'd *bet*, Detective?" He lifted a black eyebrow. "Isn't gambling what put the Ruby Gauntlet on the fast-track to where they are now?"

"You know what I mean." Commosky shot him a withering look, while Bella hid a smile behind a pale, long-fingered hand. Then, frowning, the detective looked back down at the holographic layout spread across the jade green desk. "We need a reason to get in there."

Vince transferred his gaze back to the holographic representation of the apartment as well, unconsciously mirroring the detective's frown. He understood Commosky's reasoning, but…something niggled in the back of his mind. Something about the inner workings of online games and their connection to the ComNet.

I need Brill for this, he thought with a flicker of annoyance. He tended to deal with the real world, not the virtual one, and in this case, what he—and Commosky—didn't know about the situation could probably fill the storage capacity of Bella's tablet.

But Vince was reasonably sure that Jasmine's ritzy apartment was not the Ruby Gauntlet's physical nexus. Too splashy. Too…unprotected.

Swiveling in his chair, the Finder brought his computer terminal back to life. Whatever Brill had spent the day working on, he could take a five minute break.

"What are you doing?" Commosky's voice was sharp and suspicious.

"Calling my information broker." Vince did not turn around. "He—"

A sharp gasp from Bella drew both men's attention to her. Bella mutely waved her comlink, her eyes wide with shock, and then she lunged for the nearest holoprojector.

Renji Kino's face disappeared, to be replaced by a face Vince knew well. Ninti Akawaga, one of Zyga Station's best news reporters. His best contact at Zyga Station News, in fact, the woman he'd first talked to back when he'd uncovered the *Juggernaut* conspiracy months ago.

"…breaking news story." Ninti Akawaga faced the cams, the expression on her smooth mocha face calmly concerned. She wore a bright purple pantsuit today, and her long black hair was a riot of curls. "We have received reports from credible inside sources that the abnormal blackouts Zyga Station has experienced today are in fact the work of a group attempting to put pressure on the Council for their own means."

Bella gasped again, the sound echoing the hitch in Vince's own throat. He stared at Ninti, feeling a curious settling inside his brain.

"What the—" Commosky rose from his seat. He half-squinted, half-glared at the holoprojector. "How can she possibly have found that out?" He transferred his glare to Vince. "Do you think your friend—"

"No," Vince said automatically, but then he paused, considering it. Brill *had* been angry about Starlit and Lumen putting everyone on Zyga Station at risk. Putting *him* at risk.

But angry enough to leak the situation to the media? No. Vince gave his head a mental shake. That was too bold, too direct, for somebody like Brill.

"…standing outside the Council's office on the Rim." Ninti swept a hand toward the side and the cam followed the gesture to three ornate white marble steps leading up to an equally ornate pair of double doors with elaborate metal curlicue overlays before returning to her face. "I'm sure I am not the only person aboard this space station who would like answers. The people of Zyga Station have a right to know if our lives and our children's lives are being threatened by a terrorist group."

A piece clicked into place inside Vince's mind. He chuckled, before breaking out into a full belly laugh. Commosky and Bella both turned to regard him, the one irritated and the other concerned for his sanity.

The Finder pointed to the holoprojector. "This has the Families written all over it." His grin was so wide it made his cheeks hurt. "They don't like what Starlit and Lumen have done and this is their way of making sure everybody knows about it. Council or no Council."

He dissolved into laughter again. It felt good to laugh, even if the circumstances were less than ideal.

Bella shook her head, her almond-shaped wide with something that was almost awe. "It's brilliant."

"It's demented, that's what it is." Commosky shoved back his chair and started pacing the narrow confines of Vince's office again. The energy rolling off of him in waves gave the distinct impression that at any second he might very well start climbing the walls to gain a little more legroom.

The detective locked his hands behind his head, his expression thunderous. "What is this going to accomplish other than to drag everybody into a three—no, make that *four*—four-way fight?"

Vince just chuckled again and swiveled back around to his computer terminal, ignoring the complaints. Deep down, he knew Commosky already knew the answer to that.

This? This was just the detective venting because the situation kept unraveling like a cheap sweater that had gotten snagged on a sharp corner and he was helpless to do anything about it at the moment.

Brill answered his secure comm channel call on the second buzz. His subterfuge overlay was still in place, but at this point the sight of his fake bearded persona didn't even faze the Finder.

"I take it you're seeing this," Vince said in lieu of greeting. He waved an arm to indicate the holoprojector behind him without actually bothering to look at it.

"Oh, yes." Brill's fake bearded face split in a grin reminiscent of the one Vince himself had sported just a moment before and the information broker actually rubbed his hands together. "Haven't had this much fun since…well, that's not relevant." He brushed the thought aside with an impatient flick of his fingers. "What is it?"

"Thought you would have called back before now, instead of leaving us hanging," Commosky growled over Vince's shoulder before the Finder could speak. The stocky detective had come to a halt behind Vince's chair.

Brill fixed Commosky with an unreadable look. "Some of us aren't off work for the duration, Detective."

Commosky made a disgusted sound in the back of his throat, but Vince held up a hand. "Sit down, Commosky. Brill." He gave the information broker an admonishing look. "Let's remember we're all working toward the same goal here."

He didn't wait for Commosky to settle back in his seat before he continued, "We think we've found Starlit and Lumen's real-world locations."

"Or at least Starlit's apartment on Level 1," Bella put in.

"Let me guess." Brill cocked his head, before rattling off an apartment address. "That the one?"

Vince had a split second to feel shocked. Then a dangerous grin split his face. "Good to have some confirmation."

"I've been quite busy," Brill said primly, ignoring Commosky. "I suppose then, that you've identified Jasmine and Kenji as possible suspects?"

"Yes." Vince leaned forward a little. "I was hoping you might have found out a little more about them."

"I have, but I don't know that it helps us at the moment." Brill waved a hand. "Mere corroboration." This time, he did look at Commosky. "The sort of thing that'll help you build a case later."

"Sounds like you've got nothing, then." Commosky folded his arms across his chest. "A fat lot of good your source on the inside did."

Brill narrowed his eyes. He wasn't physically present, but Vince could have sworn the temperature inside his office dropped a few degrees. "I'm getting to that, Detective."

"Boss," Bella said suddenly, the bell-like tones of her voice holding an urgency that drew all three men's attention to her. "Look."

She pointed to the holoprojector on the right. The holo still of Commosky's head and shoulders in his gray and crimson Station Authority uniform stared back at them.

This time, the tickertape at the bottom displayed the words: *SUSPECTED FOUL PLAY INVOLVED.*

CHAPTER 25

Bella unmuted the sound on the holoprojector and the dulcet, concerned tones of a female news anchor flooded Vince's office. The four of them listened in growing astonishment.

"…search continues for Detective Ron Commosky, a homicide detective in Zone 3. Detective Commosky disappeared from his home this morning and Station Authority now believes foul play may be at involved. Station Authority requests that anyone with any information regarding the detective's whereabouts please—"

"Turn it off," Commosky said hoarsely.

Bella's gaze flicked to Vince. He nodded imperceptibly and Bella muted the holoprojector again. For a few seconds, no one spoke. The only sound was Vince's airscrubber, which had been running in the background.

All eyes were on Commosky, however. The detective had bowed his head, a muscle in his jaw working. Vince could practically see the gears in his head spinning with a dozen different scenarios and possibilities.

The airscrubber shut off just as Commosky shoved his chair back from Vince's desk and rocketed to his feet. "I can't stay here."

He started pacing again the beige carpet again, but this time his movements were controlled instead of frenetic. He reminded Vince of holos he'd seen of animals in zoos on other worlds. Instead of the harried, panicked dashing back and forth of something being hunted, it was the look of something pacing the confines of its cage, searching for a way out,

All at once, Commosky stopped and whirled back around to face Vince. "If I'm such a serious threat to the Ruby Gauntlet that they've plastered me all over the ComNet," he said grimly, "then they've got somebody searching Zyga Station's cams for me."

He shook his head. "Doesn't matter if it's their people or they've conned the Council into using Station Authority resources. I'm pretty good, but they'll find me and they'll track me here." He spread his hands, a small, bitter smile playing on his lips. "Apart from bringing me in, it'll put you and Ms. Escovedo in an awkward position *and* it'll jeopardize what we're trying to do here."

Vince waved that aside. "Occasionally all in a day's work for a Finder." He did give the detective a chiding look, however. "You might have a better understanding now of why I operate the way I do on occasion."

Commosky inclined his head in the barest of nods.

"I notice," Brill said, his voice very dry, "that you don't seem concerned about me, Detective."

"You don't seem the sort who'd be in any danger from an operation like this," Commosky returned. "You'll have already taken steps to protect yourself."

Vince kept himself from rolling his eyes with a great effort. Commosky was right, but they didn't exactly have time for this. "I suggest you settle this later," he said curtly. "Commosky, I understand your reasoning, but where do you think you're going to go?

If they manage to trace you here, don't you think they'll trace you from here to wherever you go next?"

From the suddenly wary look that shuttered Commosky's face, Vince knew he'd hit a nerve. The detective didn't exactly *have* a plan—other than he knew he needed to *go now*.

Vince swiveled his chair to face Brill again. The nascent idea that had been forming in his mind, coalescing out of bits of information, took on solid lines and contours. He jabbed a finger in the direction of the blue holographic map still hovering patiently above his jade green desk. "Jasmine or Starlit, or whatever her name is, might live in a swanky apartment on Level 1, but I'd be willing to bet—" he flashed a wry smile over his shoulder at Commosky, who was still pacing, "—that's not the heart of their operation."

His gaze met Brill's, and an understanding passed between them. Brill inclined his head in the barest of nods—a note of congratulations.

"I had the same thought," the information broker admitted. "In fact, this is what I've spent a good chunk of time on today."

"We need to find their server," Vince explained to Bella and Commosky. "The Ruby Gauntlet was built into the *Everheart* game, but it runs on its own server. If we can find that..." He trailed off, a host of possibilities opening up before his mind's eye.

Commosky actually stopped pacing and stood stock-still, as though this revelation had shut his internal power off.

Good, Vince thought. *He needs a little shaking up to get his head back on straight.* Aloud, he said, "It'll be housed somewhere discreet. Somewhere relatively obscure and protected." He held up a hand palm out. "Somewhere nobody would think to look because it doesn't draw attention to itself."

"Oh!" Bella snatched her tablet up again and made a few quick swipes. She then excitedly turned the device around to show it to Vince. "You mean someplace like an apartment in the middle of Level 9 in Zone 2?"

CHAPTER 26

A QUICK, FIERCE SMILE LIT VINCE'S FACE. HE scrutinized the layout Bella was showing him. "Exactly like an apartment in the middle of Level 9 in Zone 2."

"That's…perfect." On the computer display, Brill shook his head, as though he couldn't believe he hadn't found that himself yet. "Absolutely perfect. Who owns it?"

Bella glanced back down at the tablet in her hands. "Letitia Theriot."

"Letitia Theriot?" Brill's tone abruptly sharpened. "Are you sure?"

"Yes." Bella shifted slightly to see him better on the computer display. "She—"

"I know who she is." The information broker's gaze shifted to Vince. "She's my source," he said bluntly, his mouth twisting as though he'd bitten into something foul. "Just managed to worm her name out of her. She failed to mention her apartment houses the flipping *server*."

"Remember," Vince said, shaking his head, "we don't know this for sure." He glanced at Bella, his expression thoughtful. "It's a good working assumption, but we won't know until we dig further."

Commosky's hand twitched, again reaching for a comlink he didn't have.

"You know…" Brill eyed Bella. "I've never wanted an assistant until now." He shook his head, his expression a mix between impressed and crestfallen. "Whatever he's paying you, Ms. Escovedo, I'll double it."

A brief flash of panic flooded Vince, followed by a tightening in his chest. He couldn't afford to double Bella's salary. She was worth every credit though.

Before he could think of a response, Bella beat him to it. Posting one hand on her hip, she arched an imperious eyebrow at Brill. "Attempting to poach your colleague's employees, are you?"

"Is it working?" Brill asked shamelessly. He leaned a little closer to his computer display, making his borrowed bearded face loom larger. "I've said it before, but anybody Vince Grable thinks is worth hiring is definitely a keeper."

"And I'll keep her," Vince interjected. He nodded to Bella. "As long as she'll work for me."

"Sorry." Bella offered Brill a sunny smile and a shrug. "I happen to like my job."

Commosky made an irritated sound in the back of his throat. "Can we get back on track? We're wasting time." He drew himself up to his full height, the keen spark in his eyes flaring back to life now that they had a Plan. (Or at least *something* to work towards.) "It never occurred to me that the server and Starlit and Lumen's locations might be two different places."

He shook his head slightly. "We were always more focused on finding their actual physical location. Figured if we could locate them, we'd find everything else we needed."

"Not surprising," Brill said thoughtfully, "given that you're a homicide detective looking for actual people. But this?" He circled a finger in the air. "This is my realm of expertise."

"Then start talking." Commosky glared at Brill, his black eyebrows furrowing and making him look like a thundercloud again. "We don't have time for this. *I* don't have time for this."

"Commosky," Vince began, glancing sideways at the detective, but other man ignored him.

"Are you *positive* this Letitia person is your source?" Commosky continued to glare at Brill. "The way things are shaping up, we'll probably only get one shot at this. Are you *sure*?"

That…was actually a good question. Vince leaned against the side of his desk, the edge poking into his hip, and folded his arms across his chest. He glanced at Bella, who was still clutching her tablet. Her dark eyes flicked back and forth between Commosky and Brill.

The tension was palpable. Vince felt it stretching through the molecules of air filling his office, wrapping sticky tendrils around each of them and sinking hooks into their muscles. Time was running out.

Figuratively, they were poised to jump out of the hangar bay into the vastness of space—and they had to make sure they had a cord tethering them to the Station so they wouldn't just keep falling forever.

But Commosky was right—they didn't have time for this.

Vince cleared his throat. "Detective, Brill gave us her name earlier." He nodded to Brill's bearded face on the computer display. "He doesn't do that if he doesn't have the info to back it up."

"I've been cultivating her for a while now." Brill sounded grumpy. Sometimes he was touchy about the verification of the veracity of his information.

Vince couldn't exactly blame him for that.

"Had to ask." Commosky held up both hands, though he was still frowning. "In my line of work, you have to have proof and solid evidence, remember?"

"Let's just say I'm ninety-nine percent sure and leave it at that."
Brill deliberately looked away from the detective to address Vince.
"Ms. Theriot might have failed to mention the server, but she *does*
want out. The direction Starlit and Lumen are taking the Ruby
Gauntlet scares her. I believe she'll help us."

"Understandable." Vince nodded, rubbing his hands together. A
surge of adrenaline coursed through him, setting his heart to beating
a little faster than usual.

Finally. After a day spent sifting through information and putting puzzle pieces together, a chance for some action.

He addressed Brill again. "If we find the server, we've got them.
Right?"

"Well…" Brill hesitated. "It's not that simple." He shook his head.
"It's not enough to find the server. We have to be able to access it. If
we can do *that*…then we have them."

"Are you thinking of trying to shut it down?" Vince raised a
skeptical eyebrow. If so, that was a bold move—bolder than they
probably had any chance of pulling off.

"Oh, no." Brill waved a hand. "No point. They've advanced far
enough that they've got at least one backup server somewhere else
in case the main server goes down. Probably two or three, if they're
smart."

"Then what are we doing?" Commosky growled, crossing his
arms over his chest. "How are we doing to get the physical evidence
we need?"

Brill graced him with a beatific smile that looked strange on his
bearded face. "We're doing something better." His smile widened.
"We're going to have Ms. Theriot install a back door."

Vince sucked in a breath. *Oh, boy.* He glanced sideways at Bella,
to find her looking back at him, with wide eyes.

"What—" Commosky began, his voice rising, but Brill held up
a hand.

"Have to make a call. Back soon." He abruptly severed the encrypted comm connection.

133

CHAPTER 27

Brill's idea of 'back soon' turned out to be a solid hour and a half. Commosky was practically climbing the walls of Vince's office by that time, and Vince wasn't far behind him. The forced inactivity, coupled with the fact that every minute that slipped past brought the Ruby Gauntlet and Station Authority another minute closer to tracking Commosky down, wore on them heavily.

Only Bella seemed mostly unaffected by the delay. Though, to be honestly, that was mainly because she had buried herself in yet another review of Commosky's data.

Vince had just fixed himself another cup of tea (not that he needed it; he'd lost count of how many cups he'd drunk today) and was debating whether or not to stir any of his precious honey into it when it happened. The now-familiar sound of someone calling him through an encrypted channel broke the stillness filling his small office like an oppressive invisible cloud.

The change in the atmosphere was immediate—and electric. Commosky, who had finally collapsed on the couch, dropped the tablet he'd been studying and sprang to his feet.

Bella straightened, her entire posture alert.

For his part, Vince nearly forgot his freshly-brewed tea in his haste to cross his office. He managed to slosh some of the steaming liquid onto his hand, but he barely registered the burn. This was it.

He could feel it in his bones—and in his goatee, which had startled prickly madly.

As soon as Vince tapped a command into his keyboard and answered the call, Brill's face filled his computer display. At this point, the sight of the information broker's bearded borrowed face seemed entirely natural.

"Took some doing," Brill announced cheerfully, "but I'm happy to report I talked Ms. Theriot into it."

Vince and Bella exchanged glances, before they both looked over at Commosky. They'd discussed exactly what Brill's idea of a 'back door' entailed, but they hadn't quite been able to figure out what part Vince and Commosky would play.

"In case you're wondering," Brill continued blithely, "the plan is simple. You're going to go to Ms. Theriot's apartment and hand her a datachip containing a little something I put together for just this occasion. She'll then use that to get me access to the Ruby Gauntlet's server."

Ah. That made sense. Vince nodded to himself, his eyes narrowing thoughtfully at Brill's face on his computer display. He'd been wondering exactly that would work.

Commosky made a scoffing sound. "We're just going to walk in there and hand her a datachip?" He started pacing again, running a hand over his short dark hair. "That's it? *That's* your grand plan?"

"What, did you think you'd just be able to walk in and walk out with a server computer?" Brill raised an eyebrow, his tone acerbic. "You're forgetting you don't have a warrant, Detective. You'd just be arrested as a common thief." His voice dropped to low, icy tones. "And in addition to screwing up your own investigation, you'd also make it almost impossible to nail Starlit and Lumen for what they've done."

"I don't like it," Commosky said bluntly, whirling to face them all. "This whole thing rests on a *datachip* and your—" he pointed a finger at Brill's face on the holoscreen, "—assurance that this Letitia Theriot will cooperate."

"She will."

"You still don't *know* that." Commosky glared at him. "This whole thing could be an elaborate trap."

Vince stirred, hard-pressed to keep from rolling his eyes. Hell of a time for Commosky to go paranoid on him.

"In that case," he said briskly, "you can stay here, Detective. I'll go by myself."

As he'd expected, his words caught Commosky off-guard, snapping him out of whatever strange funk he'd just fallen into. The detective's jaw dropped a little, and then he clenched his teeth. "That won't be necessary," he ground out.

Vince continued to eye him. "Don't let this get to you, Commosky. We're too close. Besides…" He quirked an eyebrow. "I don't see any other options, do you?"

A long pause ensued while Commosky considered this. He didn't seem to care that they were all staring at him. Finally, he exhaled in a long rush and his shoulders deflated as some of his tension bled out.

"Not legal ones," he admitted. "At least not until I get put back on the case."

Bella offered him an encouraging smile. "This is a good idea, Detective. If you get Letitia Theriot that datachip, she can help us get everything we need to take Starlit and Lumen down. And then—"

Her face abruptly screwed into a frown, as though she'd just thought of something truly disturbing. Bella turned that frown on Brill. "What happens to Letitia after she helps us?"

That same thought had just occurred to Vince. He, too, looked at Brill.

"Ah, well," Brill had the grace to look slightly abashed. "I was going to mention this, but you beat me to it, Ms. Escovedo." He glanced at Vince and then Commosky in turn. "There's one more component to this plan."

"Of course there is," Commosky growled, his dark eyes flashing with irritation. He sliced a hand through the air. "It'd be too much for you to give us everything straight, now, wouldn't it?"

Any other day, Vince would have come to Brill's defense. As it was, he stared at Brill, one hand on his chin. "Should have known there was more to this plan than that," he said grimly. "Just delivering a datachip? Way too easy."

"Yes, well, I was getting to it." Brill dismissed their irritation with a flick of his fingers. "Besides, I didn't even know this would *be* the plan until after I spoke to Ms. Theriot. Honestly," he added to Bella, who was glaring at him, her arms folded across her chest.

Tension flooded the office again, until Vince felt his muscles were so tight the slightest movement would snap them. He deliberately took a breath and let it out, forcing himself to relax. Then he sank down into his office chair and reached for his tea. "Better start from the beginning, Brill," he advised. "And this time, give it to us straight."

"It's quite simple." Brill lifted his shoulders in a prosaic shrug. "I convinced Ms. Theriot to install the datachip to grant me server access. She's even agreed to turn Station's evidence—"

Out of the corner of his eye, Vince saw Commosky's eyes widen in shock.

"—but in return, she wants us to help her escape from her apartment and find a safe place to stay until she can talk to the right people." Brill pursed his lips. "I really was going to get to that part."

Silence fell over Vince's office again while he, Commosky, and Bella respectively considered this.

For his part, Vince leaned back in his chair, absently reaching for his tea. He took a sip of the strong, black brew without really tasting it. *Stars. Nothing like subterfuge and a rescue mission all rolled into one.*

He took another sip. There was really only one option. Setting his tea aside, he abruptly leaned forward, meeting Brill's gaze through his computer display.

"Well, it doesn't sound like she's kidding about wanting out. We'll have to work quickly." The Finder looked at Commosky before addressing Brill again. "The clock starts ticking once she installs the stuff on that datachip, doesn't it?"

"Yes. Once she lets me know it's done, we'll have to work out a way to get her out of there." Brill scrunched his bearded face into an expression that was almost apologetic. "No estimate on the time frame, unfortunately."

"Of course not," Commosky muttered. "That'd be too easy." he frowned, his gaze drifting off in the direction of the front door beside Bella's desk. "We have to get this right," he said at last. "If Starlit and Lumen catch Letitia, they won't hesitate to kill her. Not at this point." He drew his lips into a line. "No matter how valuable she is to them."

"Brill." Another thought struck Vince; he looked abruptly at Brill again. "How are we going to get this datachip from you?"

"That would be where Ms. Escovedo comes into play." Brill inclined his head toward Bella. "You've got blank datachips handy, I hope?"

"Hold on." Bella rummaged in her desk drawer, before waving a small package in the air. "Yes. They're right here."

Brill glanced at Vince, and it was his turn to lift a questioning eyebrow. Vince nodded once and the information broker turned his attention back to Bella. "I'm going to send you an encrypted file, and I need you to do exactly as I say."

"I can do that." Bella straightened up in her seat, looking fierce and determined.

"As soon as that's ready," Vince nodded to Bella, "we'll get out of here, Commosky."

Commosky nodded, his dark eyes contemplative. "It would be best if nobody traced me to this office. But…" he frowned. "If somebody *is* watching you too, how are we going to keep from leading them right to Letitia Theriot?"

"Don't worry about that." Vince waved a hand, a knowing smile tugging at his lips. He glanced at Bella, who was prepping the data-chip. "We'll go see Mrs. Kawana first."

At the sound of that name, Bella's head popped up. "Oh!" Her almond-shaped eyes widened in realization, and then her pretty red lips curved in a broad smile. "That's perfect, Boss! Nobody will suspect that."

Vince nodded. To Brill and Commosky, he said, "I have a new client who lives on Level 8 in Zone 2."

He didn't wait for their matching dawning looks of comprehension. Instead, he downed the last of his now-cold tea and rose to his feet. A surge of energy rushed through him, making his goatee prickle again.

This *would* work.

CHAPTER 28

Beside the entrance to Mrs. Kawana's apartment, a small wreath made of an artificial spray of cherry blossoms hung just below the lock panel. Vince eyed that wreath as he reached out and tapped the intercom button on the panel. Some people couldn't help themselves—they had to decorate everything. Even if they lived on a space station.

It figured his latest client would be one of those people.

Level 8 was a mix of apartment building blocks and rows of living quarters that faced the corridors and larger boulevards criss-crossing the level and dividing it into organized sections. A couple of small cafés and eateries were scattered throughout Level 8, but for the most part, residents here had to take the main elevator bank to go up to another Level to buy food.

That meant that the air smelled a little different here than on other levels—there were fewer faint traces of food scents permeating this part of Zyga Station and more…human smells. Laundry deter-gent. Soap. Perfume and cologne.

And, on occasion, body odor from someone who *really* needed a shower.

Vince and Detective Commosky had passed one such individual a little while earlier. The stench had lent new purpose to both their strides.

Now, Commosky shifted on his feet beside Vince. The Finder had done his best to help the detective alter his appearance a little—just enough to hopefully throw Zyga Station security cams off. It hadn't been easy.

Vince didn't mind letting Commosky in on a few of his secrets—lifts for his shoes to make him look taller, extra padding under shirts to make him look bigger or more out of shape, and so on. Those were all things Vince used only occasionally, in the instances when he needed to make himself look different than even his usual unobtrusive appearance.

The real difficulty had been altering the contours of Commosky's face. His skin was swarthy, but he was still lighter than Vince. Most of the makeup Vince used on the rare occasions he applied prosthetics to his face was much too dark for the detective.

They'd almost had to give up and hope they could move fast enough that they could deal with Mrs. Kawana and reach Level 9 before Station Authority caught up with them, and then Vince had remembered he had another box of disguise makeup. It had been left over from a case he'd worked a few years earlier that had involved, ironically, keeping a young man from being found by the Bok Family until he could make it off-Station.

It wasn't the best disguise job Vince had ever done, but it would work. At least for a little while.

So far, they'd made it out of Zone 5, through the Hub to Zone 2, and up to Level 8 without any trouble. Commosky had left first, through Vince's apartment, and then Vince had departed his office a few minutes later. They had met at the elevator bank and traveled together from there.

Commosky had also removed his jacket and left it at Vince's office. He'd shaken his head when Vince asked him if he'd get cold without it. "I'll be all right." He'd then eyed Vince, who was putting his brown leather jacket back on. "Never seen you without that."

Vince had just shrugged. "I get cold," he'd said simply, and left it at that.

They lived aboard a space station, after all. Even with over a million human beings packed into Zyga Space Station, space was cold. Vince had always imagined that icy, freezing cold seeped into the very metal that held Zyga Space Station together.

"Yes?" Mrs. Kawana's high-pitched voice floated out of the intercom.

"Finder Grable, Mrs. Kawana."

The door immediately slid aside. Vince had called her earlier to let her know he was coming, and Mrs. Kawana must have been standing on the other side of the door, waiting for them. She was a petite, slender woman, barely more than a meter tall, but her size was no indication of the force of her personality.

Mrs. Kawana wrung her hands together, staring up at Vince with wide, worried eyes. Her thin face had almost an elfin quality to it. Blunt cut black bangs swept across her forehead before blending into her chin-length bob. "Thank you for coming!" She bowed her head. Then her gaze transferred to Commosky, and her worry visibly shaded into suspicion.

Vince hadn't mentioned him—deliberately.

"This is an associate of mine," Vince said, before she could voice the question brewing in her eyes. "New to the Finder business and asked to shadow me for a case or two." He nodded to Mrs. Kawana. "Everything is still perfectly confidential. Paperwork, you know."

He didn't look at Commosky to see if the detective maintained a straight face. They'd been over this already on the way here. Commosky didn't like the idea of posing as a newbie Finder, but...he didn't exactly have many other options.

The idea of Commosky filling out confidentiality paperwork in order to shadow Vince seemed to mollify Mrs. Kawana. The suspicion in her eyes faded, to be replaced with worry and a kind of anxious expectancy.

Vince wasn't exactly sure what it was about signing paperwork that comforted people, but it did. Case in point.

Mrs. Kawana stepped aside, gesturing with delicate, bird-like flutters of her hands for them to join her inside her apartment.

As soon as Commosky's stocky frame cleared the doorway, Mrs. Kawana tapped the lock panel and the door slid shut. The busy sounds of people moving up and down the corridor outside vanished, to be replaced with clear, bell-like tones of a simple melody playing in the background. Her apartment smelled like lavender, with a faint undertone of ginger and sesame oil. It was an odd combination, but not as jarring as Vince would have expected.

The Finder glanced around quickly, appraising his surroundings with a professional eye. He stood with Commosky in the middle of a small living area, which gave him a strong first impression of being stuck in a cherry tree surrounded by blossoms. The bulkheads were a faint, delicate shade of pink, and the carpet beneath their feet was so white Vince was almost afraid to take another step on it.

On one side of the room, a couch and two chairs upholstered in pale silver covered in sprays of cherry blossoms were arranged around a dark wooden coffee table, while a matching tall bookshelf filled with strange little knickknacks stood on the other side next to a large holoprojector mounted on the wall. A tranquil picture of an avenue lined with pink cherry blossoms on some unknown planet currently filled the display.

A glance through the doorway leading into the kitchen on the right and a glance down the hall jutting off to the left showed more of the same. Mrs. Kawana was a widow; Vince wondered if her decor predated her loss of her husband, or if this was how she'd chosen to redecorate after losing him so as to make moving forward a little easier. He also wondered how his client managed to keep everything so pristine.

After a second, he glanced sideways at Commosky to see what he thought. The stocky detective, his face currently unrecognizable as his own, was doing his own appraisal. He met Vince's gaze briefly, but his black eyes gave no indication as to what he was thinking.

"Please sit down." Mrs. Kawana gestured gracefully to the couch. She herself practically floated over to one of the chairs and sank into it as though she weighed no more than a feather. Her outfit matched her decor—a white long-sleeved cardigan over a pale green blouse and a silver skirt that almost blended right into her chair.

She barely waited for Vince and Commosky to ease themselves into seats before blurting out, "Have you found it yet? My grandmother's sculpture?"

Vince suppressed a wince. This was the tricky part of their plan. He had not yet, in fact, located the missing sculpture.

What he *had* determined, however, was that this sculpture meant more to Mrs. Kawana then your usual family heirloom. She was worried enough about it that his gut sense was that something else was going on with it.

What that might be, he didn't yet have a clue, but something was definitely off.

His goatee bristled; the Finder resisted the urge to rub his chin. Instead, he settled back against the surprisingly comfortable cushioned couch and offered Mrs. Kawana a frank, quizzical look. "I haven't found it yet."

He always hated this part. Telling clients bad news was never fun. The way the anxious hope died in Mrs. Kawana's face, her body visibly wilting, made something twist in his chest. It always did that. He'd just learned how to cope with it.

"Mrs. Kawana," Vince leaned forward in his seat, resting his elbows on his knees. He kept his expression gentle and open. "I have the distinct sense that you are not telling me something about this sculpture. Something important."

"It belonged to my grandmother." Tears flooded his client's high-pitched voice. "It's all I have left of her. She practically raised me."

It was a good story, but Vince's gut told him to keep digging. "Is that all?" He raised an eyebrow.

"Of course it is." Mrs. Kawana tried to huff, tried to act like it was absurd for Vince to even be questioning her, but when he just continued to look at her, his expression frank and unwavering, something crumpled in her face.

Tears spilling down her cheeks, she buried her face in her hands and mumbled something incoherent.

Now it was Commosky's turn to lean forward. One eyebrow was cocked, as though he couldn't quite believe what he thought he'd heard.

Vince was right with him on that one.

"What was that?" he asked, at the same time as Commosky said, "What?"

Mrs. Kawana dropped her hands, but she didn't lift her gaze from her lap. "There's a secret compartment. It's got a datachip that has video of me and my late husband." Her fingers twisted into the fabric of her skirt. "In...ah...in bed."

CHAPTER 29

Sympathetic understanding flooded Vince. *Oh.* One corner of his mouth quirked in what could have been a wry smile, if he'd let it live.

That…was not the sort of thing most people wanted others stumbling across. It also explained Mrs. Kawana's emotional reaction to the loss.

Aloud, he said, "I see."

"It—it was just the one time, you see." Two bright spots of color had appeared high in Mrs. Kawana's thin, ivory cheeks. "A whim, my husband had one night." She lifted one cardigan-clad shoulder in a shrug. "We'd been married a few years and he wanted to do something…daring. Something new." She almost smiled. "Afterward, we couldn't believe we'd done it. And then…when I lost him…" She shrugged again. "I couldn't bring myself to get rid of it. He was—we were so…*happy.*"

"So you hid it," Commosky said, his rumbling voice a little gentler than it had been earlier.

"I did." Mrs. Kawana tried to laugh, but it came out as more of a sob. "In my grandmother's sculpture. It was supposed to be safe there. I never dreamed—" She broke off, shaking her head in mute distress.

"How much is it worth?" Commosky looked from Mrs. Kawana to Vince. "The sculpture itself, I mean?"

"Thousand credits, easy." It was Vince's turn to shake his head. Mrs. Kawana had been forthcoming about that part. "Antique. Over seventy-five years old."

The Finder surveyed his client again, a thoughtful frown creasing his forehead. In the back of his mind, he felt that sense of urgency pushing him to just *leave* and go hunt down the Ruby Gauntlet's server room. But, this was a delicate situation.

And Mrs. Kawana *was* his client. His obligation to her predated this mess with Commosky and the Ruby Gauntlet. (At least, this *particular* stage of the mess with Commosky and the Ruby Gauntlet.)

Speaking of which, the woman was still in tears. He had to deflect that before it got worse, or they'd lose more time trying to calm her down.

Vince took a breath of lavender, ginger, and sesame oil-infused air and exhaled slowly, letting the gentle tones of Mrs. Kawana's background music wash over him. He forced himself to clear his mind, forced himself to push all thoughts of Starlit and Lumen aside. They would get to that.

Then he leaned forward and put a hand out toward his client. "Mrs. Kawana." He gentled his voice even further. "It would have been…helpful…if you had imparted this information to me earlier."

"I know." She sniffed and then brushed a tear away with the cuff of her sleeve. "I just—I didn't know how to say it."

"That's understandable." He paused. "Do you have any reason to believe anyone else knew about that datachip?"

Mrs. Kawana automatically began shaking her dark head, but then she paused, seriously considering it. After a few beats, she looked at Vince and shook her head again. "No. We didn't tell any-one. My husband—my husband kept our private life private." She half-smiled. "He wasn't one of those men who over-shared." Her smile turned tremulous. "It was ours. Just ours."

Vince nodded. That was the impression he had gotten, but he had to ask. You never knew.

"So it was probably taken by someone who has no idea about the compartment and what's inside." Commosky leaned forward as well.

Vince suppressed a smile. This might not be a homicide inves-tigation, but it *was* a puzzle and Commosky *was* a detective. Clearly, the man couldn't help himself.

"Who had access to your apartment during the time it went missing?" Commosky gruffly cleared his throat before tipping his head toward Vince. "Finder Grable has shared a few details with me, but we haven't had time to go over everything." He offered Mrs. Kawana a slight smile that softened the still-hard contours of his dis-guised face. "Besides, sometimes retelling a story brings back details you might have forgotten or overlooked the first time around."

Mrs. Kawana nodded, twining her fingers together in her lap. She stared down at the white carpet by her feet for a moment, and then began to explain. Her voice started out low and halting, but picked up speed and volume with every word.

She'd put in a maintenance call some days before for an issue with a broken glowpanel in her kitchen that she couldn't fix. The day of the theft, a woman from Maintenance had finally arrived and fixed the problem.

Only trouble was, after she left, Mrs. Kawana's sculpture had been gone too.

"I contacted Maintenance and this woman denies that she took my sculpture." Mrs. Kawana's grip on her fingers tightened even fur-ther. "I explained that she wouldn't be in any trouble, I just wanted it back because it was my grandmother's. She still denied it, rather emphatically, and that was when Maintenance told me to take it up with Station Authority." She lifted her thin shoulders in a helpless shrug. "They told me to file a report, but they couldn't guarantee that anything would come of it. Petty theft. Not very important, in the grand scheme of things."

The sadness in her voice touched Vince's heart. Situations like this were why he did what he did. He flicked a glance in Commosky's direction, to see how he was taking this criticism of Station Authority.

The detective's somber expression hadn't changed, except perhaps to tighten a little around his eyes. "It's true. Not much they can do about things like that sometimes." It was his turn to lift a shoulder in a shrug. "Too much petty theft on Zyga Station." He nodded to Vince. "Which would be why you called Finder Grable."

"Yes." Mrs. Kawana turned watery, hopeful eyes on Vince. "Please, Finder, please tell me you at least have *something*."

Vince could feel Commosky's eyes on him too. His gut twisted uncomfortably. He didn't have much for her, but he wished he did. He could hardly tell this poor woman that the only reason they were sitting here was because they were using her case as a front to conceal their real objective.

"I have feelers out in the usual black market for things like this." Before Mrs. Kawana's hopeful expression could morph into crestfallen disappointment, he added quickly, "I wanted to find out what else you weren't telling me about this, in case worst comes to worst."

"Which would be?" Mrs. Kawana asked in little more than whisper.

"Worst case is I can't retrieve the statue but I get you the money it was sold for." That had happened a few times over the course of his career. Of those four clients, only one had been completely dissatisfied and unwilling to accept monetary compensation. Most of the time, Vince had found money ultimately trumped sentimental value.

Even before he saw the look on her face, he knew that would not be the case here.

The Finder didn't blame Mrs. Kawana, either. If he'd lost a beloved spouse and someone had stolen a memory like that, he'd want to move space and stars to get it back too.

He met his client's teary gaze. "Are you still good with not pressing charges against the thief if I manage to recover the sculpture?"

Mrs. Kawana hesitated a few seconds, before nodding emphatically.

"All right. That may help." Vince rose to his feet and then inclined his head toward his client in a courteous nod. "Thank you. I'll be in touch."

Commosky rose to his feet as well, and Mrs. Kawana followed suit, wringing her hands together again.

"That's—that's it?" She bit her lip, before turning pleading eyes on Vince. "That's all you have for me?"

"That's all I have for you." Vince offered her a slight smile; he didn't want her breaking down in tears again. "Just needed more background information."

Mrs. Kawana bit down on her thin bottom lip, but she nodded and, more importantly, she didn't cry. She just fluttered along behind Vince and Commosky as they headed back to the front door.

Just before they exited, Commosky turned back to the small woman. "He'll get it back." He jerked his chin to indicate Vince. "Best Finder I know."

Mrs. Kawana's small, tremulous smile was the last thing Vince saw before her apartment door slid shut behind them.

CHAPTER 30

Dᴇᴛᴇᴄᴛɪᴠᴇ Cᴏᴍᴍᴏsᴋʏ ᴅɪᴅɴ'ᴛ sᴘᴇᴀᴋ ᴀɢᴀɪɴ ᴜɴᴛɪʟ ʜᴇ and Vince had exited the elevator bank on Level 9 and turned off the main boulevard that bisected the level to work their way toward the block that held Letitia Theriot's apartment building. This late in the afternoon, traffic was nothing more than a thin trickle of pedestrians streamed back and forth around them.

"Think you can find actually find that sculpture?" Commosky managed to raise an eyebrow at Vince while simultaneously keeping his head down a little to prevent the cams mounted at various points throughout the Station's corridors from getting a good look at his face. "Sounds like the thief has had plenty of time to get rid of it."

"Maybe." Vince lifted one shoulder in a shrug. The air here held more of a metallic smell than one of food at the moment. "Mrs. Kawana realized it was missing fast enough that this Cordero woman might not have had time to do more than stash it someplace safe."

That was his gut sense, actually. Annette Cordero, the maintenance worker, might be gutsy enough to swipe valuables from the apartments she was supposed to be helping maintain, but like most petty thieves he'd encountered over the years, she probably had a healthy sense of self-preservation. Unless she was absolutely desperate, she'd lay low for a couple of days—just long enough to let the initial fuss die down. Then, she'd fence the sculpture and get it off her hands.

The Finder frowned, absently raising a hand to rub his chin. His goatee was tingling. Beneath the part of his brain that was actively engaged in solving the Ruby Gauntlet problem, another part of his brain was eagerly sorting through options for dealing with this thief.

He shook his head. "I'd go hunt her down now, if time allowed."

"It doesn't."

Vince directed a frown at the shorter, stockier man. "You would say that."

"Hey." Commosky half-lifted a hand, though he didn't look at Vince. His dark gaze continued to sweep the sidewalks and the assorted doors lining both sides of the corridor here, assessing potential threats and problems. "Let's keep our priorities in order. The Station's safety trumps one petty theft."

"Haven't forgotten." Vince consulted his internal map. They were coming up on an intersection, and Letitia's apartment complex was down two corridors to the left. He cut across the corridor at the intersection and Commosky easily kept pace. "Just looking at it from a time management perspective."

The detective snorted as they turned left down a new corridor that was lined with nothing but entrances to apartment complexes. "You think you could get her to cooperate that fast?"

Vince took a half-second to consider. Could he? He inclined his head in a nod. "I do."

This time, Commosky huffed a laugh. "You would say that." He then shook his head. "Have to say, I almost believe you."

That wasn't worth dignifying with a response. Instead, Vince repressed the instinct to roll his eyes and kept walking.

As apartment complexes on Zyga Station went, most of ones on this Level were solidly middle-class. They featured enclosed, sound-buffered courtyards that had a few trees, some shrubs, and maybe some benches so residents could sit and pretend for a moment that they didn't live on a space station orbiting a gas giant. Most of them also had play equipment for children.

On the outside, colorful murals covered the apartment complexes' walls, turning what would have otherwise been a drab gray metal corridor into a series of bright, uplifting splashes of color. Each apartment complex had its own mural, or series of murals. Each complex's name was embedded in a mural somewhere, amidst ribbons of color, landscapes, or fanciful drawings of people working together.

Letitia Theriot lived in an apartment complex called Sunset Dreams. The reason for this name became evident as soon as Vince and Commosky neared it. Vince actually stopped walking for a second to take it in. Beside him, the homicide detective slowed as well, canting his head to one side as he also studied the mural.

"That," Vince said in quiet awe, "was painted by someone who's been on a planet and witnessed an actual sunset."

"What makes you think that?" Commosky glanced from the mural to Vince and back. "Could have been done by somebody working from a holo."

Vince considered that, before shaking his head. "No."

He didn't know how to explain it to the detective. Commosky had, as far as Vince knew, been born on Zyga Station and had never left. He'd never seen a real sunset, seen the variety of reds, oranges, and pinks that shaded the sky, before they darkened into lavenders and blues along the edges of the horizon. Technically, a sunset was just light reflecting off of clouds and pollutants in the atmosphere, but there was a majestic quality to each and every one.

The person who had painted this mural understood that.

Vince wanted to reach out and touch it, wanted to trace his fingers over the swathes of orange and pink covering the middle part of the wall. The words Sunset Dreams had been painted just below the golden setting sun in a three-dimensional matching golden yellow script outlined in black.

Compared to the murals on either side, it looked a little newer, as though it had been done more recently.

"It's pretty," Commosky conceded at last, eyeing the mural again. Then he raised an eyebrow at Vince, as though the Finder had just revealed he had a second head. "Not the time to get distracted. Got a job to do, remember?"

"Didn't forget." Vince resumed walking along the sidewalk again, his pace brisk. "Just have to appreciate art sometimes."

"You can appreciate it all you want when this is through." Commosky kept his voice low, but his warning tone was crystal clear. "Don't lose focus on me now, Finder."

It wasn't that.

Vince lifted a hand to his face; his goatee had started bristling again. The Sunset Dreams apartment complex occupied a corner block; they had to turn the corner and walk down another corridor to reach the entrance to the courtyard. The Finder cast one last look over his shoulder at the mural.

The artwork triggered something in his brain, but he couldn't quite remember what it was. The thought, or memory, or whatever it was, hovered in his brain, just out of reach.

Had he seen artwork like that before? If so, where?

They neared the open doorway that served as the entrance to the Sunset Dreams' courtyard, and Vince pushed thoughts of the artwork out of his mind. Commosky was right; they didn't have time for this right now. But he *would* come back to it later.

Something told him it was important…he just didn't know how or why.

At least, not yet.

CHAPTER 31

THE SUNSET DREAMS APARTMENT COMPLEX, VINCE DISCOVERED, was one of the few that did not cater to children. When he and Commosky passed through the open doorway that led into the courtyard, they found a large, airy space with a handful of shrubs in pots and a couple of copper-brown benches arranged beneath a trio of small ornamental trees in the corner that had been pruned to resemble green globes. Someone had thoughtfully laid out pathways in alternating shades of cream and tan tile to wind from the entrance through the courtyard to the trees and benches and up to the main entrance.

Once upon a time, Vince had lived in a city built on an actual planet and had seen apartment complexes there. It sometimes seemed strange to him that the architects of Zyga Space Station had chosen to duplicate that particular housing model here. But, as he looked at the windows and the small balconies that looked out on this enclosed courtyard, he supposed he couldn't blame them for trying to give people a small semblance of privacy and keep things from being quite so compartmentalized.

At this time of day, the courtyard was empty, save for an elderly woman who sat reading on a bench in the corner of the courtyard, beneath one of the globe-like trees. She glanced at Vince and Commosky with narrowed eyes, her dark gaze assessing them much the same way Commosky had been assessing their surroundings since the second they left Vince's office.

The Finder met her suspicious gaze, offering her a courteous nod.

After a second, the elderly woman nodded back and then returned to her datapad. Clearly, she didn't recognize them, but she'd dismissed them as possible threats. Threats weren't usually polite.

"Bet she knows every face in this place," Commosky said under his breath, as they strode up the tiled walkway to the main entrance. He darted a discreet, imperceptible glance in her direction.

"Probably," Vince replied, just as quietly. It was universal; every place he'd ever been had at least one person like that. In fact…

Struck by a sudden thought, he abruptly broke away to approach the old woman. He could practically feel the glare Commosky directed at his retreating back, but he ignored it. His instincts were screaming at him that the artwork was important somehow.

He had no idea how, much less to which case, let alone anything else, but…his gut seldom led him the wrong way.

"Excuse me," Vince said with a polite smile as he neared the elderly woman.

She had looked up from her datapad the second he started across the courtyard toward her, eying him with a frankness that would have scared a lesser man. Her light brown face was lined with wrinkles, and her long, silver hair hung loose around her shoulders in a cascade of curls, but her brown eyes narrowed at him in scrutiny. She raised an imperious brow in silent acknowledgment of his interruption.

"Do you know who painted the sunset mural?" Vince jerked a thumb over his shoulder in the general direction of the mural on the other side of the apartment complex.

The woman eyed him a second longer. Finally, she tilted her head ever so slightly to one side and uttered a single word. "Why?"

"It's phenomenal." Vince shook his head in appreciation. "Absolutely phenomenal. I think I've seen another piece of this artist's work, but I can't remember where it was. I'd like to find more." He tipped his head over his shoulder toward the main entrance. "Does he or she live here?"

"No." The woman shifted in her seat, her posture seeming to unbend a little. "And I don't know much about the artist, other than the fact it was a woman. Landlord hired her a few months ago." She lifted one bony shoulder in a careless shrug. "Kept to herself, did an amazing job, and then left. That was all."

That was all.

It wasn't nearly enough.

Especially since Vince didn't even know why the sunset mural had caught his interest the way it had. He inclined his head in a courteous nod. "Thank you."

The elderly woman waved his thanks away with a flick of her fingers, before returning to her reading.

Vince kept his senses attuned to her while he strode back to Commosky, who was waiting rather impatiently for him, but the old woman didn't seem to be paying them any further attention. That was good—if nothing else, his little inquiry about the sunset mural had killed any further suspicions she might have otherwise harbored.

"What in the stars was *that* all about?" Commosky muttered under his breath, shooting Vince a sideways glance out of the corner of his eye. "We're wasting time."

"Wasn't wasted," Vince said, but he did not elaborate further. Instead, he stretched out a hand to the panel mounted beside the smooth one-way synthglass door and tapped the intercom button. The lock panel prompted him to enter an apartment number, which he did.

Beside him, Commosky shifted on his feet. The detective was careful to keep his posture relaxed and avoid resembling an uptight Station Authority officer, but Vince could feel the tension rolling off of him in waves.

He almost told the detective to relax, but before he'd even had the chance to open his mouth, a husky woman's voice emerged from the intercom panel.

"Hello?"

Vince peered at the doorpanel, but the small holoscreen beside the intercom remained dark and blank. He knew the doorpanel allowed Letitia to see him in the matching screen set in the doorpanel beside her front door, but clearly she had no intentions of returning the favor.

"Are you Letitia Theriot?" He didn't wait for an answer, but continued, "We're here about your last Maintenance request, ma'am. May we have a moment of your time? It's important."

"I'm sorry?" Letitia sounded a little confused. And also a little wary. "My last Maintenance request? That was resolved."

Vince's pulse quickened. This was where things got a little tricky. Brill might have secured Letitia's cooperation in a venture to take down her bosses, but he hadn't actually given her a timeline for anything. For all Letitia knew, it could be days before someone showed up at her door.

Brill had calculated (sensibly, Vince thought) that their odds of keeping something from…interfering…with this plan were better if Letitia had no idea when they were coming. If something happened and Starlit and Lumen discovered she planned to betray them, she couldn't take Vince and Commosky down with her. Instead, Brill had established a codeword with Letitia to be used whenever his agents arrived.

The key was getting her to let them inside without using the codeword.

This turned out to be another area where Brill came in handy. Once the idea to visit Mrs. Kawana and use her missing sculpture as a cover story had sparked into being inside Vince's brain, Brill promptly did some quick, discreet digging. It didn't take long for him to learn that Letitia had recently submitted a Maintenance ticket.

Vince had to admit that took some of the pressure off. It would be easier to talk his way into Letitia's apartment knowing that she had recently dealt with Maintenance. He'd been prepared to fake an issue inside her apartment, but this was better.

Not surprisingly, Commosky had argued there wasn't a difference. As far as he was concerned, convincing Letitia that her apartment had an issue and convincing her to talk to them about her last Maintenance ticket were the same thing. Vince had given up trying to explain the nuances to him on their way here, but Commosky did eventually admit that this was their best option.

Now, Vince infused his voice with apologetic fatigue. "Yes, ma'am, but we're investigating a string of recent thefts. People are accusing Maintenance workers of stealing from them."

"You're investigating thefts?" Letitia asked.

"Yes," Vince answered.

"And you want to talk to *me*?"

"Yes."

Letitia paused, and even through the intercom it sounded laden with alarmed suspicion.

Vince held back a sigh. This was not the right time to use Brill's code word.

Beside him, Commosky did a good job of resembling a bored maintenance worker. He kept his head down, hiding any evidence of the impatience coursing through him.

"It won't take much of your time, ma'am." Vince cleared his throat gruffly. He'd met dozens of Maintenance workers over the years, and had learned that most of them preferred to do their jobs with as little interaction with people as possible. He used that to his advantage now.

"We just need to ask a few routine questions and we'll be out of your hair." When she hesitated again, he looked at Commosky and then back at the door panel. "Please? It'd be nice to get home at a decent time tonight."

Another, longer pause ensued.

Commosky darted a glance at Vince from beneath lowered brows. That look said, *She's not going to go for it.*

Vince ignored him. His goatee prickled, but he resisted the urge to scratch his chin. *Come on.* He focused on the blank holoscreen, willing Letitia to cooperate through the metal and wires and synth-glass. *Let us in.*

"Oh, whatever," Letitia said abruptly. "Come on up. Let's get this over with."

Relief mixed with exultation flooded Vince. He suppressed a triumphant smile as the door in front of him beeped to indicate Letitia had just unlocked it for them and then slid aside with a barely audible hydraulic hiss.

He did not look at Commosky, but strode confidently inside. They were in.

CHAPTER 32

THE SECOND VINCE SET FOOT IN THE Sunset Dream's lobby, a strong scent of citrus air freshener hit him in the face. He wrinkled his nose in distaste. Beside him, Commosky also made a face, but didn't comment. Instead, they both looked around.

Save for its particular color scheme, the lobby looked about the same as the lobby of every other apartment complex Vince had ever set foot in aboard Zyga Space Station. The walls were drab white, dotted with relentlessly cheerful artwork prints that matched the place's overarching sunset theme, and the floor tiling was a muted shade of pink. Soft instrumental music played, the sort of calming music that blended from one song to the next with no danger of a particular tune getting stuck in your brain.

The lobby was empty. A small circular reception desk made from recycled materials in a darker shade of pink stood in the center of the lobby, but there was no one seated behind it. (Vince recognized the desk's material; it was just like most of his own furniture.) Numbered doors lined both sides of the halls extending to the left and right.

Beyond the reception desk stood a small internal elevator. Vince and Commosky crossed the pink floor to it. As they stepped inside, Vince noted that the smell of citrus was even stronger in here. What had they done, doused the entire place with it?

"She's on the second floor, right?" Commosky asked, but he didn't wait for an answer before he told the elevator, "Level 2."

The elevator obligingly carried them up one floor and disgorged them into another bland hall lined with numbered doors. Vince took the lead, scanning the numbers on the doors to their right as they moved purposefully down the hall.

Twenty seconds later, he slowed to a halt in front of 218. "Here it is."

He exchanged a quick look with Commosky and then reached out a hand to tap the intercom button on the doorpanel.

To their surprise, the door slid open immediately—but the person blocking entry into the apartment was not Letitia Theriot. Instead, a tall, hulking man with olive-toned skin and coal-black eyes glared down at Vince and Commosky. He wore a tight black shirt that showed off his impressive muscled upper body, and his dark hair was close-shaved.

Vince's first thought was that this man was ex-military. But since Zyga Space Station didn't *have* a military, that meant he had to have come from someplace else. Or maybe he was a hired mercenary, or even a body builder turned security guard.

Regardless, this man was not somebody Vince wanted to tangle with unless he had to.

His goatee bristled; he resisted the urge to rub his chin. They hadn't anticipated that Starlit and Lumen would have assigned security guards to Letitia and the servers she was hosting. In hindsight, that was a glaring mistake.

Of *course* they had assigned security guards to Letitia.

Vince pasted a weary smile on his face. "We're from Maintenance—"

"Yeah, yeah, we know," the taller man cut him off curtly. Scowling, he stepped aside just enough to allow Vince and Commosky to squeeze past him into a moderately-sized living room.

Vince cast a quick look around. An ice-blue couch with white and lemon-yellow throw pillows sat against one white wall, facing a large holoscreen. Two matching ice-blue recliners framed the couch, and a low coffee table made of real dark wood stood on a silver rug in front of it. The air smelled faintly of sandalwood.

A second man lounged in one of the recliners, but he sprang to his feet as Vince's gaze fell on him. He wore the same clothes as his comrade—tight black shirt and olive green trousers with plenty of pockets—but while his dark hair sported the same close-shaved cut, he was light-skinned. He was also half a head shorter.

Vince didn't see Letitia Theriot anywhere, but he was willing to bet she'd done the decorating. The whole place had a brightness to it that made the hulking security guard and his companion stand out like a couple of rusty old bolts in a shiny new piece of metal bulkhead. Tasteful prints of famous paintings from various artists aboard Zyga Space Station dotted the living room walls, and more hung on the hall leading farther back into the apartment.

"Why are there two of you?" The tall man closed the door and frowned suspiciously at Vince and Commosky before darting a skeptical glance at his shorter companion. "You can't get Maintenance to send one guy to fix somethin' on a good day, and now they're sendin' two?"

Suspicion was nothing new. Vince could work with that.

"Accountability." The Finder didn't look at Commosky as he twitched his shoulders in a shrug, a trifle self-consciously. "Theft is bad for Maintenance's image. Makes the head honchos very unhappy." He held out a hand palm-up. "You know how it is. One guy screws up, and the rest of us take the fall."

The shorter of the two men grunted. "Sounds about right."

"You got the notes, newbie?" Vince shot a hard look over his shoulder at Commosky.

"Yes, boss." Commosky held up his comlink, his meek delivery perfect.

Satisfied, Vince swung his gaze back to the tall man. "You're not Letitia Theriot."

"You can talk to me." The tall man folded his muscled arms over his broad chest.

So that was how they wanted to play it. Vince adopted a long-suffering expression. "Listen, man. I would if I could, but if you ain't the owner, I can't talk to you. Gotta follow the rules. And I know Ms. Theriot is here—we just talked to her, remember?"

"You can talk to me," the tall man repeated.

"No, I can't." Vince waved a vague hand toward the general direction of the main Maintenance office, which was somewhere on Level 20 below them. "Main office will have my head, particularly after this theft mess. I don't want to lose my job over this." He jerked a thumb over his shoulder at Commosky. "Or his."

Commosky nodded solemnly, still clutching his comlink.

"Look," the tall man said, his dark eyes narrowing into slits. "I appreciate what you're doing here, but—"

"Rigby, I want to talk to them," said a woman's voice from somewhere off to Vince's left.

The Finder recognized the voice as that of the woman who'd answered the door buzzer. Letitia Theriot. *Finally.*

All four men turned as a woman appeared in the doorway of the hall. Vince recognized her immediately from the holos Bella had pulled up for them earlier.

Letitia Theriot looked more exhausted than she had in the holos, but there was no mistaking her. She was almost as tall as Commosky and solidly-built, with curves in all the right places. Her curly black hair was pulled back in a bun and her creamy, peach-toned skin was devoid of makeup. She wore soft black pants and an over-sized pink long-sleeved shirt.

The tall man, Rigby, transferred his frown to her. "Ms. Theriot, I think it's best if—"

"This is still my apartment." Letitia cut him off smoothly, almost tonelessly, before raising her eyebrows at him. The look in her blue eyes was steely. "And if somebody from Maintenance has been stealing things, don't you think it'd be good to know about it?"

She didn't wait for an answer, but moved forward into the bright living room to face Vince and Commosky.

"Thank you, Ms. Theriot." Vince focused on Letitia, though he kept part of his attention on her two guards. "This won't take much of your time."

He launched into the spiel he'd given her over the intercom, adding a few more details. Then he asked, "Have you noticed anything missing?"

"Missing?" Letitia frowned, before sending a confused, almost bewildered glance around her living room. "I can't say that I have." She smiled wryly. "I doubt anybody with sticky fingers would have tried anything here, anyway. Rigby and Saul here are very observant." She tipped her head slightly toward her two guards.

They remained impassive, but Vince had the distinct sense that they took this as a compliment.

"Are you sure?" Commosky spoke suddenly, his voice quiet, but insistent. "All the missing items are small enough to have slipped into a tool bag, or in some cases even a pocket." He used his hands to measure the size. "A small sculpture. An antique SilverBeard clock."

Vince watched Letitia's eyes widen at the mention of Silver-Beard. Surprise, and was that…hope? He and Commosky hadn't decided exactly who would slip Brill's code word into the conversation, but there was no denying it had been the perfect opportunity.

"I…don't know." Letitia looked around at her living room again, her eyes unfocused. "They came through here, but the problem was actually in my hygiene unit." She shrugged. "Nothing in there to steal."

"He didn't steal anything," the shorter man, Saul, said irritably. He folded his arms across his chest, mimicking his colleague. "We were watching him the whole time."

The tension in the room seemed to thicken. Vince stood motionless on the edge of the silver rug, though inside his nerves and muscles felt stretched as tight as a lifeline tethering someone to the bulkhead in an emergency crisis when all the air was being sucked out into the icy black void of space.

This couldn't be it. They were too close. There had to be something else they could do to get into the—

"Oh," Letitia said abruptly. She tilted her head to one side, her blue eyes going distant, as though she'd just remembered something. She looked at Vince, her face brightening with a sudden dawning thought. "How long ago did you say these thefts started? A couple of weeks?"

Vince had been intentionally vague, but he played along. "Yes, ma'am."

"Maintenance *did* send somebody to fix a glowpanel for me a few weeks back. I forgot about that." Letitia looked at her two scowling security guards. "It was before you—well, before." She waved a dismissive hand, turning back to Vince. "The glowpanel was in my game room."

She was making this story up out of nothing. Vince had seen the Maintenance logs; she'd had only the one call in the last six months. He looked at her, impressed by her on-the-spot ingenuity.

Not only had Letitia immediately recognized they were working with Brill, but now she was wildly inventing a means of letting them poke around her apartment…while at the same time indicating that her security guards were a recent addition.

He *really* hoped she could pull this off.

"Is anything missing?" Commosky took a step forward, the expression on his disguised swarthy face a mixture of helpful eagerness.

Vince had to hand it to him; for somebody who was usually quite the commanding force, the detective was doing a good job pretending to be a lowly Maintenance worker.

"I don't know." Letitia tapped her chin thoughtfully. "I keep a lot of things in there." She trilled a little embarrassed laugh. "It's not always the most…organized."

Behind her, Rigby huffed under his breath and Saul shook his head. Clearly, her guards agreed with that assessment.

Letitia snapped her fingers. "Come with me and we'll go check real quick. Then you can get out of here and hopefully cross me off your list." She cast a sideways glance at her guards. "I've got to get back to work."

It occurred to Vince then that he didn't know exactly what role Letitia played in the Ruby Gauntlet, other than to physically house the gaming club's servers in her apartment. He suppressed a flash of irritation. They'd been in such an all-fired hurry that he'd relied on Brill more than usual and failed to dig up as much of the background details as usual.

"Ms. Theriot…" Rigby started to growl, but Letitia glared at him.

"My apartment," she hissed in an undertone, as though daring him to contradict her. "*Mine.*"

Saul wasn't so restrained. He shot her a flat look. "Not all yours what's in here."

"All the more reason to make sure somebody didn't walk off with it," Letitia retorted. Tossing her head, she marched across the living room and beckoned an imperious hand at Vince and Commosky. "Come with me."

The two men followed, all too aware of the way the two security guards fell in behind them.

The datachip in Vince's pocket seemed to suddenly burn white-hot. Everything hinged on these two things—the datachip and Letitia.

CHAPTER 33

T HE GAME ROOM STOOD AT THE END of the hall, a former bedroom that now served a completely different purpose. A thrill of anticipation raced through Vince as he followed Letitia, Commosky close behind him. He was acutely aware of Rigby and Saul bringing up the rear. The two men were silent, but their entire aura screamed disapproval.

Letitia stopped in front of the closed game room door and entered a complicated sequence of numbers into a lock panel wired into the wall beside it. Behind her, Vince exchanged an imperceptible glance with Commosky, who had drawn up next to him. That lockpanel had to have been a new addition. Most apartments didn't have internal doorlocks of that caliber.

The door unlocked with a click and slid aside, allowing a rush of cooler air to race past them, tinged with a scent Vince could only quantify as belonging to computer machinery. Letitia strode across the threshold, and the four men followed.

Compared to the white brightness of the living room, the game room was practically pitch-black. Vince blinked several times, willing his eyes to adjust. He had a brief impression of tiny blinking blue and white lights along one wall before Letitia said, "Lights, medium."

A round glowpanel in the ceiling flickered to life, shedding a golden glow over the room's interior. It *was* a game room, that was for sure.

Instead of the white carpet that covered the floor elsewhere in the apartment, the floor here was smooth slate blue tile. A slim, shiny black version of what Vince recognized as a full-body immersion gaming rig sat in one corner. (Not that he'd ever seen one in person; they were technically illegal aboard Zyga Station. He had, however, seen holos.) The rig featured a comfortable ergonomic seat and harness with hand and feet controls suspended from a curved stabilizer arm mounted to a sturdy platform about a meter and a half wide. The gaming rig was tall enough that the person in it could stand or even jump. There was no viewscreen; Vince assumed the gamer wore special hologlasses.

Opposite the gaming rig sat a comfortable armchair with a small rectangular wooden table beside it. On the other side of the room from the gaming rig, stood a large, comfortable black desk with attached shelving. Letitia had three computer screens, connected to what Vince guessed was a single computer, but he couldn't tell for sure.

His eyes lingered on a series of shelves at one end of the desk, where several tiny computer casings sat, whirring away. Blue and white lights blinked or flickered along their edges. None of them had a computer screen attached.

Those were the servers. Had to be.

He refocused as Letitia started talking.

"…glowpanel up there." She pointed unnecessarily up at the overhead. "I stayed in here with him, though, so I don't think he had time to do anything." She cast a dubious glance around the game room, before drifting over to the desk to poke through a few loose items Vince couldn't immediately identify. "We have security cams in here, but we don't think we keep the footage more than a couple of weeks."

"Ms. Theriot…" Saul said warningly.

Vince experienced a brief flash of panic. Of *course* Starlit and Lumen would have security cams in here. The Ruby Gauntlet's servers—and Letitia by extension—were valuable enough that they'd want to keep an eye on them.

Brill, we're getting sloppy. He resisted the urge to grit his teeth. If Letitia was wrong about how long they kept the footage and they went back over it…

Vince cut the thought off before he could travel any further down that road. Best not to think about that now. Their job was to pass Letitia the datachip so Brill could do his thing. If they did that… with any luck, Starlit and Lumen would never have the opportunity to look at old cam footage.

Letitia posted both hands on her hips and surveyed the room critically. Her gaze swept over the desk, mentally cataloging the items on it, before traveling to the servers. Finally, she eyed the gaming rig, as though debating whether or not a wily, thieving Maintenance worker could have spirited part of it away.

Rigby stirred. "Ms. Theriot, is this really—"

"I don't think anything's missing," Letitia announced. "Nothing major, anyway." She turned back to Vince and Commosky. "I told you I was watching him. I'd have noticed if he took something big." She shrugged carelessly. "And I doubt he took a datachip or anything like that. Datachips are cheap and there's no guarantee he'd get anything valuable on one."

"If you're sure, Ms. Theriot." Vince inclined his head. "Thanks for letting us check. Glad you weren't affected." He jerked a thumb over shoulder at Commosky. "We just need your signature and we'll be out of your hair."

"Good," Saul said from his post beside the door. He cast a pointed look at Vince and Commosky, jerking his head for them to start moving.

Vince held back until Letitia left the game room first, and then followed on her heels. The datachip was still burning a hole in his pocket, but he couldn't risk pulling it out.

Not yet.

Saul and Rigby brought up the rear, both grim-faced. They closed and locked the game room door behind them and Vince saw his chance.

Darting his left hand into his pocket, the Finder pressed the tiny datachip between two fingertips and then withdrew his hand.

As soon as they were back in the living room, he held out his other hand to Commosky. "Comlink."

The detective wordlessly dropped his comlink into Vince's outstretched hand. Vince opened a note-taking app, though at this point he doubted the security guards would check for actual paperwork. In the process, he transferred the datachip to his right hand.

"If you'll just sign here…" Vince extended the comlink to Letitia, pressing the datachip up against one side of the device as he did.

Letitia took the comlink—and the datachip—and scrawled her name on the comlink display with the tip of her finger. "Here you go." She handed the device back to Vince—sans datachip. Her face was pleasantly blank.

"Thank you, ma'am." Vince bobbed his head in a grateful nod. "We won't need to bother you again."

"I hope you find everything that person took." Letitia pursed her lips together, folding her arms across her chest. "If we can't trust Maintenance workers, who can we trust?"

"You've got a point there," Commosky said as he followed Vince to the door. He inclined his head in a respectful nod. "Thanks, ma'am."

Vince glanced over his shoulder as Rigby closed the door behind them. His eyes met Letitia's for a split second before the door slid shut. In her blue gaze, he saw mingled fear and determination.

Phase one was complete. Now all they had to do was wait for Letitia to do her part.

Vince drew in a shallow breath. He really, *really* hoped this worked.

CHAPTER 34

Vince exhaled in relief once they had put a couple of blocks between them and Letitia's apartment. They'd done their part. It was up to Letitia now, to gather her courage and follow through with the plan Brill had concocted.

Commosky's thoughts seemed to running along similar lines. He glanced at Vince out of the corner of his eye. "Wonder how long it'll take her to get everything installed and contact your friend."

"Don't know."

"Could be a while, if she's afraid of making those two goons suspicious."

"Maybe." Vince stopped at the edge of the gray sidewalk and held up a hand to flag a passing silver transport pod. As it slowed to a stop beside them and a door popped open, he gave the detective a hard smile. "I'd say she spends enough time on her various devices that they won't even have a clue."

"That'd be preferable," Commosky said.

Vince climbed into the transport pod and took a seat on one side. Commosky climbed in after him and settled on the opposite side.

Vince sent Brill an encrypted text. ::*Done. FYI she has babysitters.*::

He then leaned back against the transport pod's green cushion and eyed Commosky across from him. Now that they'd gotten that over with, he could turn his attention to other matters.

"Don't suppose you'd be up for a little side trip, Detective."

Commosky snorted. "As opposed to hiding in your office the rest of the night? No offense."

Vince just waved that aside.

"What do you have in mind, Finder? Wait—" It was Commosky's turn to hold up a hand. "Let me guess. Maintenance."

"Got it in one." Vince allowed himself a small grin, his dark eyes glittering. "I'm thinking we should find that Maintenance worker and have ourselves a little chat."

Commosky eyed him sharply. "This ought to be interesting."

CHAPTER 35

Vince considered his options as he and Commosky headed down to Level 20 to visit Zone 5's Maintenance office. If Leanza Bonani wasn't there, they'd have to either track her down or else wait for her to come back and clock out at the end of her shift.

For expediency's sake, he hoped Leanza would be there. That would be easier than tracking her down. Although, there were benefits to that too. An official setting might make her cling to her story; if they could catch her alone, talking her into giving Mrs. Kawana's sculpture back would be easier.

If Leanza hadn't already sold it.

The thought twisted something in the pit of Vince's stomach. For Mrs. Kawana's sake, he hoped that wasn't the case. He'd told her the truth—tracking the sculpture down once it was sold would be almost impossible. The only hope they had was if the buyer lived on Zyga Station.

Vince *might* be able to track it down then. Maybe. With a lot of work…unless he got incredibly lucky.

That didn't happen often. Sure, luck was sometimes a component, but he'd learned to never, ever depend on luck to get him through something.

Better to plan for the worst and grab lucky breaks when he happened to trip over them.

Each of Zyga Station's five Zones had a Maintenance office. These coordinated with the Engineer Department office headquarters on the Rim to keep the Station running smoothly. In theory, the Core had a Maintenance office too, along with the Authorized-Access-Only levels at its heart that contained the Station's engine, life-support systems, and other important systems. In practice, however, the Core didn't get much in the way of Maintenance, particularly the lower levels.

It was one of the smaller injustices of life aboard Zyga Space Station, Unfortunately, like other things—such as the Families' insidious influence—there wasn't much the average citizen could do about it. You lived in the Zones if you could afford it, and if you couldn't, you lived in the Core.

Vince's pulse quickened as they neared the nondescript office complex that held Zone 5's Maintenance main office. From the outside, it certainly didn't look like much. It was Maintenance—they didn't get fancy signage or decorative architecture. They were simply there.

It reminded him of many of the people who worked in Maintenance, who were simply there, in the background, going about their jobs without drawing a lot of attention to themselves. It was the sort of essential work to keep the Station running smoothly that nobody noticed until something broke or otherwise stopped functioning.

"If it weren't for the lettering," Commosky said dryly, indicating the black letters spelling out 'Maintenance' above the main entrance, "I'd have walked right past this place."

"It does blend in."

Vince led the way up to the double doors, which were inset with opaque, one-way synthglass, and Commosky matched his pace.

"You been here before?"

"Couple of times. Not recently, though."

As they approached the entrance, the doors automatically slid aside. A rush of warmer air met them, tinged with the scent of oil and overlaid with a faint metallic machinery smell. Vince crossed the threshold and turned to the left without breaking stride.

"No security?" Commosky cast an incredulous look over his shoulder. "Anybody can just walk in here?" He kept his voice low, but his astonishment threaded through every syllable.

Vince was surprised by how gratified Commosky's surprise made him feel. He'd had that same thought for years, but had always assumed that Station Authority knew—or assumed—something he didn't.

Although…they still didn't know how Starlit and Lumen were affecting the Station's power grid. They'd probably bribed or coerced someone with clearance high enough to allow them to tinker with things, instead of unauthorized people sneaking inside to cause mayhem.

"There's a little security." Vince nodded to the receptionist's desk—such as it was—against the left wall beside the entrance to a short hall that looked like it had sprouted a number of offices.

"That's nothing." Commosky shook his head in disgust. "You'd think they'd want to keep access to the Station's mainframe a little more secure."

"Bureaucracy at its finest," Vince said lightly, moving toward the receptionist's desk.

Behind this desk sat a middle-aged woman with a pale, thin face and dark hair pulled back into a loose bun. She was currently fielding a call; as Vince and Commosky approached, they heard her patiently explaining to the person on the other end that they couldn't get someone from Maintenance there that moment, but that someone would be dispatched as soon as possible.

Vince politely waited until the receptionist ended the call. When she did, she looked at him and Commosky, pursing her lips and giving her head a slight shake.

"I swear, it never fails. People think we're some sort of immediate fix." She rubbed the bridge of her nose wearily. "Like we don't have an entire Zone to take care of."

Vince wisely said nothing, merely nodded in understanding. Commosky followed suit.

The receptionist eyed them over her desk. Her gaze lingered on Commosky; Vince hoped his disguise was sufficient to stand up to close scrutiny. "What can I help you with?"

Vince offered her a smile. "My name is Finder Vince Grable. I'm looking for Leanza Bonani."

"Oh, yeah?" The receptionist's gaze hardened fractionally as she leaned back in her seat.

Of course it couldn't be easy. Vince suppressed a sigh. Instead, he withdrew his wallet from the breast pocket of his brown leather jacket and showed the receptionist his Finder's license. "I'm sure you've heard about the report that was filed against Ms. Bonani."

"Yeah." There was absolutely nothing friendly about the woman's voice.

Vince noted that as quite interesting. Either this woman didn't care for Station Authority officials or Finders poking into Maintenance's business, or she liked Leanza Bonani and considered her a friend.

He leaned forward a little, lowering his voice. "Look, the woman who filed the report is my client. The missing item has a lot of sentimental value and my client just wants it back. There's no need to involve Station Authority any further."

"Leanza denies she did anything wrong." The receptionist folded thin arms across her chest; she didn't have much in the way of a bosom.

"Well, in that case," Vince spread his hands, "she's innocent and she has nothing to worry about talking to me."

The receptionist gave him a flat look that told him exactly what she thought about *that*. But then, something sparked in her dark eyes. She jerked her chin toward Vince's chest, where he'd tucked his wallet back his jacket breast pocket. "What did you say your name was?"

"Vince Grable." A spark of hope ignited in his chest.

"You're the guy who was one the news a while back? Found out what happened to the *Juggernaut*?"

"That's me."

Vince didn't look at Commosky, standing at his elbow. He kept his attention on the receptionist, who was thawing marginally. The hard wariness in her eyes faded into something that was almost respect, tinged with a hopefulness that surprised him. *This Leanza must be a good friend of hers.*

Either that, he thought shrewdly, *or she's leery of Station Authority for an entirely different reason.*

The receptionist pressed her lips into a thin line, her gaze darting from Vince to Commosky and back. "You're absolutely *not* with Station Authority?"

"I am not." Vince put as much quiet assurance into those three words as he could. He readied the story they'd developed for Commosky, but it wasn't necessary.

All at once, the older woman seemed to make up her mind. Glancing around as though checking to see if they were being watched, she leaned forward and pitched her voice lower. "I don't want to get anybody in trouble. Understood?"

Satisfaction mixed with quiet triumph curled through Vince. *Gotcha.*

CHAPTER 36

Aloud, Vince said, "Understood." He leaned toward the receptionist, resting an elbow on the desk and dropping his voice to match hers. "Look, Ms…" He tilted his head. "What *is* your name, by the way?"

"Mariska," she said grudgingly.

"Mariska. We—" Vince waved a hand between Commosky and himself, "—don't want to get anybody in trouble either. I just want to find my client's missing item. It belonged to her grandmother."

Mariska's dark eyes flickered, but the wary, concerned, strangely hopeful look on her face didn't change.

Vince had worked with people like this before. They wanted to help, wanted to do the right thing, but they also couldn't bring themselves to come right out and talk about what they knew. This conversation would require a little delicate finesse.

"We've narrowed the possible list of suspects down to Leanza," he said gently. A pause, and then, "This isn't the first time she's been accused of theft."

It wasn't a question.

Reluctantly, Mariska shook her head. "But," she held up a hand, "I honestly don't think she *did* do it every time."

That was interesting. Vince leaned in a little farther. "Really? Why?"

"Because Leanza likes her job. She's good at fixing stuff." The receptionist shrugged a thin shoulder. "And I've heard her talk about how much better the pay is here than it is back in the Core."

"She's from the Core?" This from Commosky.

The receptionist shot him a look, staring longer than either of them liked. "Yeah. What of it?"

"Nothing." Commosky held up both hands in the hopes of ameliorating her suddenly hostile tone. "It's just…there's a tough crowd in parts of the Core and sometimes good people get towed under by them."

The receptionist glared at him a second longer before switching her attention back to Vince. "And, no, before you ask, she's not a gamer either. Not like *that.*"

That had actually been Vince's next question. He acknowledged the answer with a nod and moved on. "So what makes you think she's responsible for *part* of the thefts?"

A guilty look flashed over the older woman's face; she pressed her lips together to seal them shut again.

"Look, Mariska…" Vince exhaled deliberately. "The best thing you can do to help your friend is help me." He met her eyes, his brown gaze steady and clear. "My client would like to avoid any legal trouble, but the next person Leanza swipes something from might not be so understanding."

Mariska held his gaze a moment longer, and then she broke. "She's not a klepto. She's paying off a debt or something. I think. I'm not totally sure." Her words tumbled out rapidly, as though she was afraid she'd stop talking if she let herself think about them for a second. "And the payments, or whatever they are, aren't all the time. Every couple of months, kind of random."

Vince exchanged a glance with Commosky out of the corner of his eye. That was interesting too.

"That's not just petty theft," he said quietly.

Mariska shook her head vigorously, her fingers turning a stylus over and over. "She's hard to get to know, but she's not a bad person." She looked at Vince, her eyes wide and pleading. "Something else is going on."

"I believe you." Vince offered her a reassuring smile. This just kept getting better and better. "Where can we find her?"

"Her shift ended about twenty minutes ago. She came back here, but she hasn't clocked back out yet. She's through there." Mariska pointed her stylus toward a door at the far end of the room.

Both men turned, following the direction of her stylus. Vince narrowed his eyes slightly as he took in the bold lettering on the door proclaiming: 'Authorized Personnel Only'.

Of course it was restricted. Nothing could be that easy.

He rubbed his goatee, quickly considering his options. He could have Mariska page Leanza, but that would almost certainly tip the other woman off. She'd either hide or else she'd take another way out of the building—and even if Vince knew this place well enough to know where all the exits were, he didn't have the manpower to cover them all.

No, this called for another option. Vince leaned in toward Mariska again, propping his hip against the brown recycled material of the desk, and jerked his head toward the door. "Think you could get us a couple badges?"

Mariska's breath hitched in her throat, her eyes widening fractionally. Obviously, ratting Leanza out to help her in the long run was one thing, but letting two unauthorized strangers into a secure part of the Maintenance office was completely different. In that instant, Vince knew that everything hinged on this moment.

Either Mariska would help them...or they'd have to do things the hard way.

The hard, much more time-consuming way.

Stars, Vince thought as he held Mariska's gaze, his heart thumping a little faster in his chest, *don't balk on me now.*

He opened his mouth to say something…anything…but Commosky beat him to it.

"We'll be discreet." The detective leaned forward as well, his voice solemn and earnest. "In and out. Nobody will be in any trouble."

Mariska bit her lip. Her dark eyes were suddenly huge in her thin face. "I'm not—I'm *supposed* to run visitors past my boss." She tipped her head vaguely to the right, which, since it was a wall, probably meant her boss's office was somewhere above them.

A thrill of anticipation slid through Vince's veins. He could hear the 'but' coming.

"But…" Mariska visibly swallowed and then rummaged through a drawer to her left. She pulled out two lanyards with rectangular white badges. The word 'Visitor' was written in large red letters. Solemnly, she handed them to Vince and Commosky in turn. "You have an hour. Tops."

"Thank you." Vince slung his lanyard over his neck.

Mariska extended a tablet. "Sign here, both of you." Once they did (though Vince had no idea what name Commosky had put down), the receptionist drilled Vince with a look that was equal parts solemn resolve and nervous trepidation. "Don't make me regret this."

The Finder offered her a confident smile. "We won't."

CHAPTER 37

As they approached the door marked 'Authorized Entry Only', Commosky gave his head the slightest shake. "You certainly know how to pick 'em, Grable. An open and shut case of petty theft would be great on a day like today, but, no. That's too simple."

Vince didn't answer. Privately, he agreed, but, well, there wasn't any point in admitting it out loud. Either way, he was committed.

In the back of his mind, he spared a thought to wonder if they'd stand out in street clothes, but he needn't have worried.

They were halfway across the room when the Authorized-Entry-Only door opened and a stream of people emerged. Maintenance workers who'd just clocked out, and all of them were dressed in street clothes.

Vince and Commosky stepped aside to let them pass, out of courtesy, but they both kept a sharp eye out for Leanza.

The two men spotted her at the same time. Leanza came through the doorway in a clump of three women with a large tote over one shoulder. She was dressed in street clothes—a cerulean blue long-sleeved shirt over light-wash jeans. A few brown curls straggling out of her ponytail and her light-skinned face looked tired.

That fatigue vanished as soon as she glimpsed Vince and Commosky cutting across the stream of departing workers to reach her. Her fingers tightened on the strap of her bag. For a second, Vince thought she would make a run for it.

She didn't. She narrowed her eyes at them, her expression turning stony and positively forbidding.

"Leanza? Vince kept his voice pleasant, even as he matched her pace. "I'd like a moment of your time."

"Yeah, well, I'm busy." Leanza tried to push past him, but Vince stood his ground. When she attempted to cut around him, Commosky blocked her path as well.

She stopped short in the middle of the lobby, looking beleaguered and more than a little irritated, and folded her arms across her chest. "Get out of my way or I'm calling security."

Vince was intimately familiar with this tactic. Draw as much attention to yourself as possible, in the hopes of making a problem go away. Unfortunately for Leanza, he was perfectly fine with drawing attention.

"That would be good, actually." He offered her a polite smile. "They'll be able to offer us a private room to talk."

Her stony expression flickered, confusion warring with a hint of fear. "I'm serious. They'll kick you out faster than you can say 'Security.'"

"I think you'll find you want to talk to me, Miss Bonani." Vince pulled his Finder's license from his inside jacket breast pocket and showed it to her. "My name is Vince Grable. Mrs. Kawana hired me to find the sculpture you stole from her."

"*Allegedly* stole." Leanza huffed, her annoyance deepening, before she unfolded her arms long enough to jab a finger toward Vince. "You can't just walk around accusing people of stealing things. I don't care what that old freighter said. I. Didn't. Do. It." She punctuated each word with a jab of her finger. "Now, you better get out of here before—"

"Mrs. Kawana is willing to let the whole matter drop if you return her sculpture," Vince said smoothly, as though Leanza wasn't still speaking. "She won't press charges. She'd just like the statue returned. It belonged to her grandmother and has sentimental value."

Leanza rolled her eyes dramatically. "Like I haven't heard that before." She shot Commosky a sour look. "Who's this? Your sidekick?" Without waiting for an answer, she shoved past him. "I'm out of here. You don't have any authority."

"This is the fifth complaint that's been lodged against you in the past six months." Vince raised his voice, so that his words carried above the chatter and tired conversations filling the lobby. A few of Leanza's coworkers glanced their direction. "If people can't trust Maintenance not to steal from them—" a few more people looked their way, "—Zyga Station has a big problem."

Leanza's steps faltered as she registered the attention they were drawing. She shot Vince a nasty look over her shoulder, but before she could say anything, he continued loudly, "How many theft complaints does it take before they—"

"Stop it." She stomped back over to Vince and Commosky, her eyes blazing and her hands balled into fists. "Stop it. Shut up. You can't just—" she waved a hand, "—say all that stuff at the top of your lungs like that." She posted her hands on her hips, an angry flush rising in her pale cheeks. "I work here. I like my job."

"Then why are you stealing from people?" This, from Commosky.

"Is there a problem here?" interrupted a stern voice from behind Vince.

All three of them turned to see that a security guard in a light gray uniform had materialized in the lobby. He looked from Leanza to Vince and Commosky and back. Clearly, he knew Leanza was an employee.

Vince was willing to bet that even if he didn't know about the formal complaints lodged against Leanza, he could probably find out. He held out a hand to the security guard. "Vince Grable. I'm—"

"Leaving," Leanza blurted out. "With me." She grabbed his arm. "Bye, Martin."

Before Vince could say anything else, Leanza had steered him around and was tugging him in the direction of the door. Commosky sauntered after them, his hands in his pockets.

As they passed the receptionist's desk, Vince glanced at Mariska, who looked a little sick, and gave her an encouraging nod. She'd done well, even if she felt at the moment like she'd betrayed her friend.

In the long run, this was better for everybody, especially Leanza.

Leanza didn't stop tugging Vince after her until they were outside the Maintenance office and halfway down the block. Only then did she drop his arm as though the brown leather of his jacket had burned her and whirl to face him. She looked angry enough to spit bolts.

"Was *that* really necessary?"

"You could have cooperated." Vince lifted his shoulders in the merest of shrugs. "You chose to do things the hard way."

Posting her hands on her hips again, Leanza raised her chin. "You don't have nothin' on me." She snorted scornfully. "Station Authority don't have nothin' on me, or else they'd have done somethin' after that Kawana woman complained."

"I'm not Station Authority." Vince shrugged again. "I'm a Finder." He eyed her. "That means my job is to find things and get them back to my clients."

"He's good at it," Commosky said in his deep, rumbling voice.

Leanza's gaze flicked to him, before returning to Vince.

"You have two choices." Vince kept his body language open and non-threatening, but he let a stern note slip into his voice. "You can cooperate with me and this entire thing will disappear."

"Or you'll harass me until you find the sculpture, blah, blah, blah." Leanza waved a dismissive hand, the sarcasm in her voice biting enough to pierce a hull. "I'm not scared of you."

"Oh, no," Vince said genially. "I won't harass you." He waited until she glanced at him, confused, to smile. "But I will comb through every bit of your life, for as long as it takes until I locate my client's sculpture. Whatever you're hiding, whatever trouble you're in, I'll find out what it is. And when I'm done, I'll take everything to Station Authority."

He shook his head. "You won't get another job on Zyga Station."

"You'll be lucky if you're not on a transport to the mines," Commosky added.

Vince shot him a look. *Was that really necessary?*

Commosky only shrugged, completely unrepentant.

To her credit, Leanza managed to keep a mostly stoic expression, but a little of the blood drained from her face. It made her brown eyes seem even darker against her light skin.

"But," Vince continued lightly, "as I said, if you cooperate and return the missing item, Mrs. Kawana will drop all charges." He made a little 'poof' with his hands. "This whole mess will disappear and you'll go back to life as normal."

"It's just a little statue!" Leanza burst out. "What's the big deal?" Irritated, she waved a hand. "Somebody like her can afford to replace it."

"That's not the point," Commosky said sternly, even as Vince said, "It's not the statue itself."

Caught off-guard, Leanza blinked. She stared at Vince, visibly confused. Her confusion turned to suspicion. "What?"

CHAPTER 38

OUT OF THE CORNER OF HIS EYE, Vince saw Commosky shoot him a look—the kind of look that said he couldn't believe Vince had just given away that piece of information.

Vince didn't care. Commosky had his way of running an investigation, and Vince had his own. Sometimes, getting results called for unorthodox methods.

Like using the truth to hook a suspect's interest.

"This isn't about the statue," Vince repeated. He held a hand palm up. "Oh, sure, Mrs. Kawana would like to have it back. It *was* her grandmother's. But—" he shook his head, "—she's more concerned about what's *inside* the statue."

"It has a secret compartment?" Leanza asked, before she could stop herself. "No wonder—" she cut herself off abruptly.

Commosky raised a stern eyebrow, but Vince ignored this lapse. (For now.) Instead, he blithely continued on as though he hadn't heard a word. "Mrs. Kawana lost her husband a while back, but before he died, they made a little recording of themselves." He raised his eyebrows suggestively.

It wasn't necessary to say any more. Leanza reared back a little. "Okay. Wow." She made a face. "*Wow.*"

"So, as you can imagine, that's why this—" Vince motioned to her, "—won't go away. My client would like that memento of her husband back and she's willing to keep paying me until I find it."

Leanza had recovered a little of her savoir faire. She hoisted her bag a little higher on her shoulder and shrugged breezily. "Really wish I could help, but I can't. Didn't do it, like I said."

"That's how you're going to play it?" Commosky asked, his voice low and cold.

The woman spared him a dismissive glance. "Yeah." She shook her head. "Told you, ya ain't got nothin' on me."

She started to turn away, but Vince said, "Not yet, maybe, but I will." Her steps faltered and he raised his voice a little. "I'm going to start with the payments you've been making somebody."

Leanza froze in her tracks, just as he'd hoped. Her shoulders rose and fell once, and then she whirled around and stalked back over to Vince.

Uncaring that technically she was outnumbered and that both of these men were bigger and taller than she was, she jabbed a finger in his face. Her face was white with fury. "You stay outta my business. Don't you *dare* go messing around in things that don't pertain to you."

Vince held his ground. He'd hit a nerve. "That's my job. Whatever pertains to my clients pertains to me." he spread his hands, careful not to touch her. "If you won't make things easy on yourself, I'll have to keep digging." He held her gaze, thought behind the fury he thought he saw tears sparkling. "And you may not like what I find."

"My life is none of your business." Leanza punctuated each word with a jab of her finger.

"It is now that you're my best lead for recovering my client's property."

Commosky shifted on his feet. "I'd think about this, kid. We go down this space lane, you may end up on the hook for more than just one statue."

Leanza whirled on him too, venom dripping from every syllable. "Both of you can pound meteorites." Her eyes dropped to the 'visitor' badge still hanging from Commosky's neck and her lip curled in disgust. "You've been talking to Mariska, haven't you?"

It wasn't a question. She snorted, shaking her head. "Can't trust anybody around here to keep their mouth shut."

"She's your friend and she's looking out for you." It was Vince's turn to shake his head. "Although at the moment I can't say what she sees in you."

"Yeah, well, whatever she told you is wrong."

Vince raised an eyebrow. "You're not making regular payments to somebody?"

People streamed along the sidewalks, giving the three of them a wide berth. A couple of them shot Leanza concerned looks, but she just shrugged and waved them away.

"Even if I was, it ain't any of your business." Her face hardened. "Couldn't do anything anyway."

"Maybe not." Vince lifted a shoulder in a shrug. "But who's going to make those payments when you're in jail for theft?"

Leanza glared at him. "You can't prove nothin'."

Vince held her gaze. "I will."

"You *do* realize who you're talking to," Commosky said unexpectedly. He tipped his head toward Vince. "Guy who found the *Juggernaut*."

To her credit, Leanza mostly managed to keep a straight face. Mostly. Her eyes widened a little, but she said nothing.

Impatience set its claws into Vince, but he forced it back. Patience was everything in this business—even if he could feel time slipping through his fingers.

At last, Leanza set her jaw. "Don't need you digging into my business. Or anything connected with me," she added for good measure. She jerked her chin toward Vince. "You saying you'll walk away if this statue shows back up? Charges all get dropped and nobody pokes around anymore?"

"That's what I'm saying." Vince just waited. It *sounded* like she was wavering, but…he didn't trust this woman not to decide she'd rather risk an investigation.

Leanza propped her hands on her hips, fixing a scowl on something beyond Vince's right elbow. The Finder could practically see the gears in her head turn, see the mental calculations she was performing to weigh the pros and cons.

At last, she folded her arms across her chest. "We may be able to work something out."

"Glad to hear it." Vince smiled, but he didn't relax. There was more. There was always more.

"Meet me at Le Bouf's in an hour or so." Leanza's dark eyes narrowed to slits. "No cops, and you better keep your end of the deal." She unwound her arms to point a threatening finger at Vince. "Otherwise, your name won't be worth space dust when I'm through with you."

Commosky opened his mouth—probably to say something along the lines of her not having much influence in the mines—but Vince held out a hand. "Understood." He smiled genially. "Thank you."

Leanza just huffed and pivoted on her heel before stalking off. She cast one suspicious glance over her shoulder—probably to make sure they weren't following her—and then disappeared around the corner.

Vince let out a breath. Relief and satisfaction mingled with sadness. That girl had a weight on her shoulders, no mistake about it, but even if he offered to help, he doubted she'd let him.

"You sure letting her walk off is the best option?" Commosky asked under his breath.

"Can't hold her." Vince shook his head. "Might be able to follow her, but I can't say I want to trek all over Zone 5. She'd run us ragged."

"Looks like you were right about her sitting on that statue." Commosky snorted. "Unless she's already fenced it and this was just her way of buying time."

"It's a possibility," Vince conceded. "I think the odds of her showing up are pretty good. Whatever she's got going on, she's more afraid of having somebody shine a light on it than she is losing the statue." He unslung the 'visitor's badge from around his neck and held out a hand for Commosky's. "Better return these."

The detective handed his badge over. "And then what?"

Vince smiled. "We got to Le Bouf's and get some dinner while we wait."

CHAPTER 39

Le Bouf's was a little eatery on Level 8. It wasn't much more than a handful of wooden tables and chairs inside a large, surprisingly dim compartment next to a laundromat. It smelled good, however; the air laden with the comforting scent of onions, garlic, and basil. The bulkheads were covered in pictures of scenes from someone's homeworld—green rolling hills, an ocean view from a rocky beach, autumn leaves in gold, scarlet, and orange on trees Vince didn't recognize.

Only two other tables were occupied; one by a couple, and another by a family with three small children. Vince and Commosky chose an unoccupied table in the corner.

Commosky studied the worn wooden table for a few seconds before frowning at Vince. "Where's the menu button?"

In answer, Vince jerked his thumb over his shoulder in the direction of a large black chalkboard that hung on the bulkhead beside the counter and a small pay station. The names of three soups were written on the chalkboard in slightly crooked white lettering.

"They only have three options a day."

In today's case, the three soups were corn chowder, minestrone, and gumbo.

Commosky blinked, before shaking his head and resting his arms on the table. It creaked a little under his weight. "I'd ask how you already knew about this place, but I suspect I already know the answer." He lowered his voice further. "I don't like this."

Vince followed the glance the detective darted at their surroundings. "It was our best option," he said in an undertone. "You're supposed to be missing. Nobody will expect you to be having dinner here. Besides, Leanza didn't recognize you either."

Commosky squinted at the menu. "What's gumbo?"

Vince smiled. "Phenomenal. A little pricey, but it's worth every credit."

"I'll try that, then."

Vince got up and went up to the counter to place and pay for two orders of gumbo. When he returned, he found Commosky still regarding the table with a dour expression. "Now what?"

"Haven't done much undercover work." The detective gestured to their surroundings, shaking his head. "Not used to being on this side of an investigation. Still feels wrong."

Especially when the stakes are this high, Vince thought, but he kept it to himself. Commosky wasn't the only one risking everything. He kept anticipating his comlink to buzz, letting him know that Letitia was ready to go.

"Marv," called a tiny lady from the counter.

With an internal jolt, Vince remembered that Marv was the name he'd given earlier. Pushing back his chair, he rose swiftly to his feet and went up to collect their food.

"Marv?" Commosky raised an eyebrow when Vince returned bearing a tray with spoons, napkins, and two steaming bowls of gumbo.

"First name that came to mind." Setting the tray down on the table, the Finder carefully lifted one of the bowls of gumbo and set in front of his own seat. He grabbed a spoon and a napkin, and then slid the tray across to Commosky. "You'll like this."

"Is that shrimp?" Commosky stared down at his bowl. "And chicken?" He glanced at Vince. "How much did that set you back?"

"Don't worry about it." Vince waved a hand. "Going on my expense report."

"Your poor client," Commosky said, but he was smiling.

Vince just snorted and stirred his gumbo, mixing the hearty stew into the rice it had been served over. Commosky knew full well that Vince's Finder fees were reasonable.

"What is this?" Commosky held up his spoon, eying a round slice of something green with little white seeds inside.

"Okra," Vince said, holding back a laugh at the odd look on the detective's face. "You've never had it before?"

"No." Commosky's tone implied he'd been just fine with that up to this point.

"You'll like it."

"You keep saying that," Commosky muttered, but he ate the piece of okra. After he swallowed, he shrugged. "A little slimy, but not bad."

Vince held up his spoon in a kind of salute, as if to say, *See?*

They had nearly finished their dinner when the door opened and Leanza marched in. She'd changed clothes—she now wore a burnt orange sweater over black leggings—and she had a small black backpack slung over one shoulder.

Shoulders square, chin up, almost in defiance, Leanza paused at the entrance just long enough to ascertain where Vince was. Then, face resolute and eyes hard, she made straight for him.

This surprised Vince, for two reasons. One, he'd have thought that she'd be averse to drawing unnecessary attention to herself, given she was returning stolen property. And two…most people, when they'd been caught doing something illegal, had the grace to at least act like they felt ashamed.

This was…brazen. Like Leanza was doing *them* a favor by returning Mrs. Kawana's statue.

He studied Leanza, trying to reconcile this version of her with everything he'd learned so far. The results didn't quite match up. Something was off.

He narrowed his eyes a fraction. Or, at the very least, something else was going on.

"Here." Leanza unceremoniously dumped the backpack in the middle of the table, nearly sending it into Vince's all-but-empty bowl.

Vince half-expected her to turn around and stalk out, but she knew better. Posting a hand on her hip, Leanza stood there, waiting. Her gaze flicked from him to Commosky and back, her dark eyes angry and resentful.

"Thank you," Vince said calmly, sliding his bowl to one side and pulling the backpack toward him so he could inspect its contents.

Mrs. Kawana's pale stone statue gleamed in the depths of the backpack. He was sure it was the original, but he checked it anyway. Reaching down into the bag, he felt for a tiny, invisible indentation in the side of the base. When he pressed it, a small drawer popped out of a slot. A glance inside told him that it held a tiny datachip.

Pressing the tiny drawer back into place, Vince looked up at Leanza. "I trust you haven't fiddled with anything?"

Her lip curled in a sneer. "Do I look that stupid?"

"No." Vince offered her a small smile. "You understand I have to ask."

"Yeah, yeah." She waved her free hand, the resentment in her eyes deepening. "Are you satisfied? Gonna leave me alone now?"

Out of the corner of his eye, Vince noticed they were drawing attention from Le Bouf's other patrons. Leanza wasn't shouting, but she wasn't being particularly careful to keep her voice down, either.

His goatee bristled; he resisted the urge to rub his chin. There was a reason for that. There had to be.

"If you've held up your end of the bargain and returned Mrs. Kawana's property intact," he nodded to the backpack, "then she will follow through with her end and contact Station Authority to drop all charges." He waited a beat. "That will happen tomorrow during regular business hours."

"Fine."

Vince expected Leanza to toss her hair and stalk out at this point, but again, she surprised him by holding out her hand. "I want my backpack back."

Across from Vince, Commosky made an affronted sound in the back of his throat.

The Finder ignored him. Several pieces slotted into place, revealing the answer—or at least a partial answer—to the riddle that was Leanza's behavior. *She wants everyone to see me walk out of here with this statue.*

There could be only one reason for that—she wanted plenty of witnesses so that either the person she owed money to or the statue's prospective buyer knew she no longer possessed it.

There's a third option, he thought wryly. *She could be hoping that I'll encounter difficulties with Station Authority—or somebody else—on my way back to Mrs. Kawana.*

If so, that was just petty aggravation. It wouldn't get Vince into any real trouble. No, it was far likelier that Leanza was using his to make a very public announcement that she no longer possessed the statue.

"Well?" Leanza demanded imperiously.

In answer, Vince reached into the backpack and withdrew the statue. He held it carefully in one hand and proffered the backpack to Leanza by its straps. "Thank you."

She snatched the backpack from him, but he held on for a moment, until she glared at him.

Vince held her gaze. "It's possible," he said quietly, "that I can help you."

Leanza just sneered at him. She tugged on the backpack again, and this time Vince let go. The young woman slung the backpack over her shoulder, turned on her heel, and stalked out of the eatery in high dudgeon. She let the door slam behind her.

Vince noticed that everyone in the eatery watched her go. He couldn't help wonder if there was someone here, watching her. She'd been very specific about this place, and she'd made a scene.

Across the table from him, Commosky shook his head. "For someone who's getting a break on a theft charge, you'd think she'd be a little more grateful."

"You'd think," Vince agreed, but his goatee was still tingling. He rubbed his chin, looking down at the statue he still held in his other hand. "You done? Let's get this back to Mrs. Kawana."

He didn't say, 'before something else happens.'

He didn't have to.

Commosky picked up on that loud and clear. Smiling wryly, the detective rose from his chair. "You're the boss."

CHAPTER 40

THE ENTIRE TRIP BACK TO MRS. KAWANA'S apartment, Vince felt like he had a target indicator painted on his back. Marching through Zone 5 carrying an expensive statue made him uncomfortable—which had been part of Leanza's purpose, he knew—but it was more than that. He couldn't shake a gut feeling that something was about to go wrong.

Again.

Vince could tell Commosky felt it too. The detective's eyes kept darting around, constantly assessing their surroundings. He was too experienced to jump at the slightest oddity, but he was even more on edge than he'd been earlier.

Thankfully, Mrs. Kawana opened her apartment door on the first buzz. Her eyes immediately fell on the statue in Vince's arms. She pressed both hands to her mouth, her shoulders shuddering and her almond-shaped eyes widening and filling with tears.

She stood aside, almost in a daze, as Vince and Commosky slid past her into her apartment. The stocky homicide detective immediately hit the door release, sealing them off from the corridor outside.

Vince cast a quick look around as he turned toward his client. Her apartment looked no different than it had earlier. Same pale pink bulkheads, same pristine white carpet. The only difference was that something that smelled like macaroni and cheese now mixed with the scent of lavender that permeated the air.

"You found it." Mrs. Kawana finally found her words. Tears of happiness dripped down her cheeks, but she wasn't sobbing. She moved toward Vince, her hands outstretched. "I can't believe you actually found it."

Vince held the statue out to her and she took it tenderly, almost reverently. Cradling it in her arms, she stared at it for a few seconds before she looked up at Vince. "That Maintenance woman had it?"

"Yes. She agreed to your deal. I told her you'd call Station Authority tomorrow."

Mrs. Kawana nodded and looked back down at the statue. Slowly, as though she still couldn't quite believe it was real, she turned the statue around until she found the hidden button in the base. A second later, she dumped the tiny datachip that had been inside into her palm.

"I have no reason to think she tampered with anything," Vince said, "but I'd recommend that you check that datachip to be sure it's yours."

Wordlessly, Mrs. Kawana nodded again. She drifted out of the room, still carrying the statue.

Vince exchanged a glance with Commosky, but neither of them spoke. They just continued to stand on the white carpet in the middle of the living room.

A moment later, Mrs. Kawana returned. Her cheeks still glistened with tears, but she was smiling. "It's here," she said, setting the statue back on the end table where it had been before.

She then turned to Vince, holding out both hands. "I can't thank you enough, Finder Grable." She grasped his hands, squeezing tightly. "Thank you, thank you, *thank you.*"

"You're welcome." Vince inclined his head. "I'm glad I—we—" he tipped his head toward Commosky, "—could help." He held the older woman's gaze. "Just make sure you call Station Authority. Important to hold up your end of the deal."

"Yes, yes. I'll take care of it." She let go of his hands to turn to Commosky. "Thank you."

Commosky ducked his head in a gruff nod.

Mrs. Kawana turned back to Vince. "Send me your bill, Finder."

"I will."

She showed them to the door, all smiles and gratitude. Just before he stepped out onto the doormat, Vince gave the tiny woman a conspiratorial smile and lowered his voice. "You might want to find a safer spot for that datachip in the future."

Mrs. Kawana returned his smile. "That's a good idea."

She closed the door behind them and Vince glanced up and down the corridor. Nothing out of the ordinary jumped out at him, but he still couldn't shake the feeling that something was off. His goatee refused to stop bristling.

If they were being tailed, whoever was following them was good. Really good.

He and Commosky started back toward the main elevator bank. After a moment, the detective nodded over his shoulder in the direction of Mrs. Kawana's apartment. "Glad we're not carting that thing around anymore." He shook his head. "You see the looks we were getting?"

"Yeah."

"Wasn't sure if somebody would try to jump us or we'd get reported to Station Authority." A muscle in Commosky's cheek twitched as he briefly clenched his jaw. "Under normal circumstances..." He trailed off with a shrug.

They were passing a block of apartment complexes now. Vince glanced sideways at the shorter man. "Isn't there some law of the universe about that? 'Whatever can go wrong will'?"

Commosky shot him an irritated look. "Don't jinx us. We've made it this far."

Huh. That was an interesting wrinkle. Vince raised an eyebrow at Commosky, genuinely surprised. "I wouldn't have thought you'd go for that kind of thing."

"Yeah, well…" Commosky's shoulders drew up, making him look a little bit like a turtle drawing its head into its shell, before he forced himself to stand tall. "When you've seen as much as I have, you realize there are a few things in the universe that can't be explained."

That prompted a smile from Vince. "Just a few?"

Commosky opened his mouth to answer, but at that moment two silver transport pods veered out of their designated traffic lane in the center of the corridor. Neatly, they glided to a halt along the sidewalk just ahead of Vince and Commosky. Both doors opened and two burly men with short haircuts and nondescript dark clothing stepped out.

A couple that had been walking toward Vince and Commosky on the sidewalk quickened their pace and scurried around the two men, shooting the transport pods uneasy glances.

Something concrete settled into the pit of Vince's stomach. Ah. Here it was. He stopped and turned to face the two men, acknowledging that they probably wanted to speak to him.

Beside him, Commosky also stopped. His posture was relaxed and open; only a faint tightening around his eyes betrayed the tension that gripped him.

"Finder Grable?" The shorter of the two men gave Vince a brusque nod. He gave Commosky an assessing once-over, but his attention returned to Vince.

"That would be me," Vince said easily.

"Will you come with us, please?"

The 'please' surprised Vince. The kind of people who showed up out of nowhere and pulled individuals into transport pods weren't usually terribly polite. He cocked an eyebrow at the man. "Who's asking?"

"Does it matter?" the other burly man growled, but his comrade shot him a quelling look.

"Polite," he said through gritted teeth. "Supposed to be polite."

His companion just narrowed his eyes to slits and folded his arms imposingly across his chest. The movement made his biceps look huge and he knew it.

"'Our…employer would like a word with you, Finder." The shorter man gestured to the transport pod. "It's urgent."

"I'm sure it is, if he or she has sent you to collect me." Vince remained where he was. Late evening traffic flowed up and down the corridor, but pedestrian traffic had lightened considerably. This wasn't the best time to snatch somebody off the sidewalk, but it also wasn't the worst.

They did say 'please'. He turned to Commosky. "Why don't you—"

"Grable," Commosky growled, but the shorter man interrupted.

"Your friend can come too." He waved a calloused hand toward the interior of the closest transport pod. "In fact, we insist."

Vince glanced at Commosky. In the detective's eyes, he saw a reflection of the thoughts going through his own mind. If this wasn't Family-related, he'd eat his brown leather jacket.

Well, there was only one real way out of this. He smiled genially at the two men. "All right. Never let it be said this Finder isn't accessible to prospective clients."

He started toward the closest transport pod. Behind him, Commosky made a noise in the back of his throat, but he followed.

They both climbed inside. The shorter of the burly men climbed in after them and shut the door.

It was only then that Vince realized they weren't the only occupants. A slim woman occupied the corner opposite him, dressed in a long-sleeved turquoise blouse and a knee-length black skirt. A translucent silver scarf wrapped around her black hair, and the transport pod was filled with the sweet, fruity scent of her perfume.

The woman greeted them with a smile, holding up a tablet. "Good evening. Mr. Oswari would like a word with you."

Vince's goatee bristled again. The Oswari Family. *Well, that answers* that *question.*

Beside him, Commosky went very still. Vince was sure the detective was torn between professional curiosity and a desire to keep his identity a secret, given that all of Zyga Space Station had been put on alert to the fact that he was 'missing'.

Vince made a show of settling back against the transport pod's cushions. Whatever their exterior appearance, these were personal transport pods. The cushions were covered in gray leather and lacked a payment device.

He spread his hands. "At the moment, I am at Mr. Oswari's service." The Finder felt the hard look Commosky darted at him, but he ignored the detective. The best thing they could do was keep up the pretense that Commosky was a new Finder seeking advice.

The shorter burly man stirred in his seat next to the woman in turquoise. "Much appreciated." He tapped a button on the transport pod's onboard AI panel and they began to move, the pod merging smoothly back into traffic.

At the same time, Vince heard the distinct 'click' of the door locks. His senses sharpened, but he maintained a pleasant expression. His eyes fell on the tablet in the woman's hands. "I take it we won't be speaking to Mr. Oswari in person tonight?"

"No." She gave him an indulgent smile, her fingers tapping out commands. A second later, she turned the tablet around.

Oswari's face filled the display. In a thick, cultured voice, he said, "Good evening, Finder Grable."

"Oswari." Vince inclined his head in a nod.

The head of the Oswari Family turned his gaze toward Commosky. "Good evening, Detective Commosky."

CHAPTER 41

I N THAT INSTANT, THE TENSION FILLING THE transport pod shifted, changing from wary curiosity to something fraught with danger. The confines of the transport pod suddenly seemed too close, the woman's perfume too cloying.

Shock flooded Vince like a jolt of electricity. *He knows. How does he know?*

A pit opened up in his stomach. If the head of the Oswari Family knew that his companion was Ron Commosky in disguise, who *else* knew?

To his credit, Commosky managed to keep a straight face. He tilted his head to one side in polite confusion. "Beg pardon?"

"Ah, it is a good act, but—" Oswari shook his head, "—no good, I'm afraid, Detective."

The tension inside the transport pod shifted again. Vince couldn't explain it—and it made no sense at all—but…he had the strangest feeling that they weren't in any real danger. He rubbed his chin thoughtfully, drawing attention from both the burly man and Oswari himself.

"I must commend you on your creativity, Finder Grable." Oswari inclined his head in a respectful nod. "I doubt most people would recognize the detective here. But if you are, like I am, in possession of certain facts, it becomes an almost inescapable conclusion."

"Certain facts?" Commosky asked gruffly.

Oswari waved a hand. "Your association and collaboration with Finder Grable here in the matter of the Ruby Gauntlet, of course."

Vince's mouth went a little dry. The Oswari Family knew about *that* too? He didn't dare look at Commosky. Again, he couldn't help but wonder, if *they* knew, who else did?

Commosky doggedly shook his head. "Don't know what you're—"

"Please, Detective." On his end of the vidcall, Oswari held up a hand. "Any other day I might be inclined to humor this little farce and allow it to play out to its inevitable conclusion." He shook his head. "Not today."

Out of the corner of his eye, Vince noted that the transport pods were turning down a boulevard that led deeper into the residential section of Level 8. *Where are they taking us?* He'd have expected them to head toward the main elevator bank.

That they were going a completely different direction was at the same time both alarming and intriguing.

"The entire Station is looking for you, Detective, and yet here you are, out wandering around Zone 5 in disguise—albeit a good disguise, I must admit—with Finder Grable here." Oswari shook his head again, leaning toward his screen. His dark eyes tracked back and forth between Vince and Commosky, as though he hoped he might find the answer to his questions written on their faces. "That begs the very obvious question: why?"

Vince wanted to laugh, but he didn't think Oswari would take it well at the moment. "If you've had people following us, then you know I was working a case."

"Yes, yes, the trivial theft of that statue." Oswari impatiently brushed that aside. "Hardly anything worth a homicide detective's time and effort, even if you *are* avoiding Station Authority."

It wasn't worth arguing that his client hadn't considered the case trivial. Vince settled back against the transport pod's remarkably comfortable cushion. *He has a point about Commosky.*

He didn't look at Commosky, who had turned as motionless as…well…Mrs. Kawana's statue. Instead, the Finder spread his hands. "Why don't you get straight to the point and tell us what it is that you want, Mr. Oswari? Since you've made it a point to tell us how short on time you are."

Oswari regarded him with those flat, cold dark eyes, and then he smiled. It would have been a pleasant, almost friendly expression—if it had gone anywhere near his eyes. "I'm sure you already know this, but the owners of the Ruby Gauntlet are behind today's troubling… power outages."

"We're aware," Vince said. Beside him, Commosky remained silent, regarding the tablet as though he expected Oswari to jump through the display and attack them.

"Good. What else do you know?"

Vince did laugh then. "Oh, no." He shook his head, smiling. "I'm not playing that game. *You* picked *us* up, Oswari. You tell me why we're here."

The temperature inside the transport pod plummeted. The woman holding the tablet did not move, but Vince heard her breath catch in her throat. Beside her, the shorter burly man tensed.

Even Commosky looked askance at Vince, his gaze darting sideways as though he didn't know whether to be impressed or alarmed at the Finder's tenacity.

Vince held firm. This was a calculated risk. Oswari *had* come to them—and he'd instructed his minions to be polite. Ergo, he wanted something pretty badly.

After a long few seconds, Oswari let out a barking laugh and leaned back in his chair. "I like you, Finder. You're good at your job. That is why you're still alive."

He probably wasn't wrong, but Vince brushed that aside with a flick of his fingers. "I don't have all night, Oswari." He smiled shrewdly. "And from the sound of it, neither do you."

"Get to the point," Commosky interjected, deciding to speak at last.

The burly man across the seat from them shifted uneasily, but Oswari just switched that flat, cold gaze to Commosky and considered him for a second before returning his attention to Vince. "If you've been investigating the Ruby Gauntlet, you must know its owners, Starlit and Lumen, are raking in a considerable amount of illegal money from their little Diamond Club."

"Yes," Vince said.

Oswari glanced at Commosky. "And, you, Detective, are currently attempting to link them to several homicides that have occurred aboard Zyga Station in past several years."

"That's confidential information." Commosky narrowed his eyes at the head of the Oswari Family, apparently deciding it was no longer worth attempting to deny his real identity. "How did you come by it?"

"That is not relevant." Oswari waved a brusque hand. "The important thing is that if you take all of those things and put them together, a rather disturbing picture emerges."

For someone who claimed to be in such a hurry, the head of the Oswari Family was certainly taking his time getting to the point. Vince resisted the urge to shift in his seat. He opened his mouth, but Commosky beat him to it.

"And what picture would that be?" The detective didn't bother keeping the brusqueness from his voice.

Vince watched Oswari's eyes narrow at Commosky's tone, but his voice, when he spoke, was calm. "Starlit and Lumen are attempting to put pressure on Station Authority and the Council to recognize them as a legitimate operation."

"So?" Commosky raised his chin. "Why would that bother you?"

Oswari briefly pressed his lips into a thin line before he said, "All the evidence points to them attempting to become a third Family here on Zyga Station."

There it was.

Vince had been beginning to think that Oswari wouldn't actually say the words aloud. He raised his eyebrows in polite surprise. "A third Family?"

"Yes. Not officially, of course, but that is the net result." Oswari's thin lips stretched in a smile. "You needn't pretend to be surprised. Given the amount of work you and the detective here—" he nodded to Commosky, "—have put into this case, I would be shocked if you hadn't arrived at the same conclusion."

"It crossed my mind." Vince glanced from Oswari to the burly man and the woman, who had yet to say a word, before returning his attention to the head of the Oswari Family. "What I don't understand is—"

"—what this has to do with us." Commosky folded his arms across his chest, staring grimly at the head of the Oswari Family.

CHAPTER 42

EVEN THROUGH THE TABLET DISPLAY, THE LOOK Oswari gave the detective was glacial. "You are fortunate, Detective, that you are not in my employ. I do not suffer people to speak to me as you do."

Commosky didn't miss a beat. "No, you just make people suffer. You and the Bok Family both." One corner of his mouth turned up in a sneering smile. "And you don't want competition. Starlit and Lumen forming another Family will cramp your style."

"There is a…delicate…balance to life aboard this space station, as I'm sure you are well aware, Detective." Oswari's dark eyes glittered with impatience and something that almost looked like…fear.

Interesting. Vince filed that away for future reference as well. Aloud, he said, "I believe I'd classify it more as a delicate balance of power."

"Be as that may," Oswari shook his head, "I think we can all agree that Starlit and Lumen becoming a Family bodes ill for the rest of us." He waved a hand, indicating the Station around them. "They actually had the audacity to shut off the *power*. More than once."

"The Families have standards?" Commosky shook his head, his arms still crossed over his chest. "Who knew?"

Vince glanced at him out of the corner of his eye, surprised that the detective was being so antagonist. *Is he just frustrated, or he working some other angle I can't see?*

Aloud, he said, "They crossed a line."

"Yes." Oswari's voice grew very cold. "Bok Chul and I may have our…disagreements…when it comes to our…business practices in the Core, but we have no desire to harm Zyga Station itself and its population."

If the subject wasn't so dire, Vince might have let himself audibly snort at this. Just because Oswari was desperate enough to enlist the aid of a Finder and a homicide detective didn't mean he'd taken complete leave of his senses. The head of the Oswari Family wasn't about to openly *admit* he was the head of the Oswari Family. That would be illegal, of course, and it would probably give Commosky grounds to arrest him.

"By shutting the power off," Oswari continued, "they proved that they have no qualms about putting the Station in danger." He shook his head again. "They cannot be allowed to continue down this course."

Commosky regarded the head of the Oswari Family with hooded eyes. "You think the Council will give them a Casino license?"

"If the alternative is Zyga Station losing power again?" Oswari gave the detective a chiding look. "What do you think, Detective?"

"I think it's interesting that there's actually a line you say you won't cross." Commosky lifted his chin.

Vince inclined his head in a nod of agreement. He'd never really considered the fact that the Families had never openly jeopardized the Station's wellbeing. It threw Starlit and Lumen's actions into even starker relief.

Oswari smiled thinly. "You cannot make money if there's no one to frequent your business. And I am in the business of making money."

An understatement if Vince had ever heard one. He glanced around the interior of the transport pod again, assessing the shorter burly man and the woman in turquoise still patiently holding the tablet so they could see Oswari. Both of Oswari's minions were expressionless, though the tension in the transport pod remained.

The Finder eyed Oswari. "What exactly is it that you want from us?"

"What do I want?" Oswari smiled that thin smile again.

Vince narrowed his eyes a fraction. Was it his imagination, or did the older man's shoulders relax a little, as though Vince's questions had relieved him of a burden?

"I want you to help me stop them." Oswari glanced sideways, looking at someone beyond Vince and Commosky's view. "

"*We* want you to help us stop them," said a familiar voice.

Vince tensed. He knew that voice. That was—

On Oswari's end of the vidcall, the cam pulled back to show Oswari seated in a chair side by side with Bok Chul. The head of the Bok Family had been there the whole time, quietly waiting for his moment to interject.

Beside Vince, Commosky made a small choking sound.

Vince knew the feeling. That the two Families were apparently working together was shocking enough, but *both* Family heads in the same room? As far as he knew, that had only happened a few times in the past several *decades*.

Bok Chul looked from Vince to Commosky and back. "The danger Zyga Station faces from Starlit and Lumen transcends any of our…past…disagreements. It transcends the distinction between citizen and Station Authority official." His wrinkled face settled into grave lines. "They need to be stopped."

CHAPTER 43

*T*HEY NEED TO BE STOPPED.

Those words seemed to hang in the close confines of the transport pod. Vince sat very still, his back pressed against the comfortable gray leather of his seat. He couldn't say he was *surprised* the Families were taking action against Starlit and Lumen, but…

He *was* surprised they had deigned to join forces for the endeavor. And that Oswari and Bok Chul had come to the two of *them* for help.

Beside Vince, Commosky apparently had the same thought. He let out a short, disbelieving laugh. "All those resources between the two of you and you're coming to *us* for help?"

The two Family heads exchanged glances.

"Yes," Oswari said. "In this current state of emergency, we determined this was the most expedient course of action."

Bok Chul smiled. "You might say, Detective, that we are using every resource at our disposal. As far as we can determine, you—" he nodded to Commosky, "—and Finder Gable currently have the most knowledge of the Ruby Gauntlet and its workings."

It was flattering, but… Vince narrowed his eyes, raising a hand to rub his chin. His goatee was bristling. "I agree with—" he caught himself before he said Commosky's name, "—my colleague here. I don't buy it."

Oswari's eyes narrowed in displeasure, and his mouth thinned, but beside him, Bok Chul merely continued to smile. "I wouldn't expect anything less from you, Finder." He leaned forward in his seat, reaching for something out of sight. When he sat back in his chair, he held a glass of dark red wine. "The answer is simple." He took an appreciative sip of his wine and swallowed. "We don't have time to mount an in-depth investigation of our own."

Commosky laughed again. "Meaning, you didn't think they were that much of a danger to your various operations until it was too late."

Dead silence greeted these words.

Vince glanced sideways at the detective with something akin to awe. If the idea of the power and corruption these two men represented frightened Commosky, he didn't let it show. He just continued to drill both of the Family heads with a hard, keen look.

"I would not," Oswari said at last, "put it quite that way, but—"

Bok Chul interrupted him. "No, no, he's right." He took another sip of his wine. "You didn't see this coming, Oswari, and neither did I."

Oswari bristled, but then he calmed himself. "They threatened the very wellbeing of the Station itself. Put that way, I don't believe *anybody* could see it coming."

Vince's goatee was still bristling. He rubbed his chin again, thoughtfully. "What exactly is it that you're hoping we can do?" He turned his free hand palm up.

"Stop them, obviously," Oswari said at once. He pointed to Commosky. "You've been investigating them for months. There has to be *something* in all of that data that could help us."

"We have friends among the information broker community," Bok Chul said. "Our resources are at your disposal." He raised his wine glass. "Anything you need."

The hair raised on the back of Vince's neck. Resisting a sudden, strong urge to shudder, he glanced at Commosky. The detective was studying the two Family heads, his expression thoughtful.

A pit formed in Vince's stomach. In that instant, he felt as though a chasm had suddenly opened at their feet. The slightest misstep would send them tumbling into it, never to return.

If he—or Commosky, *especially* Commosky—took what Bok Chul and Oswari were offering, there was a good chance that the Families would end up pulling them into something worse. A good chance that they'd ended up being *owned* by the Families. That the detective was actually considering this offer told Vince how badly he wanted to bring Starlit and Lumen to justice.

If they did this…if they reached a compromise with the Families to keep the Ruby Gauntlet from taking over Zyga Space Station…

Well… Vince drew in a breath, almost imperceptibly. He didn't think Commosky's conscience would allow him to live with himself afterward.

He might take Starlit and Lumen down, but at the cost of losing himself.

There has to be another way.

Out of the corner of his eye, Vince saw Commosky open his mouth. *Now or never,* he thought, before straightening in his seat and drawing everyone's attention. "What if we're already working a plan?"

Commosky sent him a sharp look, but the way Bok Chul and Oswari both looked at him, without even a hint of surprise, told Vince everything he needed to know. *They were hoping we were already working an angle on this.*

"Given how short our time is," Oswari said finally, "that would be ideal." He exchanged a glance with Bok Chul beside him. "Is there any way we can be of assistance?"

Was there anything they could do that Vince wouldn't hate himself for later? His mind raced, sifting through possibilities.

At that moment, his comlink buzzed in his pocket. "Comlink," he said, by way of warning, before he reached into his pocket and withdrew the device.

Across the pod from him, the short, burly man twitched a little, but otherwise remained calm.

It was a text from Brill. ::*She's ready. Will be heading out for 'boba tea' soon.*::

A wave of calm clarity settled over Vince. This was it. The final piece of the plan was falling into place.

He looked at Commosky, who was watching him with an expression that said if he didn't start talking soon, he wouldn't be responsible for the outcome. "Our asset is ready."

Instead of looking relieved, Commosky's entire posture tensed, ready for action. One of his hands clenched into a fist. "Finally."

"How can we help?" Oswari leaned forward, making his face loom larger in the tablet display.

Vince looked at Commosky again. He didn't trust the Families as far as he could throw any of their members with one hand tied behind his back, but… They did need some help.

Commosky narrowed his eyes, tilting his head to one side. "What are you thinking, Grable?"

In answer, Vince turned to the two Family heads. "We need a couple of transport pods and a distraction. A good one."

It was Oswari and Bok Chul's turn to exchange glances. "We can help with that," Bok Chul said, swirling his wine absently in his glass.

"Yes." Oswari nodded, a little more enthusiastically than Vince would have expected. "I know exactly how to distract Starlit and Lumen."

"How's that?" Commosky asked gruffly. He looked a little wary, and Vince couldn't blame him. The Families weren't exactly known for their upstanding contributions to Zyga Space Station society, after all.

"We give them what they want." Oswari spread his hands, smiling beatifically. "We give them you, Detective."

CHAPTER 44

THE BOTTOM DROPPED OUT OF VINCE'S STOMACH. The gumbo he'd eaten earlier stirred uneasily. He turned his head to look at Commosky, who sat absolutely motionless in his corner of the transport pod.

It was the last thing the Finder wanted to do to close this case… and yet…it made an awful sort of sense. Thanks to Starlit and Lumen, the entire space station was on the lookout for Commosky, thinking he was in some sort of trouble. Even with his disguise, the detective was bound to be recognized sooner or later.

Commosky flicked his gaze sideways to meet Vince's. His expression had gone flat and cold, making him look more like the version of himself Vince had first encountered on the other side of an interrogation table in a Zone 4 Station Authority homicide division all those years ago. He didn't react with outrage or anger.

He was, Vince realized, seriously considering this.

Finally, Commosky snorted and turned his attention back to the Family heads. (Vince felt a little sorry for the woman stuck sitting there patiently holding the tablet.) "If this were any other occasion,

I'd be sure you were selling me out to get rid of me. As it is, I haven't quite worked out if you're getting ready to screw us over some other way."

Neither Oswari nor Bok Chul answered this.

Smart men, Vince thought.

"Think it's doable, Finder?" Commosky shifted his attention to Vince. "Will you be able to protect our asset alone?"

At this, Oswari sniffed. "Alone? He'll have our help, won't he?"

Commosky transferred a flat stare to the man, but continued to address Vince. "Like I said, Finder, can you do this alone?"

Could he? Vince paused, giving the question the consideration it was due. Rubbing his chin thoughtfully, he shrugged. "Barring Family interference, it shouldn't be an issue."

His answer spurred a sharp-toothed smile from Commosky, but Oswari bristled. "Barring Family interference?" The Family head glared at Vince, his voice growing very cold. "You're treading on dangerous ground, Finder, making insolent comments like that."

Bok Chul, Vince noted, said nothing. He merely remained seated, taking the occasional sip of wine from the glass he held loosely in one hand.

Vince met Oswari's irritated gaze, suppressing his own irritation. "I'd be remiss if I didn't exercise caution." He twitched his shoulders in a casual shrug. "I don't think I have to remind you that you do have a reputation in certain quarters of Zyga Station."

Oswari's glare could have frozen a shuttle's engines, but he was on the wrong side of this and he knew it. Even so, he still seemed inclined to go on the offensive.

Vince filed that away for future reference. This was the first time he'd ever personally encountered Oswari, and the differences between him and Bok Chul were quite striking. He reminded Vince of an angry hornet buzzing around, while his counterpart in the Bok Family was more like a lazy viper. Both were dangerous, in their own way, but one was vastly more annoying that the other.

Commosky held up a hand. "I have conditions."

"You're not in any position—" Oswari began, bristling, but Bok Chul interrupted him.

"Of course he is." Bok Chul regarded his rival Family head with a thin-lipped smile. "Let's not forget the position *we* are in, my friend."

Even through the tablet display, Vince could feel the temperature drop again.

More to save face than anything else, Oswari shrugged. "That is a good point." He smiled, but it was all sharp edges. "Neither one of us is accustomed to asking for help."

Bok Chul acknowledged that with a nod, before waving toward Commosky. "Your conditions, Detective."

"One." Commosky held up a finger. "It hasn't escaped me that you'll be reaping goodwill from Station Authority and possibly even the Council itself for bringing me in." His voice grew stern. "You will *not* spin this to imply that I was in any way, shape, or form involved in something illegal."

"Done," Bok Chul said lazily, before Oswari could even open his mouth.

"Two." Commosky held up a second finger. "You will not interfere with Finder Grable here collecting our asset and doing what needs to be done." He glanced at Vince, jerking his chin in a faint nod to indicate the Finder should chime in.

"We have a good plan," Vince said, sweeping his gaze around the transport pod. "It's taken a lot of careful maneuvering to get to this point, but we're confident we can pull it off." In his mind's eye, he saw Brill, heard the fear and anger in his voice when he talked about Starlit and Lumen going too far when they jeopardized the Station.

"Don't interfere," Commosky said coldly. He drew himself up in his seat, regarding Oswari and Bok Chul with thin-lipped disdain. "If you two have managed to set aside your usual squabbles to work together on this, don't stop now. You want to keep Starlit and Lumen from forming a Family? Don't ruin this investigation."

His dark eyes glittered with a storm of emotion. "If you do, they'll walk and we'll all be stuck with them."

"We do not want that," Bok Chul murmured.

"Neither do we." Oswari shifted in his seat.

"Good," Commosky said firmly.

Silence filled the transport following this—silence tinged with a sense of camaraderie, even as the wrongness of it pressed on Vince. Because it did feel wrong—he couldn't remember a time when he'd knowingly teamed up with one Family, let alone both of them.

The Finder waited a beat, and then cocked an eyebrow at Commosky. "Anything else?"

"Yeah." Commosky rubbed a hand over his face, before frowning. "I need to clean this off first so I look like myself."

"That can be arranged, Detective," Oswari said.

"Quickly," Bok Chul advised, his gaze focused somewhere offscreen. "We don't have much time left."

Vince met Commosky's gaze. A sense of understanding passed between the two of them. Neither man trusted the Families…but at the moment they didn't have another choice.

This wasn't the best option, but it *was* the option that stunk the least.

Vince felt something settle in his chest. Regardless, they'd have to watch out and make sure they didn't get double-crossed. He glanced at the tablet in the hands of the woman seated across from him. The display showed that Bok Chul and Oswari had leaned their heads together and were conferring quietly.

He frowned. That would be easier said than done, with this crew.

CHAPTER 45

An hour later, Vince loitered at a back table inside a little tea shop on Level 9, drinking his second cup of tea since his arrival. At this time of night, the tea shop was not busy, but it still did brisk business. Being the only tea shop on this entire level that was open twenty-four hours a day had its perks.

Leaning back in his recycled wood chair, Vince stretched his back and breathed in the comforting scent of tea permeating the air. The tea shop was not large; it only held a handful of tables, including several corner tables where group of five or six people could gather. It should have felt cramped, but the soft lighting from little lamps suspended from the overhead combined with soft instrumental music and that wonderful smell of tea created a cozy atmosphere instead, like everyone here had crowded into a dear friend's living room. The staff was small, but quiet, though they were friendly enough when they needed to be.

In all, it was an introvert's dream. Even with what little Vince knew about Letitia Theriot, he could see why this place was a favorite of hers. Brill doubted a late night boba tea run would raise any flags with her…bodyguards…and Vince agreed.

While he waited, the Finder had divided his attention between the interior of the tea shop and his comlink. It was unlikely that either of the Families would interfere, or that Starlit and Lumen would have any reason to interfere at this point, but that didn't mean he could let his guard down. Plus, he had to work out the best way to whisk Letitia out from under their collective noses.

To that end, Vince pulled up a few maps of Level 9 and studied them to augment his memory. He then sent a message to the shorter burly man, whose name was Udo, requesting a transport pod to be on standby to meet him around the corner when he gave the signal. Udo's comm frequency most likely belonged to a burner comlink, but that was all right. Vince expected that from the Families.

His comlink abruptly vibrated with an incoming text. Brill. ::*Asset is on the way.*::

Before Vince could respond, Brill sent him a second text—a comm frequency for Letitia.

Vince's eyebrows rose in surprise. That would be helpful. He saved Letitia's frequency as a secondary number for Mrs. Kawana—probably overkill on the caution side of things, but he *was* dealing with Families and a group of people who'd shown no compunction in shutting down the entire space station.

After Vince responded to Brill with an affirmative, he thought for a second, and then placed a request with Zyga Station's transportation system for a transport pod of his own to arrive around the corner in a few minutes.

He smiled grimly to himself. Just in case. Couldn't be too careful, in a situation like this.

When the tea shop's door opened with a gentle tinkle a few minutes later, Vince didn't raise his head to see who had entered. Instead, he studied the newcomer from beneath his lowered brow. A knot in his chest simultaneously loosened and then tightened again.

Letitia Theriot had arrived—and she was not alone.

Vince swallowed the flare of annoyance that swirled through him. Of *course* she hadn't been able to get away by herself. He was willing to bet that before the events of the past few days Letitia had wandered wherever she pleased around Zyga Station sans escort, but no more.

Starlit and Lumen had enough sense to put an end to *that*.

On the table, Vince touched a finger to his comlink, pressed the 'send' button on the message he'd already composed to Udo. ::*Now.*::

Lifting his nearly-empty cup of tea to his lips, he watched Letitia and her bodyguard—the shorter, light-skinned man, Saul—out of the corner of his eye. Letitia's peach-toned skin seemed a little paler than it had been earlier, and she still looked tired, but she strode up to place her order with the sure familiarity of someone who had been here many times before. She wore the same clothes as earlier—soft black pants and that overlarge pink shirt—but she'd wrapped a soft gray sweater around herself. A medium-sized black purse hung over her shoulder.

Shrewdly, Vince eyed that purse. There was no telling what she'd stashed in there—and he'd be willing to bet that her bodyguard hadn't touched it. Not if Letitia was one of those women who routinely carried a purse with her.

If she was smart, she'd brought a few of the things that were most important to her. Should everything go well, there was no telling when she'd be back in her apartment again.

Her bodyguard, Saul, took up a position at a table near the door. Vince avoided eye contact as the man's cold, dark gaze swept around the tea shop's dimly-lit interior. He watched Saul out of the corner of his eye, poised to jump and run if necessary, but the maintenance uniforms he and Commosky had worn earlier had done their job. Saul's gaze now skimmed over the Finder without an ounce of recognition and returned to a casual surveillance of the tea shop.

Without looking at Letitia, Vince triggered the text he'd already composed to her. ::*Back corner by the secondary exit. We're exiting through the kitchen.*::

In his peripheral vision, he watched her dig her comlink out of her purse and glance at it. The Finder was pleased to see that she managed to keep her cool and not draw attention from her handler. Dropping the comlink back into her purse with neither a word nor a look in Vince's direction, she continued to wait patiently by the counter for her boba tea.

Vince suppressed a frown, thinking rapidly. Whisking Letitia out through the kitchen wouldn't work. There was no way he'd be able to get her out to a transport pod without having to fight Saul off. The element of surprise would be ruined, and even at this hour the resulting brawl would draw far too much attention.

No… He narrowed his eyes slightly. This called for a different plan. One he'd have never been able to use by himself, but since the Families were oh, so eager to help…

He texted the short burly man again. ::*Asset isn't alone. Require assistance with handler.*:: He gave the man a brief description of Saul and then a few specific instructions.

He then texted Letitia again. ::*Outside.*:: She wouldn't know exactly what he meant, but she'd get the gist of it.

At that moment, the tea shop worker handed Letitia a plastic cup of purple boba tea with a large straw. Letitia thanked her with a smile and took a sip of her drink before she glanced at her phone again. Once more, Vince had to commend her on her casual nonchalance.

He picked up on the faint strain underlying her movements and expressions because he was trained for it; the Finder doubted Saul would notice. His job was to guard Letitia and the servers from outside threats, not a threat from Letitia herself.

Letitia drifted toward the door, taking another sip of her purple boba tea along the way. Vince sent another rapid-fire text to Udo. ::*They're coming out.*:: He then casually rose from his table, picking up his now-empty cup.

Saul did not open the door for Letitia, but instead followed her through it. Vince trailed after both of them, disposing of his trash along the way. He trusted Udo just enough to be sure he'd do as Vince asked—but the Finder did not trust him enough not to attempt to scoop Letitia up in the process.

No matter how desperate the Families might be, old habits were hard to break. Betrayal was, unfortunately, one of those habits—and Vince could think of several ways Oswari and Bok Chul could use Letitia against Starlit and Lumen.

CHAPTER 46

Nearing the tea shop's exit, Vince slowed his steps. Not enough for the employees or the few remaining patrons to notice he was loitering, but just enough to put a little space between himself and Saul's no doubt paranoid instincts. A few extra heartbeats, that's all.

As the Finder stepped out onto the corridor sidewalk and the dimmer light of the glowpanels set to their night-cycle settings overhead, he saw Saul and Letitia just ahead of him. Letitia walked slowly, sipping her boba tea, and Saul had to adjust his stride to keep with her. He said something to her that Vince didn't quite catch, his tone just this side of irritated.

Letitia merely gave her ersatz bodyguard a flat look, the oversize straw between her lips. Then she tossed her head and turned away from Saul. She wasn't as calm as she pretended; Vince read tension in the lines of her shoulders.

She was ready, expecting…something. Even if she didn't know what the plan was yet.

Vince's gaze darted toward the corner. *Come on*, he urged Udo silently. *Get over here.*

As if his thought had carried to the burly Family man telepathically, a transport pod zipped around the corner and slammed on the decelerator beside Saul and Letitia. The door flew open and two men in dark clothes jumped out.

To his credit, Saul reacted immediately. Swearing loudly, the bodyguard reached into his coat for a weapon with one hand, while he pushed Letitia behind him with his other hand.

This was the moment Vince had been waiting for.

As the two newcomers converged on Saul, Vince darted forward to take Letitia by the elbow and hurry her along the sidewalk toward the corner.

The woman started, nearly dropping her boba tea when he touched her, but a flash of recognition passed through her eyes as Vince met her gaze. Her lips pressed into a thin, firm line and she quickened her pace to keep up with him.

He gave her a minute nod. *Good girl.*

The two of them rounded the corner just as Saul let out an aggravated shout. A little jolt of adrenaline pumped through Vince. *He's realized she's gone.*

They didn't have much time. The plan entailed keeping the Families from knowing where Letitia was going as well…though of course the *Families* didn't know that.

Just ahead, the transport pod Vince had scheduled earlier waited against the curb, its smooth silver surface glistening in the dim light from the overhead glowpanels. Vince steered Letitia toward it. In three strides, they had reached the pod and climbed inside.

Vince immediately shut the door. "Lazula Game Shop," he told the pod's onboard AI, glancing out the rear viewport at the corner. It was still clear—no one had emerged around the corner yet.

Just as he'd calculated.

Obediently, the transport pod pulled away from the curb. It glided up the corridor—away from the tea shop and the three-man altercation no doubt still raging behind them. A moment later, the transport pod picked up speed as it settled into the fastest route to their destination.

"Wow." Across from Vince, Letitia slumped back against the dark blue cushion of the transport pod's seats, clutching her taro boba tea. Her hands, he noticed, were trembling. She shook her head from side to side, her blue eyes wide in her pale face. "It worked."

"Yes." Although they weren't in the clear yet. Vince kept that observation to himself, however, and extended a hand to her. "Finder Vince Grable."

She accepted his hand and they shook. Her fingers were cold.

"Letitia Theriot, but you know that already." She flashed a wry, self-deprecating smile, before nodding behind them. "That was pretty slick back there."

"Had some help." Vince glanced over his shoulder as well, though it was too early to tell if anybody was tailing them. "The Families *really* don't want your bosses joining their ranks."

"The Families?" Letitia jolted upright so fast she nearly came out of her seat. Her purple tea sloshed alarmingly in her cup; the lid the only thing keeping it from splashing everywhere. She gaped at Vince. "You're working with the *Families*?"

He saw real fear in her eyes and hastened to reassure her. "No, no, no, it's not like that." He shook his head. "More like they see the writing on the bulkhead and they wanted help from us to keep the Ruby Gauntlet from becoming another Family."

When the horrified expression on Letitia's face did not change, Vince changed tacks. They didn't have time for misunderstandings that could jeopardize everything.

In a few brief sentences, he outlined how the Families had decided they needed to join forces to combat Starlit and Lumen—and how they'd enlisted Vince and Commosky for help.

Letitia's horror faded, to be replaced by a bewildered sort of awe. "That guy who was with you is the homicide detective everybody on the entire Station is looking for?"

"Yeah."

"Wow." She blinked, sitting back against the cushion again. "That was some disguise."

"That was the point."

Letitia shook her head. "And the Families basically sacrificed him to make themselves look good with Station Authority." Her lip curled in disgust, even as remnants of her earlier fear filled her blue eyes. "Typical."

"More or less." Vince shrugged. "In their defense—" the words tasted bad even in his own mouth, "—Commosky *does* make a good distraction." He fixed Letitia with a level look. "As far as your bosses know, Commosky's the main threat to them, and not you."

Letitia nodded, drawing in a shaky breath, and ran her fingers through her ponytail. All at once, the enormity of what she was doing seemed to hit her. Setting her tea aside in a cupholder next to the door, she buried her face in her hands and hunched over. Her shoulders rose and fell as she sucked in breaths in rapid succession.

"Oh, my God, I can't believe I'm actually doing this." Her voice, though muffled, was clear enough for Vince to understand her.

Compassion swelled in his chest as he watched her struggle to contain herself. "What you're doing is very brave."

"Or incredibly stupid," she retorted through her fingers. "When they find out what I've done…" She didn't finish, but trailed off, her shoulders shaking with suppressed emotion.

Vince frowned, a hint of concern sliding into his compassion. They didn't have time for emotional meltdowns right now, either.

All at once, Letitia dropped her hands and straightened. Though her face was chalk white, her expression was set, resolute. "I helped create this mess. I have to help fix it. Your friend said that he and Station Authority can protect me."

Vince nodded and remained silent, sensing there was more.

"I don't know that I *believe* Station Authority can actually do that, but…" Letitia drew in a deep breath and nodded shortly. "I believe SilverBeard."

"He's generally a man of his word." Vince glanced out the transporter's back viewport again and told the transporter's onboard AI to make a left turn at the next corridor intersection. The traffic in this boulevard was moderate at this time of the evening; he wanted to make doubly sure they weren't being followed.

Even if it was by one of the Families.

Maybe *especially* if it was one of the Families.

Across from him, Letitia abruptly frowned. "Are you taking me to a *game* shop?"

As Vince watched out the back viewport, two transport pods split off from the main flow of traffic to make a left turn after them as well. He narrowed his eyes. *Interesting.*

To Letitia, he said, "It's not our final destination."

He gave their transport pod's AI directions for two more turns, both last minute. One of the pods following them went on its way, but the other continued to trail them.

"Comlink," he said to Letitia, holding out a hand. "Don't want your bosses tracking you."

She shook her head stubbornly, one hand possessively on her purse, the other clutching her sloshing boba tea, which she'd picked up again. "I have two. Left the work one behind." She jerked her chin toward her purse. "They don't have access to this one."

"Are you sure?" Vince eyed her, weighting the likelihood of this.

A cold smile stretched across Letitia's still-pale face. "I'd bet my life on it." Her lips twisted into a pained grimace. "I *am* betting my life on it."

Vince held her gaze a second longer, and a wave of understanding passed between them. He inclined his head. "All right."

He'd trust her. For now.

CHAPTER 47

As their transport pod hurtled through the still-busy corridors of Level 9 past shops and apartment complexes, Vince kept a sharp eye on the rear viewport. As far as he could tell, that other transport pod was still trailing them. It gave him an itchy feeling, like invisible bugs were crawling over his skin and he couldn't do anything to brush them away.

"What is it?"

Vince glanced at Letitia. She was watching him, her face taut with anxiety. Before he could open his mouth, she shrugged one shoulder defensively.

"Hey, just because I work with computers all day doesn't mean I don't know how to read people." She jerked her chin toward the rear viewport. "Doesn't take a genius to figure out something's up."

Vince conceded that point with a nod and glanced out at the less-bright corridor behind them once more. The pod was still there.

Still, he hesitated. "Could be nothing."

"You don't really believe that," Letitia said flatly.

Vince suppressed a grimace. No, he didn't. The real question was whether the people inside that pod belonged to the Ruby Gauntlet or one of the Families.

His credits were on one of the Families.

Vince narrowed his eyes. He needed to recalculate a few things. To that end, he pulled out his comlink to send a quick update to Bella and Brill.

"Who are you talking to?" Letitia's voice was sharp, borderline aggressive.

The Finder glanced at her coolly. He didn't owe her an explanation, but in the interests of keeping her amenable to giving up her bosses… "SilverBeard." Without breaking eye contact, he tipped his head toward the pod tailing them down the corridor. "I think whoever's in that belongs to one of the Families."

"And you don't think they're just making sure I make it to our destination safe and sound?" Letitia lifted her chin, trying to maintain a brave face.

Vince paused. "Honestly? I'm not sure what to think. There are a lot of moving parts to this operation."

At that moment, his comlink vibrated in his fingers. He glanced down. Here was one of those moving parts now.

Bella had texted him. ::*It's all over the Station that Commosky's been found. Two of Oswari and Bok Chul's lieutenants are getting the credit for finding him and bringing him back to Station Authority. Not that Station Authority officially knows who they are.*::

Starlit and Lumen had to be congratulating themselves now. Vince's gaze flicked to the rear viewport again. That was part one and part two of this operation, done.

So why are the Families following us? he wondered. *To make sure Letitia gets there safely?*

Or did they have another reason? One more nefarious and in keeping with their general reputation?

Vince squashed a flash of irritation. He didn't have time to figure that out.

The plan he, Brill, and Commosky had hastily concocted was a good plan, but the Finder knew better than most that 99% of all plans fell apart within the first few minutes. This plan wasn't the exception—and he'd prepared himself for its inevitable collapse.

That didn't mean he had to like it. At the same time—

"They've turned your friend in." Letitia's voice broke through Vince's rapid-fire thoughts. She'd pulled out her own comlink and now glanced up at him. Her boba tea sat forgotten in the cupholder. "How much time do we have now?"

"Not enough." Vince sent a quick response to Bella and then made a snap decision. A good Finder knew when the unexpected was the best option.

Sometimes the only option.

Resolve settling over him like a well-worn, comfortable jacket, he looked at Letitia. "I'm supposed to take you to a safehouse SilverBeard arranged here on Level 9 until we can smuggle you to the Station Authority precinct in Zone 4."

Her expression didn't waver. "But?"

"I just can't bring myself to trust the Families," he said grimly.

"On that front, Finder, I agree with you." It was her turn to glance over her shoulder. "So where are we going now?"

"We're taking a little detour. I have a friend who can help us."

Letitia fixed him with a piercing look, an unspoken question in her eyes.

"I trust her with my life."

Rychek could help them. *Would* help them, even if she'd give Vince one of those looks and lecture him about Station Authority protocol in the process. That was really for appearances' sake only.

They both knew protocol didn't mean a rusted bolt to the right— or wrong—people.

"Looks like I don't have much of a choice," Letitia said, her voice very dry. "There aren't many good choices, when you do what I'm about to do."

Vince met her gaze and held it, reassuring her with the weight of his stare. "You're doing the right thing."

"I know." She swallowed visibly, before shaking her head. "Doesn't mean I don't feel like I just dove out an airlock without a spacesuit on, though."

"I've found that the things worth doing—really doing—are like that." Vince smiled wryly. "Terrifying, even when you know without a doubt that you're doing the right thing."

"Something like that." Letitia pressed her lips into a thin line, her expression growing distant as her mind's eye turned someplace far away.

Keeping half his attention on her, Vince leaned forward in his seat. If at all possible, he wanted to lose their tail before they headed to their final destination. To that end, he input a series of commands to their transport pod's onboard AI that set them on a winding, meandering course throughout this section of Level 9.

With any luck, that would be sufficient.

Letitia's voice—quiet and flat—broke into his thoughts. "You probably think I'm a horrible person."

"What?" Vince shifted his full attention back to her.

"It's okay." One corner of her mouth twitched in what was supposed to be a self-deprecating smile, but ended up looking more like a pained grimace. "I know it's true."

"Ms. Theriot—" Vince began, though he wasn't quite sure what he was going to say. He trailed off as her expression grew pensive, like she was holding an internal debate with herself. Her free hand clenched and unclenched in her lap.

All at once, like a dam breaking, words tumbled out of her. Halting at first, and then in a rush. "I didn't—I didn't know Starlit and Lumen were going to turn the Ruby Gauntlet into what it's become."

She shook her head. "I don't honestly think *they* even thought we'd all ever end up here."

Sensing a reply was not necessary, Vince remained quiet.

Letitia waved her free hand. "In the beginning, we were just this fun little part of the *Everheart* game world, and then we grew. We grew a *lot*." She set her jaw. "And, I'll be honest, we got a little greedy. The idea of a casino that went around all the rules and regulations? Well, it had a lot of appeal."

She shrugged one shoulder. "You know as well as anybody how tight money is for most of us on the Station. Having a little extra come in was good, and we weren't hurting anybody. Not really."

"Except when people came in and lost everything," Vince said coolly.

He wasn't surprised when Letitia just shrugged again. "Hey, gambling is gambling. If you don't know what you're getting into when you walk into a gaming club and put up credits, it's not our fault. Winning isn't guaranteed."

Her expression darkened. "I didn't know about the extortion and the…other stuff until recently. You have to believe me." She leaned a little closer to him, her blue eyes wide and intense, a sense of urgency thrumming in her voice.

That urgency sent an answering frisson through Vince. It made his goatee bristle; he had to resist the urge to rub his chin. Instead, he inclined his head in a nod. "And that's when your conscience started bothering you."

"Something like that." Letitia shook her head, dropping her gaze to her lap. "I couldn't believe it, at first." She twisted the corner of her sweater between two fingers. "Part of me still doesn't want to believe it, but…" She twitched her shoulders in a helpless shrug. "The more I dug into it, the more dirt I found. And I—I couldn't live with that."

She swallowed audibly. "We were supposed to be *different* from the Families. We were supposed to be *better*. But—" a bitter little laugh gurgled up from her throat. "We're not any different, and, if anything, we're *worse*. At least the Families, for all their many sins, have had the sense to avoid putting the entire freaking *Station* at risk."

"Can't argue with that." It was Vince's turn to shake his head, before glancing over his shoulder to check on their tail through the rear viewport. Near as he could tell, that lone transport pod still doggedly followed them.

His eyes narrowed. *Not for long.*

A sudden thought occurred to him; he turned back to Letitia. "What *did* tip you off that something wasn't right?"

For a second, she just looked at him. Then that wry, bitter smile twisted her lips again. "You're going to think it's selfish."

Vince quirked an eyebrow at her. "Try me."

"They told me they were putting a security detail on my apartment."

CHAPTER 48

VINCE BLINKED AND SAT BACK IN HIS seat, a frown creasing his forehead as he digested this. The *security detail* was her tip-off?

Correctly interpreting his confusion, Letitia elaborated. "You have to understand, Finder, up until this point, we'd made—well," she shook her head, "let's just say we'd made a *lot* of money and leave it at that—and apart from making sure my apartment had great security, Starlit and Lumen never worried about my 'safety.'" She hooked her fingers into air quotes. "Or the safety of the servers I take care of." She clenched her jaw. "They *trusted* me. Our arrangement was perfectly discreet, and unless Station Authority had some reason to come poking around—which they did not—everything was fine."

In her lap, her hands clenched into fists. "And then I got a call that those two would become my permanent houseguests. Well, semi-permanent. They rotate out with a couple of others."

Comprehension dawned like a cargo freighter full of ore plowing into a pleasure yacht. Vince nodded slowly. "And that told you something had changed."

"Big time." Letitia narrowed her eyes, her expression taking on a cold, distinctly ugly cast. "When I asked them why, they just said that they'd decided we were past due upgrading our security system." She laughed shortly. "We did need an upgrade, but nothing as drastic as *that*."

Vince nodded. "Can't say I'd appreciate having two strangers take up residence in my apartment either."

"I know!" Letitia threw her hands into the air in frustration. "The nerve of them—violating my privacy and making me live with strangers? Well, I told Starlit and Lumen I wouldn't stand for it. If they were so worried about the Ruby Gauntlet's servers, they could move them someplace else. One of their own apartments or something."

Even if he hadn't already known Letitia had failed on this front, Vince would have still known this approach was doomed from the start. He cocked an eyebrow at her. "Let me guess—they thought their apartments were too high profile and figured keeping the severs buried on Level 9 was safer?"

In the middle of drawing breath to continue her rant, Letitia stopped to give him a sharp look. "You know who they are, don't you?"

It wasn't a question.

Vince considered her for several seconds, debating how much to say, before he inclined his head. "I've got a pretty good idea. But," he waved a hand for her to continue, "don't let me stop you."

"There isn't much more. They basically told me that I had two choices—cooperate or get kicked out." Letitia clenched her jaw, her eyes full of bitterness. "They were actually willing to kick me out. *Me*. After all the years we worked together. After everything I did to help them build the Ruby Gauntlet."

Swallowing what had to have been a bitter lump in her throat, she lifted her shoulders in a good facsimile of an airy shrug. "Well, I caved, obviously. Laid out a few ground rules for my bodyguards, which Starlit and Lumen agreed to, thankfully, and I just put my head down and kept working."

"But at that point you started digging," Vince said sagely.

"Yes, I did. Because I couldn't figure out what had happened to make my friends turn on me like that." Letitia shook her head. "The money wasn't enough for them. I don't know *why* it's not enough—it certainly is for me—but it's not."

"They moved on to a different currency." It was Vince's turn to shake his head, his own expression turning grim. The same currency used by both of the Families. "Power."

"Yeah, and look what they've done with it."

Vince had no answer for that. He just shook his head once in silent acknowledgement and turned his attention to the rear viewport once more. That transport pod was still following them.

Sinking back against her seat, Letitia let out a shaky breath. "I appreciate your help, Finder."

"Don't thank me yet. Wait until we get through this." Vince filled his voice with as much assurance as he could muster. They *would* get through this.

In the meantime… He narrowed his eyes. That transport pod was setting off not-so-tiny alarm bells inside his head.

CHAPTER 49

Over the next few minutes, Vince kept a sharp eye on the transport pod tailing them and realized that his gut feeling of something being off was correct. No matter how many twists and turns their transport pod took, they just couldn't seem to shake their pursuers. The other transport pod seamlessly copied every move he'd instructed their pod's onboard AI system to make.

It was like their two pods were connected by some invisible form of magnetism, with one drawing the other inexorably after it.

An irritated rumble rose in his throat; he choked it back. No sense in scaring Letitia further.

Across the seat from him, his charge's expression was cool and imperious, but behind the facade Vince glimpsed signs of strain. Despite her excellent front, Letitia was well and truly terrified. She knew what the Families were capable of…and she knew now what her erstwhile friends were capable of as well.

"They're still following us, aren't they?"

"Unfortunately."

"What if we change pods?" Her voice only trembled a little as she spoke.

"Already thought of that." Vince shook his head. "We'd have to time it just right—and even then, it's a gamble."

"We could do it." Letitia leaned forward to study the little holographic map being projected beside the chip reader near the passenger side door. She pointed to a side corridor a little way ahead of them. "There. Call another pod and have it waiting for us."

"I would if we had time." Vince ran a hand over his goatee, smoothing the still-pickling bristles. "I was trying to lose them before we did anything else, but—" He shook his head again. "I think we're just going to have to go for it."

"Go for it?" For the first time, a hint of panic slid into Letitia's voice. She shot him a sharp look. "What do you—"

He held her gaze. *Trust me*, he said with his eyes, before tipping his head knowingly toward the front of the transport pod.

It might be a reach, but he couldn't say it was outside the realm of possibility that whichever Family was tailing them had also cracked this particular transport pod's internal system and was listening to their entire conversation.

Once, Vince would have laughed at the idea. Not now. He knew better. The Families' corrupt tentacles seeped into all aspects of life aboard Zyga Space Station.

The Finder made a mental note to ask Brill to investigate that possibility later before drawing in a breath. Time to stop worrying about the Families and their machinations and focus on his main mission. *We can't let the Ruby Gauntlet become a Third Family.*

The only way to keep that from happening was to get Letitia to Station Authority.

"Main elevator," he told the transport pod's onboard AI system. "Fastest route possible."

They could outrun the transporter pods tailing them.

A grim smile spread across his face. He doubted even the Families would anticipate his next move.

That was the thing about life, whether you lived on a rock hurtling through space in orbit around a star, or you lived on a man-made construction floating in the black of space like Zyga Space Station. The unexpected happened on a regular basis. You only had two options: adapt or die.

Vince chose to adapt. Life first. Always.

Glancing down at his comlink, he composed another text. ::*Need your help. Urgent.*::

To his relief, Rychek's response came almost immediately. ::*What can I do?*::

Despite everything, Vince felt a smile tug at the corners of his mouth. There was a reason Rychek was his favorite Station Authority official. He sent her a quick list of instructions as their transport pod whipped through an intersection with another corridor.

She didn't ask questions, she just sent back a single word. ::*Understood.*::

Adrenaline pumping through his veins, Vince caught Letitia's eye and held her gaze. "We'll make it."

CHAPTER 50

When Vince caught sight of the gleaming synthglass shafts of Level 8's main elevator bank looming ahead of them a few minutes later, he felt a small twinge of relief. He ruthlessly forced it down. They weren't out of this yet, not by a long shot.

Beside him, Letitia seemed to be holding her breath. Her gaze was fixed on the elevator bank, her hands clutching her oversized purse to her chest. Her abandoned boba tea still sat in the cupholder.

It was only when their transport pod began its approach to the open area lined with silvery railings that served as the entrance to the elevator bank that she turned to Vince, her blue eyes full of apprehension. "Do you seriously think we can make it to an elevator cab without those guys—" she jerked her head toward the transport pod still trailing them, "—grabbing us? If that's what they're planning?"

"No."

"Then what—"

Vince just lifted his eyebrows at her.

It only took a second before comprehension bloomed on Letitia's face. Her jaw dropped. "You're serious. We're going to ride the elevator up in *this*?" She jabbed a finger at the transport pod's floor beneath their feet.

"Yes."

"Oh, wow." She blinked once, twice, and then sat back against the dark blue seat cushion and waved her hand airily. "Okay, then. Carry on."

Despite the situation, Vince found himself smiling. "Ever done this before?"

"Nope."

"First time for everything."

Letitia snorted once, but otherwise didn't reply. She only braced herself against her seat, as though she expected this next leg of their journey to be rough and bumpy.

Vince didn't have time to assure her it wouldn't be that bad. Leaning forward to peer through the transport pod's front viewscreen at the gleaming synthglass elevator bank rising above them, he waited until the pod neared the curb. Then he instructed the onboard AI, "Transport pod elevator cab, please."

Instead of stopping to let them depart, the transport pod smoothly glided around a short curve and entered a queue leading to the less-populated—and more expensive—elevator cabs that had been constructed to ferry transport pods between Levels in each Zone.

"With any luck," Vince said, peering over his shoulder again, "they won't know exactly where we're going."

Letitia glanced through the rear viewport as well, biting the inside of her cheek. "They're still following us, though."

"Let 'em."

In his hand, his comlink vibrated against his fingers. Vince spared a glance at the display. Bella, wanting an update.

He didn't have time to give her one.

Their transport pod passed through the queue—Vince swiped an unmarked credit-chip with a speed that still felt too slow—and then the gate opened, allowing them to slide neatly into a large, silvery elevator cab wide enough for two pods side-by-side.

One window rolled downward.

"Destination?" asked a cool female voice.

Vince leaned toward the door and the open window. "Level 1."

A pause ensued.

Vince held his breath, calculating how close that other transport pod had been to them. He'd not used these particular cabs often, but he did know that they operated on a timer with a motion sensor just the same as the pedestrian elevators. If someone was close enough to trigger the sensor, the doors would stay open long enough for them to hop aboard.

Beside him, Letitia clearly had the same thought. "Oh, I hope they're not close enough to join us." She gave an involuntary shudder at the mere idea.

Vince didn't reply, but stared through the rear viewport at the elevator doors as though the weight of his gaze could force them to shut.

Beyond their elevator, he glimpsed the transport pod tailing them now pulling through the queue. It didn't stop to pay. His goatee bristled. That was a personal transport pod, then—with a travel plan set up with the Zyga Transportation system. And while Starlit and Lumen definitely had the money to travel from Level to Level in transport pods, his credits were still on one of the Families.

Behind them, the elevator doors finally—mercifully—slid closed. A second later, their transport pod jolted slightly as the elevator cab began to rise.

"Oh, thank God." Letitia released a shaky breath, slumping against her cushioned seat. In the bright light washing in from the gleaming glowpanels set in the elevator cab's ceiling, her face had gone pale white again.

"We're almost there." Vince offered her an encouraging nod, and then—finally—sent Bella a quick response.

::In an elevator headed for Level 1.::

He didn't have time to include anything else—but Bella was smart. He had every certainty that his assistant would put the pieces together and figure out where they were going.

Less than a minute later, the elevator eased to a halt and the silver doors opened on Level 1's elevator bank exit. Their transport pod glided out of the elevator and down a gleaming white marble exit ramp.

Just beyond the point at which the ramp met the wide silvery metal boulevard beyond, Vince glimpsed an official Station Authority transport pod with lights flashing sitting beside a couple of large potted trees. A tall, slim, dark-haired woman in a gray uniform leaned up against the sleek silvery surface, her arms folded across her chest.

Beside him, Letitia gasped, but Vince just grinned. He knew he could count on Sergeant Anita Rychek.

He offered Letitia a bright smile that made his teeth flash white in the darkness of his face. "It's all right, Letitia. She's a friend."

CHAPTER 51

VINCE DIDN'T KNOW WHERE RYCHEK HAD BEEN when he'd texted her or what kind of strings she'd had to pull to get up here as fast as she and her partner had, but they were here and he was grateful. Profoundly grateful.

Beside him, Letitia lifted her eyebrows pointedly. "You didn't mention your friend was Station Authority."

Vince just smiled at her. "Who else was going to be able to help us?"

She stared at him, her expression tight, and then a little of the tension flooding her seemed to ease. Only a little. She knew as well as he did that they were probably still being followed by that transporter pod.

"Pod, pull over here," Vince instructed.

Obediently, their transport pod pulled up next to Rychek's transport pod. Through the door viewport, Vince glimpsed the sergeant's partner, Talum Ano. He was a short, compact man with light brown skin and straight black hair.

Currently, Ano's square-jawed face bore a mixture of boredom and suspicion—part of Vince's instructions had been to leave him out of it unless Rychek was *absolutely* sure she could trust him—but his expression changed to one of sharp interest as he recognized Vince.

Catching the man's eye, Vince offered him a curt nod.

Outside the Station Authority transport, Rychek straightened to her full height as Vince and Letitia climbed out of their own transport pod. Her angular face was calm, but her dark eyes were sharp and alert.

Vince immediately swiped his unmarked credit-chip to pay for their fare, and the transport pod glided away without a second's hesitation.

Behind them, a few pedestrians continued to stream back and forth from the entrance to the gleaming synthglass elevator bank down the sidewalks on either side of the broad avenue, passing the ornamental trees interspersed with tall posts topped with glowing balls of white-gold light. At this point in the night cycle, the strips of glowpanels that ran all the way around the distant edges of the atrium had been dimmed, but the glow posts provided sufficient illumination to enable everyone to see their surroundings clearly.

A handful of meters away, water poured and gurgled from one of dozens of beautiful fountains scattered across Level 1, providing a welcome hint of humidity to the otherwise dry air. Far above their heads, the blackness of space pressed in against a synthglass-and-metal atrium that stretched from the point where Zone 5 met the Rim all the way along its length to the Hub. The sight usually never failed to remind Vince of the stark difference between life up here and life everywhere else aboard Zyga Station, but today he barely noticed.

He immediately moved to put himself between Letitia and the elevator bank, though he shifted slightly to keep the exit in his peripheral vision.

Just in case.

At the same time Ano climbed out of the Station Authority transport pod and took up position beside his partner. His gaze darted back and forth between Vince and Letitia, no doubt trying to figure out what was going on.

Vince wished him luck with that.

For her part, Rychek flicked a wry glance at Vince before holding out her hand to Letitia. "Sergeant Anita Rychek, Station Authority."

"Letitia Theriot." Letitia held out her own hand and shook Rychek's hand firmly. She looked a little pale around the edges, but her voice was steady as she continued, "I'd like to turn Station's evidence regarding an online gaming club called the Ruby Gauntlet and the people who own it."

"The Ruby Gauntlet?" Ano asked sharply.

"Yeah." Letitia spared him a glance. "You know the power outages we've experienced?" She gestured to Level 1 around them with her free hand. "They're responsible."

Ano eyed her dubiously. "And you can prove this?"

A cold, bitter smile curled Letitia's lips. "I can prove a lot more than that. A *lot* more."

Rychek arched an eyebrow at Vince. "This is related to Detective Commosky, isn't it?"

It wasn't a question.

"It's a long story." Vince eyed the elevator bank out of the corner of his eye—and stiffened. A silver transport pod had just emerged and was gliding down the exit ramp. "We need to get out of here." He nodded toward Letitia. "She's in a lot of danger if Starlit and Lumen realize she's switched sides before we get her to safety."

"Understood." Rychek swiftly reached over to open their transport pod's door. "If you'll join us, Ms. Theriot…"

Ano shot her a cool glance. "What have you gotten us into now, Anita?" His words were quick and he kept his voice low. "What is going on?" He turned his half-reproachful, half-suspicious gaze onto Vince. "What have *you* gotten us into?"

"We'll explain everything," Vince said brusquely, shepherding Letitia toward the transport pod. "*After* she's safe."

Across the boulevard, he watched as the transport pod stopped and hovered at the end of the exit ramp. Tension flooded him. What were they—

Rychek and Ano noticed the pod at the same time. Both Station Authority officers reached for their laser pistols, moving automatically to put themselves in the line of fire—if it came to that.

"Get in the transport pod," Rychek directed. "Now."

Letitia wasted no time obeying. She scurried inside, disappearing from view.

"Now you, Grable."

Vince hadn't been on the receiving end of Rychek's command voice in a long time. He didn't quibble, just slid into the back seat of the transport pod next to Letitia. He did not, however, take his eyes off that lone transport pod.

For the span of a few seconds, the transport pod just hovered in place. Vince had the strangest feeling that whoever was in there was making sure he'd seen it. Then, all at once, the transport pod glided forward to merge into traffic—

—and abruptly made a U-turn to return to the elevator bank. Seconds later, it whipped into the gleaming entrance and disappeared from sight.

Vince would have laughed, if he wasn't so relieved. Whoever was in that transport pod was headed back down…somewhere else in Zone 5.

Beside him, Letitia had hunched down on the seat where she couldn't be seen through any of the viewports, clutching her bag to her chest. She peered up at Vince, her blue eyes wide. "Are they gone?" Her voice was barely more than a whisper.

The Finder's gaze flicked to her; he nodded in reassurance. "They're gone."

"What was *that* all about?" Rychek demanded, as she and Ano ducked inside the pod and shut the doors. Both Station Authority officers stared from Vince to Letitia and back.

"I think—" Vince peered thoughtfully through the pod's rear viewport at the elevator bank, "—that pod was escorting us up here, believe it or not."

"Really." Letitia sounded skeptical. She straightened up in her seat, tossing her head. "*Now* you think that?"

"They left." Vince shrugged. "No point in doing that unless their job was finished." He snorted softly. "They could have *said* something."

"Back up." Ano held out a hand, before giving Vince a stern look. "Grable, we've put up with a lot from you because you're an excellent Finder and usually fairly trustworthy, but this is—"

"Talum." Rychek leveled a quelling look at him. "Did you *not* hear the part about the Ruby Gauntlet? And the power outages?"

The shorter man frowned. "Anita—"

Rychek deliberately glanced away from him to raise a questioning eyebrow at Vince in the seat opposite her. "What's the plan, Grable? Irongates?"

"Yes," he confirmed, with a glance at Letitia. "I think he's our best bet."

Plus, given Vince's past dealing with him, the Detective Inspector was likely to give him less hassle than if the Finder attempted to take Letitia straight to the Rim Division and the Council. Not to mention the risk involved with something like that.

No, Detective Inspector Irongates would make a much better bridge.

"Irongates?" Ano looked sharply at his partner, his expression a mix of disbelief and surprise, before he turned that incredulous stare on Vince.

Vince answered the question implicit in that look. "Even if we had time to get Ms. Theriot all the way to the Rim—which we don't—it's too dangerous. I trust that Irongates will know exactly what to do."

"That's not the issue." Ano waved that away before fixing his partner with a hard look. "Does he know she's—" he tipped his head toward Letitia, "—coming?"

Rychek shook her head, and then grinned. The expression made her look younger, lending a sparkle to her dark eyes. "That'd defeat the purpose of being stealthy, wouldn't it?"

Ano looked like he wanted to respond, but then he just sighed and leaned back against his seat. The resigned look he gave Rychek said he hoped she knew what she was doing.

"Letitia." Vince caught Letitia's eye and offered her a bracing smile. "Detective Inspector Irongates is the best person for you to talk to. He's hard, but he's fair. He'll help you with the next stage." He paused. "It's almost over."

This first stage, anyway.

She nodded wordlessly.

Ano glanced once more between Vince and Rychek before shaking his head and commanding their pod to take them to the Level 1 Station Authority Precinct. He trusted his partner—even if he didn't understand what was going on. He cleared his throat. "I'm sure we'll get this all sorted out."

"Yes, we will." Letitia's voice was soft, but she lifted her chin, her expression growing resolute as she looked around the inside of the transport pod. "Hopefully before more people are hurt."

"Sounds good to me." Rychek nodded her thanks to her partner, before giving Letitia a firm nod. "Don't worry, Miss Theriot, we'll get you there in one piece."

CHAPTER 52

IT ONLY TOOK A FEW MINUTES TO reach their destination. As the Level 1 Station Authority Precinct loomed in the distance, an imposing structure of gleaming white stone and impossibly clear glass, Vince realized with a start that the last time he'd been here had been a few months back, after that business with Orion Lab. He and his best informant, Rav, had uncovered a hidden gaming lab that was kidnapping people from the Core to use for test subjects.

Something heavy settled in his chest. Bella's current state was a product of that lab, though she hadn't been kidnapped for the same reasons. Grimly, Vince pushed those thoughts aside. He didn't have time for a waltz down memory lane just now.

At the same time, he couldn't help but reflecting wryly that it had been late in the evening that night as well.

Beside him, the Finder felt Letitia tense. A sideways glance at her told him that what little color had returned to her creamy cheeks once that transport pod stopped following them had drained away again. Her expression now resembled that of a woman who wanted to throw up at the earliest available opportunity.

He nudged her with an elbow. "Ever been here before?"

Letitia startled, before throwing him an incredulous glance. "Are you kidding?"

"This is only my second time." Fully aware that Rychek and Ano were both listening, he dropped his voice. "It'll be all right. Just remember—they put their pants on the same way we do—one leg at a time."

This prompted a smile. The barest of smiles, but a smile still the same. Letitia gave him a minute nod and then her gaze snapped back to the Precinct as though captured by a tractor beam.

Across from Vince, Rychek pulled out her comlink, but paused long enough to catch his eye. She lifted a dark eyebrow in a silent question.

The Finder shook his head fractionally in response. He wasn't taking a chance on sharing any salient details inside a Station Authority transport pod. Rychek had never told him one way or the other, but he didn't know what kind of surveillance Station Authority kept on their officers—and the people they transported.

Rychek accepted this with a tiny nod of her own and turned her attention back to her comlink.

The appearance of the comlink broke the spell that had fallen over Letitia, drawing her attention like a magnet. She stared suspiciously at the sergeant, her fingers tightening on her tote bag.

Vince couldn't exactly blame her on that front, but he wasn't sure how much Letitia understood about how many moving parts an operation like this had.

Before he could open his mouth, Rychek glanced up and offered Letitia a reassuring smile. "Just talking to a couple of people at the precinct."

"And?" Ano asked, before either Vince or Letitia could get a word out.

"They'll meet us at the door." Rychek's smile widened encouragingly. "You'll have an escort all the way up to see Detective Inspector Irongates."

Letitia exhaled in a shaky rush, and then nodded.

They were nearly to the Precinct now. Vince couldn't help but think that the building looked even more imperial against the backdrop of star-studded black space visible beyond it through the synth glass stretched above them.

Seconds later, their transport pod glided to a halt in front of the wide stone steps leading up to a couple of ornate double doors. Above the double doors, the Station Authority logo was emblazoned in red, while gray letters beneath it proclaimed the building to be Station Authority Precinct #5.

Vince brushed Letitia's elbow with a finger to catch her attention. When she looked at him, her blue eyes wide with a combination of fear and determination, he said seriously, "Get an attorney before you give them anything. Just in case. And remember—without your evidence, they don't have much of a case. That makes you important."

Letitia's face grew a little paler, but she nodded.

"Also, it's imperative that you tell Irongates that you need to talk to Detective Commosky. If you want to take your old friends down, you need him."

Letitia nodded again. "I've already thought of that, but thank you."

Vince turned his attention to Rychek and Ano, including both officers in his grateful nod. "Thanks for getting us here. Glad you could make it as fast as you did."

Ano shook his head. "Didn't know what was going on at first," he said frankly. "All I can say is that interesting things happen when you're around, Finder."

Despite himself, Vince grinned. "Hasn't been that bad." He shrugged carelessly. "Just a couple of cases."

"Big cases." Ano snorted a laugh, shaking his head. "You never do anything by halves, Grable."

"Life's too short to let it be boring."

"There's no doubt about *that*."

Rychek cleared her throat, drawing both men back to the present. "You coming with us, Grable?"

Vince looked over at her and their gazes met and locked. "No. I think it's best if we minimize my involvement." He smiled slightly, to take the clinical edge off of the words. "I've done my job. It's your turn now."

He glanced at Letitia, the thought occurring to him that she might not like him leaving her by herself, but he needn't have worried. The younger woman was already nodding in agreement.

"I'll be fine." Letitia gave him a tight smile. "Thank you for your help, Finder Grable." She looked across the transport pod, her blue gaze encompassing both Rychek and Ano. "Thank you."

"Thank *you* for coming forward." Rychek shook her head, a muscle in her jaw working. "The things that have happened the past two days…"

"Will hopefully never happen again," Letitia said firmly.

Ano blew out a breath. "I'll drink to that."

"Ready?" Rychek asked, her hand hovering over the doorpanel.

"Ready. Letitia set her jaw resolutely, slinging her tote bag over her shoulder in preparation to depart.

Just before Rychek opened the door, she looked at Vince. "I'd offer to let you know how things turn out, Grable, but…" She trailed off with a shrug.

Laughter, the first genuine amusement he'd felt in what seemed like days, welled up in Vince's chest. He mastered it, however, and only permitted himself a crooked smile. "Oh, don't worry. I'm sure it'll be all over the Station in short order."

"Why's that?" Some of Ano's good humor evaporated. He leaned forward to stare at Vince with narrowed eyes.

Vince met that steely glaze unflinchingly. The answer was obvious, but he wasn't about to point that out. Instead, he said calmly, "Because Zyga Station has some pretty good reporters, and a story like this is too big to keep under wraps for long."

Ano held his gaze a couple of beats longer. "Just so long as you're not the one feeding them information, Finder," he said at last.

"Talum…" Rychek's voice was a halfway between a sigh and a reprimand, but Ano's stern expression remained undaunted.

Vince flattened a hand over his heart. "Wouldn't dream of it. I want Starlit and Lumen behind bars as much as anyone."

Ano nodded curtly and that was that.

"Good luck," Vince said, and watched as Rychek and her partner hustled Letitia out of the transport pod and up the wide stone steps. A second later, they vanished through the ornate double doors.

Vince's part in the plan had, indeed, come to an end.

CHAPTER 53

IN THE FUTURE, VINCE WOULD LOOK BACK on the following day as being one of the longest of his life. Waiting for the Ruby Gauntlet to implode was excruciating painful. All he could do was putter around his office, unable to put his mind to anything in particular when the fate of the entirety of Zyga Space Station hung in the balance.

He had heard nothing from Commosky or Brill. Nor did he hear anything about Letitia, other than a cryptic text from Rychek some time after Vince had departed the Precinct the night before.

::*She's safe.*::

Under normal circumstances that would have been all Vince needed to know, but…nothing about this case had been normal.

Nor was it wrapped up—by his standards, at least.

One of the aspects of his job that Vince loved most was solving puzzles. The rush he felt when he put the last piece of information together to reveal the solution to whatever mystery he was currently solving kept him coming back for more.

This particularly case might be *solved*, but it wasn't *finished* by any stretch of the imagination.

There were too many threads left dangling for Vince's peace of mind, too many things left unexplained. He wanted—needed—a resolution, and so far he hadn't gotten one.

It was enough to drive a man to drink tea…and Vince did.

Pacing the confines of his office, Vince drank his way through the equivalent of a box of tea. All different flavors—he was so distracted he barely tasted any of them He drank black tea back to back with cinnamon apple tea, green tea, and an herbal lemon tea.

Through this waiting period, Zyga Station's power remained fully functional. That, Vince knew, was a good sign.

In those immediate twenty-four hours, the Finder also heard nothing from either of the Families. He wasn't sure what to make of this. Part of him thought that was the way it should be, but part of him was surprised they hadn't attempted to pump him for information.

That they did not question him at all was telling. Either they didn't care (extremely unlikely, given the events of the past few days), or they had their own inside source feeding them information.

Considering past history, Vince thought this by far the more likely scenario. Still, it grated that Bok Chul and Oscar knew more about what was going on than he did.

For the thousandth time, he wondered if he ought to call Brill and ask for an update, and for the thousandth time, he dismissed the idea. If Brill hadn't sent him an update yet, it was probably because he was either busy or *he* didn't know enough yet.

Probably.

"You're going to wear a hole through the carpet," Bella observed candidly, two hours after Vince had eaten a distracted dinner subsisting of hummus, crackers, and a few raw vegetables at his desk.

His assistant was leaning back in her chair, regarding him over her desk. She held a stylus, which she'd been rolling between her fingers in a deliberate attempt to get back into the very human habit of idly fiddling with things.

Bella was as anxious as he was to learn what was happening, but being a human mind trapped in an android shell, she handled her burning curiosity differently. Her android body simulated things like hormones and adrenaline, but the process was still a good deal more cerebral than visceral.

"I can't settle."

"That's obvious, Boss."

Vince sent her a rueful smile over his shoulder. "Not knowing is killing me."

"Nothing's broken on Zyga Station News yet." Bella tipped her head toward the nearest large holoprojector mounted on the wall. "I've got news alerts out."

"I do, too." Vince ran a hand over his close shorn hair.

Bella canted her head to one side, her dark, almond-shaped eyes narrowing thoughtfully. "I think this is the most distracted I've ever seen you, Boss." When Vince didn't answer, she said, "Of course, it's not like the lives of everyone aboard Zyga Station are at stake or anything."

Despite himself, one corner of Vince's mouth pulled up in a smile. "No, not at all."

He stopped pacing long enough to make himself another cup of tea—Chamomile, this time. Decaf and calming. He could definitely use that.

Vince was in the middle of stirring a dollop of honey into the fragrant, steaming liquid when several loud dings broke the stillness that had fallen over his office.

He and Bella both started. Vince froze as his brain registered the unexpected sounds. Two of the dings were from their respective comlinks, indicating that some sort of news about the Ruby Gauntlet had finally popped up.

As for the other sound…

Dropping his spoon with a clatter on the credenza's jade green surface, Vince whirled around and practically dived across his office to reach his computer terminal.

Someone was making an encrypted call to him.

It had to be Brill.

His heart pounding with anticipation, Vince dropped into his chair.

At the same time, Bella charged around his desk. She stopped short beside his chair, but lost her balance, teetering on the balls of her feet. At the last second, she caught herself by slapping a hand down on his jade green desk.

"I'm fine, I'm fine," she said breathlessly, before Vince could even react. She leaned against the desk, just out of view of his computer's cam. "Who is it?"

"Let's find out," Vince said, and accepted the call.

To his combined relief and satisfaction, Brill's face instantly filled the computer display. His real face, not the disguised version he'd shown to Commosky. The information broker was smiling broadly, and his pale round cheeks looked a little flushed.

"Evening, Finder." Brill inclined his head in a nod.

After twenty-four hours of complete suspense, Vince had no patience for social niceties. "Well?" he demanded, drilling the information broker with an intense look.

The smile on Brill's pudgy face grew even wider. "We've done it."

Relief threatened to break over Vince, but he held it at bay. "Details, man. I—"

"—we," Bella interrupted, leaning toward him to wave at Brill.

"—need details."

"Have you seen the news?" Brill inquired.

Hearing the smug note in the information broker's voice, Vince experienced a brief, intense desire to reach through the computer display and shake the other man by the shoulders. He restrained the impulse, however, to level Brill with a flat look. "Brill, you know full well the story just broke."

He jabbed a thumb over his shoulder in the general direction of his holoprojectors. "We only now got the news alert."

Brill's brilliant smile did not lessen, but he inclined his head apologetically. "I'm afraid I can't help myself tonight, Finder." He did not wait for a response, but continued, "They've arrested Starlit and Lumen on charges of fraud on a massive scale and charged them with recklessly endangering the entire Station."

He paused for one impressive beat, clearly unable to resist the urge to foster more dramatic suspense. "My source also informs me that murder charges are pending."

CHAPTER 54

Vince sat very still in his comfortable office chair, letting those words soak into him. *Murder charges are pending.* A wave of relief swelled in his chest, mixed with a hefty dose of satisfaction—and he finally allowed himself to experience it.

Brill let him savor the moment. Even through the computer display the man was practically vibrating with excited energy, but he contained himself while Vince absorbed this news.

After a few heartbeats, Vince leaned back in his chair. "Best news I've heard all day."

Beside him, Bella looked from Brill to Vince's profile and back. "I'm sure Detective Commosky is very happy they're being charged with murder."

"Undoubtedly." Brill seemed unable to stop smiling.

"Relieved, are you?" Vince raised a wry eyebrow at the information broker.

"Aren't you?" Brill demanded. "Those two maniacs won't be able to wreak havoc on the rest of us any longer." He rubbed his long-fingered hands together in satisfaction. "No more power outages. No more possibility of them forming a Third Family to terrorize the general population."

"I'm glad about that," Bella said, propping her hands on her hips.

Vince was, too, but… He folded his arms over his chest, regarding the information broker through slightly narrowed eyes. He understood Brill's relief and satisfaction—taking Starlit and Lumen down had definitely become a vendetta for the man—but at the same time… Brill was almost *too* happy about this.

"All right," Vince said abruptly, interrupting Bella's comment about being excited to watch the news reports shortly. He shot her an apologetic look, but immediately refocused on Brill, watching the other man's face carefully. "What'd you do?"

"What?" Brill's smile dimmed and he blinked innocently at Vince.

"You know what." The Finder leaned forward, bringing his face closer to his computer display, dark brown eyes narrowed again. "You're entirely too smug about this. So…" he turned a hand palm up. "What'd you do?"

For a second, Vince thought Brill might deny it. But then that slow, satisfied smile spread across the other man's pale, pudgy face again. He really couldn't help himself.

"Nothing much." Brill sighed theatrically, and then that smug smile widened even further. It was his turn to hold up a hand. "I… may or may not have facilitated the media getting a nice, anonymous info dump to help them create their press releases tonight."

Bella leaned in closer as well. "Which news stations?"

Brill's smug expression did not alter. "All of them."

"All of them?" Bella gasped. She nearly fell over in her shock, but caught herself on the back of Vince's chair. "Was that really necessary?"

Vince answered before Brill could even open his mouth. "Yes." He tipped his head toward his assistant, but his gaze remained fixed on the information broker. "Didn't want to take the risk that one of them was in somebody's pocket, did you?"

"On this space station, that's not outside the realm of possibility." Brill shrugged prosaically, his eyes glittering. "At least this way they all get a fair shot." He grinned. "I *am* an information broker. What they *do* with the information I gave them is up to them."

A sudden though occurred to Vince, chilling him to the core. He narrowed his eyes again, leveling a hard stare at Brill that had intimidated lesser men in the past. "You didn't give them Letitia's name, did you?"

The look Brill sent him in return could have frozen Vince's forgotten mug of tea. "Of course not. What kind of stupid do you take me for?" On the computer display, he seemed to draw himself up stiffly. "I only told them that Station Authority had a credible inside source."

"Is that a normal thing to include in a scoop of that magnitude?" Bella eyed Brill as well, her beautiful face creased with concern. "Should you have said that?"

"It's perfectly fine." Brill waved a dismissive hand. "Happens all the time." He glared balefully at Vince, though his next words were directed to Bella. "The trick is to give the media enough credible information to point them in the right direction."

Instead of responding, Vince turned on both of his holoprojectors, though he left the sound muted. Both of them, turned to different Zyga news stations, currently displayed reporters stationed outside of the Council's office on the Rim. He recognized the ostentatious entrance behind them.

A ticker tape along the bottom of one newsfeed read: *Origin of mysterious power outages discovered. Owners of infamous gaming club allegedly responsible for terrorizing Zyga Station.*

Vince shook his head. "Oh, I'd say you did that."

"Needed to be done," Brill said briskly. It was his turn to narrow his eyes, his expression turning pugnacious. "Had a feeling that if left to their own devices, the Council might attempt to sweep all of this under the proverbial rug."

"That's an awful lot to downplay." Bella looked askance at him, her glossy black hair swinging like a curtain as she shook her head. "Are you sure?"

"My dear Ms. Escovedo." The smugness faded from Brill's expression as he pursed his lips. "Never underestimate the desire of people in positions of power and authority to sidestep embarrassment and/or responsibility."

Vince couldn't argue with that.

Brill then directed his attention to Vince. "Finder Grable, it was, as always, a pleasure to work with you." He paused, and then added, a little too casually, "If you do hear more from your friend Detective Commosky…"

At this, Vince suppressed a rush of satisfaction. Brill might deal in information, but even he didn't know everything. He inclined his head in a courteous nod. "I'll see what I can do."

"Excellent." Next, Brill addressed Bella. "Ms. Escovedo, it's been a pleasure. Should you ever find yourself in need of a job…"

Vince ended the call before the information broker could finish his sentence. "The nerve of some people," he said without heat.

Beside him, Bella just threw back her head and laughed.

CHAPTER 55

IT WAS ANOTHER FULL DAY BEFORE VINCE had the satisfaction of receiving the resolution he so craved. During that time, he contented himself with scouring Zyga Station news channels for any further scraps of information about the ongoing Ruby Gauntlet story.

Everyone was talking about it—but no one knew much more than what Brill had sent out. The Council and Station Authority officials all remained tightlipped, giving only the barest of press releases.

Early that morning, Vince and Bella watched vid footage of Starlit and Lumen—their real identities now officially revealed as Jasmine Nerhti and Renji Kino—being arrested and transported to the Station Authority Headquarters on the Rim.

Beneath their haughty, sullen defiance, Vince thought he glimpsed an undercurrent of bewilderment. Neither of these would-be Third Family heads had any idea what exactly had transpired to topple their growing empire.

Yet.

It would all come out eventually. Even knowing as much as he did about this case, Vince already knew he'd be following that court case as it unfolded.

Now late in the evening, Vince stared blankly at an email he'd received from a prospective client about tracking down his missing brother and tried to decide if he should bridge the gap and attempt to contact Commosky, or if he should continue to be patient and wait.

"Zyga Station to Boss, come in, Boss."

Bella's clear, musical voice broke through Vince's ruminations. He looked up with a start, before turning his head to blink at her. "Excuse me?"

Bella raised expressive eyebrows at him. "You've been staring at that screen for more than five minutes." She nodded to the tablet still clasped loosely in his hands. "New case?"

Vince made an uninterested sound in the back of his throat and slumped back in his chair. His thoughts circled around this potential missing person's case before darting back to considering Commosky, Letitia, and the scandal now rippling across Zyga Station in ever-increasing waves.

Under the present circumstances, was he absolutely crazy to consider contacting one of the Families—say, Bok Chul—for information? Was it worth—

"Boss."

Blinking, Vince snapped out of his thoughts and returned his attention to Bella.

His assistant was smiling at him, but there was a distinct note of amusement threaded through her patient expression. She gestured to his desk, her long, silvery fingernails glinting in the light from the overhead. "The case?"

"Shouldn't be difficult." Vince dismissed it with a wave of his hand. "Have a feeling the brother decided to take a couple of days off from life and forgot to mention it to his family."

Bella raised an impressed eyebrow. "You got all that from that email? I read it and I didn't get that far."

"Read between the lines. This guy said that his brother is an aspiring rock musician, and I saw a headline about a huge music convention going on in Zone 1 right now." Vince shrugged. "I'll call this guy in the morning. If his brother hasn't shown up by tomorrow night, I might need to hunt him down." He shook his head. "Hate to take money for something like that."

At her desk, Bella shrugged prosaically. "Sometimes peace of mind is worth paying for."

"Sometimes. And sometimes a case like this is just the product of an overactive imagination."

Vince half-expected Bella to argue with him, but she didn't. A little suspicious, he glanced over at her to find her giving him the sort of sappy smile she usually reserved for pictures of cute little animals.

"What?" The word came out a little gruffer than he'd intended.

"You have a good heart, Boss." She shook her head, still smiling. "Nobody will ever be able to accuse you of taking advantage of your clients."

Despite himself, at those simple, heartfelt words Vince felt heat climb into his dark cheeks. To cover his embarrassment, he gave his assistant the side eye. "Shouldn't you be going home now? It's well past business hours."

Bella's jaw dropped. Not as dramatically as it would have a few months before, but her face was an absolute picture of disappointed shock. "Boss! You can't send me home now. Detective Commosky might drop by tonight! I can't miss that."

"If he did," Vince said dryly, "I'd be sure to tell you everything."

"Not the same as hearing it for myself." Bella folded her arms over her chest, scowling.

"There's no guarantee he'll stop by tonight."

"There's no guarantee he won't, Bella retorted. "Besides," she lifted a wry eyebrow. "It's not like I have to sleep." She turned one hand palm-up, indicating the office at large. "No reason I can't just stay here."

"Bella…" Vince sighed, but he already knew he'd lost. Even if Bella really *had* needed to get some rest, he didn't have the heart to deny her the opportunity to find out what had happened. She'd put in a lot of hard work on this case as well.

The Finder opened his mouth to tell her this, but found himself interrupted by the door chime. Unbidden, his eyes met Bella's, the same thought reflected in both their expressions. Was it Commosky?

Bella made to get up from her desk and answer the door, but Vince shook his head once. He'd do it himself. Just on the off-chance that it was someone else.

He did not, after all, know how far Starlit and Lumen's influence stretched throughout Zyga Station—or how much power they had even from a jail cell facing murder charges.

To Vince's surprise, not one, but two people stood outside his office door. A short, compact man with broad shoulders, and a tall, lanky woman. Both wore hats pulled over their eyes, but even before he'd gotten a good look at their faces, the Finder knew who they were.

Detective Ron Commosky and Sergeant Anita Rychek.

It was the work of a moment to run through his security protocols in order to unlock the door.

They didn't wait around.

The instant Vince swung the door open, Commosky made a little gesture to Rychek. "After you," he said in low, gruff tones.

Rychek immediately slipped into the bright light filling Vince's office, and Commosky followed.

As he passed Vince, the detective darted a piercing look at him from beneath the brim of his hat—a black fedora this time. "Shut the door, Finder. Now."

Vince was way ahead of him. Commosky had barely cleared the threshold before Vince shut—and relocked—the door. The Finder shot a glance at Bella, who stood behind her jade green desk, looking excited, and turned to greet his guests.

Anticipation thrummed through his veins. *Now, maybe we'll get some real answers.*

CHAPTER 56

If Vince hadn't had prior experience in dealing with Commosky, he might have been irritated by the length of time it took the detective to get settled. As it was, the Finder managed to squelch his burning impatience and watched the proceedings with a clinical eye.

The first thing Commosky did after setting foot inside was scrutinize the interior of Vince's office. His suspicious gaze swept over Bella—to whom he nodded curtly—before examining the rest of the office. Apparently satisfied that no one was hiding under either of the desks or Vince's couch cushions, he finally removed his hat and brown jacket and allowed Vince to hang them on a couple of hooks that protruded from the bulkhead by the door when Vince pressed an unobtrusive nearby button.

Anita Rychek, meanwhile, immediately removed her dark gray ball cap and shrugged off her matching jacket without more than a casual glance around at Vince's office. She smiled at Bella before giving Vince her outerwear when he extended a silent hand to her. Like Commosky, she wore civilian clothing. Medium-wash jeans and a comfortable-looking emerald green sweater that hugged her slim form.

Vince eyed both of his guests discreetly while he disposed of their hats and jackets, trying to work out if they'd arrived together or separately.

Before he could ask, Commosky swung around to face him, rubbing his hands together briskly. "Evening, Finder."

"Detective."

"Ms. Escovedo." Commosky nodded to Bella, who smiled back at him. He turned back to Vince. "First chance I've had to come to Zone 5 since everything went down. Couldn't slip away any earlier."

"You've been a busy man," Vince said, before turning to greet Rychek with a smile. "Anita." He held her gaze. "Thank you."

Rychek's smile softened around the edges. Her dark eyes were clear and full of something that almost looked like affection. "You're welcome." She lightly punched him in the arm before saying to Commosky, "Grable's my favorite Finder, Detective."

Commosky nodded. "Understandable."

Vince waggled a finger from one to the other. "Do you know each other?"

"Not officially." Commosky regarded Rychek for a second, his dark eyes keen. "Although I've known *of* you for quite some time, Sergeant. And—" he offered her a solemn nod, "—obviously I know what part you've played in the Ruby Gauntlet affair."

Rychek shot a wry look at Vince—a look that said she hoped Commosky was referring to her bringing Letitia Theriot in and that he didn't know *exactly* what role she'd played—before she returned Commosky's nod. "Well, Detective, I know who you are, too." Grinning, she spread her hands to the side. "Your face *has* been plastered all over Zyga Station lately."

An exasperated look flickered over the detective's craggy face. "Yeah, well, thankfully most of that's over with." He looked at Vince, his expression considering, and then he smiled. "In case you're wondering, Grable, no, we did not randomly run into each other."

"He called me," Rychek interjected. "On my *personal* comlink." She leveled Commosky with a severe look. "And you never answered me when I asked how you'd gotten it."

Commosky only raised an eyebrow at her, his expression perfectly straight. "As you said, my face is plastered all over Zyga Station."

At her desk, Bella laughed, and then quickly slapped a hand over her mouth. "Sorry," she said though her fingers.

Commosky waved a hand. "No, no. I understand." A rueful smile tugged at the corners of his mouth. "If I'm honest, none of this played out the way I ever thought it would. But…" his expression hardened into righteous satisfaction. "We got them. That's what matters."

That same swell of satisfaction rose in Vince's own chest "Yes." He arched a dark eyebrow at the detective. "I'm hoping you're here to tell me the rest of the story, Detective. Coffee?" He gestured to his drinkmaker on the jade green credenza.

"Please." Commosky strode over to one of the chairs in front of Vince's desk and tugged it around to face the couch. "Officially, I can't tell you a thing." He started to move the second chair around as well, but paused, a glint of grim humor dancing in his dark eyes. "Off the record? I think you deserve to hear the end of the story."

In the process of brewing coffee for his guests, Vince turned and caught Rychek's eye. A look of mutual understanding passed between them.

"Is that why you called me?" Rychek crossed the beige carpet and settled into a corner of the brown couch. The shade of the brown leather seemed to set her green shirt off perfectly, and for a second, Vince had the strangest thought that she looked like she belonged there.

Bella followed suit, sinking down onto the other end of the brown couch and clasping her hands around one knee.

Commosky didn't answer at first. He took a seat with the air of a man sitting down at the end of an impossibly long day, his expression temporarily going distant. Then he glanced at Rychek. "Obviously, without doing some digging, I can't prove you were the one who tipped us off to the fact that Station Authority reported me missing." He smiled, and it changed the entire contour of his craggy face. "Entirely circumstantial. But—I'm grateful." He twitched his shoulders in a shrug. "Very grateful. And your assistance in getting Letitia Theriot to Station Authority?" He inclined his head in a solemn nod. "You demonstrated admirable initiative, courage, and quick thinking."

If Rychek's cheeks tinted a little at this calm praise, she could later blame it on the lighting in Vince's office. She didn't duck her head or stammer thanks, but merely inclined her head in an answering nod. "Thank you, sir. Although, to be fair, I have a good partner." It was her turn to smile. "Talum trusted me even though he didn't exactly understand what was going on."

Silence descended on the office for a moment, broken only by the quiet gurgling sounds of Vince's drinkmaker. A moment later, he carried steaming mugs of coffee to both Rychek and Commosky. He then glanced at his assistant. "Bella?"

The gesture was half-unconscious, half-purposeful. Vince had decided it was best to make an effort to treat her as though she functioned like a normal human being—for appearances, if nothing else—and the funny thing was that at times he forgot she *wasn't* exactly human.

"I'm good, Boss." Bella held up a hand, smiling. "But, thank you."

Vince quickly brewed himself another cup of tea—not that he needed more tea. After adding a dollop of honey (he thought he deserved it, given everything), he carried his steaming mug over to the chair next to Commosky's. "All right," he said briskly. "Where do we begin?"

"I was just considering that." Commosky took a careful sip of his coffee, his eyebrows knitting together as he frowned at the carpet in the center of the open space between their chairs and the couch where the women sat. His dark gaze flicked to Rychek. "How much do you know, Sergeant?"

"If we're off the record, sir," she said with a hint of humor, "by all means call me Anita. And apart from my role in getting Ms. Theriot to the Council, I only know Station scuttlebutt and whatever the media is circulating."

Commosky accepted this without blinking; he'd clearly expected that much. "Well, then, I'll give you a brief overview."

In brisk, concise terms, the detective laid out the basics of the case he'd been building against the Ruby Gauntlet for months. He sketched a picture of Vince's previous involvement after Dent Antwerp was murdered—which had turned out to have nothing to do with the Ruby Gauntlet despite Antwerp's work as an informant—and brought Rychek up to speed on everything that had occurred prior to the moment she and her partner took custody of Letitia Theriot. Vince jumped in occasionally when the story called for it.

By the end of this introduction, Rychek was leaning forward in her seat in rapt attention, the coffee mug she cradled in her hands completely forgotten. Bella, too, was absorbed in the story, regardless of the fact that she played a role as well.

When Commosky paused to take another sip of his coffee, Vince asked, "What happened to you after we talked to Bok Chul and Amal Oswari?"

Commosky snorted. "They took me to a safehouse long enough for a couple of their higher-level goons—lieutenants, I'm guessing—to show up." His face twisted as though he'd tasted something foul. "Went back there after the fact, but of course they'd abandoned it by then." He waved a hand. "At any rate, they bundled me into a transport pod and whisked me back to my precinct in Zone 4."

"What did they tell Station Authority?" Bella leaned forward even further, her almond-shaped eyes wide and bright with interest.

"Made up a story. Said they'd found me in a bad spot and stepped in to help." Commosky's face wrinkled with disgust. "The idea of it leaves a bad taste in my mouth, but I didn't have much of a choice. Couldn't tell anybody the truth until I knew Letitia Theriot was in custody."

Vince smiled. "I would have loved to have been a fly on the bulkhead when *that* call came through."

"It caused quite a furor in the precinct, I'll tell you." Commosky snorted a laugh. "Fastest trip I believe I've ever made between Zones before." He turned a considering look on Vince again. "Much as it pains me to think that the Families assisted us, I don't know that we could have done it without them."

"No." Vince had already considered this question. "Definitely not that quickly." He shook his head, swirling the remains of his tea in the bottom of his mug. "I couldn't have whisked Letitia away from under their noses without a good deal more planning."

"Speaking of planning…" Commosky narrowed his eyes, an expression of dawning realization washing over his craggy face. "I'm surprised you didn't ask to call your… *friend*…so he could be in on this conversation."

CHAPTER 57

VINCE MET—AND HELD—THE DETECTIVE'S GAZE. THOUGH COMMOSKY'S tone was level, Vince understood the unspoken nuances in those words. Commosky might be grateful to have had the information broker's help in his moment of crisis…but that didn't mean he necessarily *approved*.

"He's got his own sources," Bella said, before Vince could decide how to answer. She turned her hands palm-up, smiling wryly. "Naturally."

"Naturally," Commosky echoed, before shaking his head. "I should have known."

Rychek finally remembered she had coffee. Raising the mug to her lips, she took a tentative sip. If the fact that it had cooled bothered her, she didn't let it show. After she swallowed, she nodded to Commosky. "How long did it take you to convince Irongates that Letitia was telling the truth?"

"That's the beauty of it." A broad, genuine smile broke across Commosky's craggy face. "With her evidence and the knowledge, she had of certain things, combined with the story I told, you've never seen Station Authority move so fast. They had us all in an armored transport pod escort to the Rim before you could say 'leverage.'"

Vince could well imagine that. "I'm sure they did." He swirled the dregs of his tea around in the bottom of his mug, but did not drink. His attention was wholly focused on Commosky. "What then?"

"Well, I'd managed to convince them that Letitia's arrival needed to be kept on the down-low, and, really, I must say Irongates was particularly helpful on that front."

"He's no fool." Rychek nodded sagely from her seat on the couch. "Occasionally more obstinate and hard-nosed than perhaps necessary, but definitely not a fool." Her dark eyes were thoughtful. "The Inspector didn't want to run the risk of tipping anyone off, either."

"No."

The two Station Authority officers, detective and sergeant, shared a significant look while Vince and Bella watched.

"In fact," Commosky continued, after taking a sip of his coffee, "Irongates escorted us to the Rim himself."

Vince nodded. "I expected that."

"For two reasons." Rychek allowed herself a wicked smirk. "One, he didn't want anything getting bungled, and two…" She trailed off, raising her eyebrows at Vince.

"Let me guess." It was his turn to smile. "He didn't want anyone else taking credit?"

"Exactly." Rychek lifted her coffee mug to him in a little toast.

"Can't really blame him on that front." Commosky twitched one shoulder in a prosaic shrug. "Given his position, it's only natural."

Vince regarded him curiously. The detective's voice was bland—almost *too* bland. "If you had to choose between justice and acclaim, you'd take justice. You think Irongates wouldn't?"

"Not saying that," Commosky countered smoothly. "It just worked out that in this case he'll get both."

"So will you," Bella's soft, melodic voice chimed in. She blinked as all eyes turned to her, but straightened in her seat and focused on Commosky. "This is your case, Detective. You're the one who's put months and months of effort into it. You spearheaded the entire operation." She spread her hands to the sides. "Won't this be a good thing for your career?"

For a second, Commosky said nothing. Then a small smile creased his craggy face and he inclined his head toward Bella. "When you put it like that…"

"Hold on." Vince held up a hand, narrowing his eyes at the detective. "Are you implying there's some question about whether or not you're to get credit for this operation?"

Commosky hesitated. "Not exactly. Everything's been a muddle, and it's taken a few days to sort out the chain of events and whether or not I did everything by the books."

"Because otherwise Starlit and Lumen's attorneys are going to argue you didn't have the authority to do anything you did." Rychek's face puckered as though she'd bitten into something tart—and foul-tasting.

"Something like that."

For the span of a few heartbeats, a black cloud fell over Vince. Disappointment hovered around the edges of his consciousness. Surely, *surely*, all of their hard work couldn't be for nothing. It was—

A ray of clarity broke through his suddenly jumbled thoughts, like a ray of sunshine through a ship's cockpit viewport as it veered from the blackness of deep space toward the sun in the Cartha system.

The Finder looked sharply at Commosky. "That might be a problem, except that—" he almost said Brill's name but caught himself at the last second, "—my friend the information broker is involved. *He's* actually the one who cultivated Letitia as an inside source and convinced her to turn on Starlit and Lumen."

Vince had the satisfaction of watching Rychek's eyes widen in surprise tinged with admiration. Meanwhile, curled up in her corner of the couch, Bella beamed.

Commosky's sober expression, however, did not change. "That *is* what happened." He shrugged again. "It should all play out that way."

"Not very trusting of your department, are you?" Vince lifted an eyebrow at the detective.

Commosky merely shrugged again. "Stranger things have happened."

"Particularly when there's money involved," Vince said shrewdly, speaking the thought reflected on both Station Authority officers' faces.

Rychek dropped her gaze, frowning into her coffee mug. She tilted it this way and that, her lips pressed into a thin line.

Vince would have given a hundred credits to know what was passing through her mind. He set his curiosity aside, however, to address Commosky again. "Getting back to the story—what happened when you got to the Rim? Did you go straight to the Council or…?"

"No." Commosky shook his head. "Precinct. Irongates knew better than to go straight to the Council. We hustled Letitia straight into a secure room in the Precinct, explained everything to Commissioner Zisk, and set up a debrief."

"I'm sure she enjoyed being debriefed again," Vince said dryly. Commissioner Antoin Zisk might be in charge of Station Authority across the whole of Zyga Station, but he had a good bit of the politician in him. He wouldn't suffer accusations of that nature lightly… but neither could he dismiss them, given the actual power outages the Station had suffered. Any interrogation he headed was bound to be intense.

"Part of it." Commosky waved that aside with a dismissive flick of his fingers. "She had to know what she was getting herself into." He turned his head, his dark eyes glinting in the light from the glowpanels in the overhead as he regarded Vince. "Either your friend the information broker prepped her pretty well, or else she did her own research."

"Or both," Bella interjected from her seat on the couch, glancing around at the other three. "She seems pretty smart."

"Oh, she is." Commosky shifted in his seat. "No doubt about *that*." He shook his head. "I have to hand it to her—she never got worked up the entire time Zisk questioned her. And he was thorough—extremely thorough."

Vince directed a look at Rychek. "Were you there for that part?"

The dark-haired sergeant shook her head regretfully. "As far as the Commissioner was concerned, once I was debriefed and gave a statement, my job was finished. He debriefed Talum too, but he knew less than I did."

Her eyes met Vince's and their gazes locked. Vince raised his eyebrows in the slightest question—had Rychek informed her superiors that she'd been the one to tip Vince off to Commosky's disappearance in the first place?

To his surprise, Rychek answered verbally.

"My superiors know that you and I have worked together before." One corner of her mouth tilted up in a smile. "They understand why you called me."

"There wasn't any need to inform them of anything else," Commosky said smoothly. The expression on his craggy face turned hard and implacable. "If the sergeant here happened to have an off-the-record conversation with a civilian colleague on a matter of public record...well..." he shrugged. "Officers *are* allowed friends."

"In other words," Bella said shrewdly, flicking a glance at Commosky from beneath long black eyelashes, "you didn't see the need to stir up any more potential trouble."

Commosky inclined his head in her direction, but did not answer directly.

It made the hair on the back of Vince's neck pickle a little to think that going forward Detective Commosky would know that he and Rychek occasionally exchanged information. He immediately dismissed his unease as ridiculous. If anything, Commosky was in the same situation. *He'd* contacted Vince outside of his purview as a Station Authority officer as well.

It comes down to a matter of trust.

Could he trust Commosky the way he trusted Rychek? Vince suppressed a snort. Of course he could. The detective had proven that.

And he, Vince, had proven his trustworthiness as well. In the end, that was really all that mattered.

He stood up, rubbing his hands together. "Before we hear the end of this, who wants another drink?"

CHAPTER 58

Five minutes later, everyone settled back down in their seats with fresh, hot coffee or tea. This time, Bella accepted a mug of piping hot tea, which she pretended to sip daintily.

Commosky glanced around Vince's office, frowning thoughtfully. "Where was I?"

"Letitia Theriot's debriefing," Rychek said from her corner of the couch.

"Ah, yes." Commosky's frown deepened.

"How did that go down?" Vince nodded toward his holoprojectors. "I know what the media reported—"

"And they knew a lot," Commosky said, an odd note in his voice. "A lot more than they should have."

"—but I'd like to know what really happened." Vince quirked a rueful smile at the detective. "It wasn't me who tipped them off, by the way."

"No, I never thought it was." Commosky made a sound that was halfway between a chuckle and a snort. "If I had to lay odds on a culprit—which is, I'll admit, a terrible way of putting it, given the nature of this case—I'd say it was your friend the information broker."

Vince only shrugged, as if to say he could neither confirm nor deny that.

"But that's beside the point." Commosky swept his hand through the air, dismissing the topic. "It took some negotiation—Letitia wouldn't hand over the encryption key on the data she'd brought with her until she had an immunity deal in writing." He shot Vince a wry look. "Your fault, I understand."

Vince just shrugged a second time. It had absolutely been the right advice to give her.

"I have to hand it to her—she stood her ground." Commosky shook his head in admiration. "I've known some grown men who couldn't go toe-to-toe with Commissioner Zisk."

"How long did that take?" Bella beat Vince to the question.

"Not long." Commosky flashed a quick, grim smile. "We all knew the clock was ticking. God only knew what kind of a deal the Council was hammering out with Starlit and Lumen. The Commissioner caved pretty quickly. Said that he was convinced by the nature of Letitia turning herself in that she'd never intended to have anything to do with anything nefarious." He waved a hand again." You know how it goes."

Vince nodded as he took a tentative sip of his tea, which was still far too hot. Green tea, this time, and decaf. He'd had enough caffeine the past two days to keep him up for a week under normal circumstances.

"Anyway," Commosky said with a shrug, "once we had access to Letitia's information, the Commissioner immediately procured a warrant for Jasmine Nerhti and Renji Kino's arrests."

Bella leaned forward, completely captivated. "Did you get to be there?" she asked breathlessly.

Commosky's dark eyes glinted with triumph. "Yes, I did."

Vince could imagine the satisfaction the other man must be feeling. Just picturing the scene and imagining the look of shock on Starlit and Lumen's faces brought *him* a vicarious thrill. He inclined his head toward the detective. "Congratulations."

"Thank you." Commosky leaned back in his chair as though some of the weight of the galaxy had been lifted from his shoulders. He raised his coffee mug to his lips, but paused to say over the rim, "They'll fight it, of course."

"They won't win." Rychek shook her head. "Too much evidence against them."

Vince snorted. "That and the Families won't let them."

A pall momentarily fell over his office at these words. The Finder took a breath. He hadn't meant for that statement to sound as grim as it did. However…that didn't mean it wasn't true.

The silence was broken a second later by the sound of his airscrubber dutifully kicking on, and then Commosky stirred.

"I suppose," he said slowly, staring down into the dregs of his coffee, "that on this one occasion, I don't much mind the Families' interference." He looked up, a cold, grim smile flickering across his face. "Off the record, of course. And just this once."

"I know the feeling," Rychek said wryly. She looked at Vince, her dark eyes thoughtful again. "It feels odd to be on the same side."

"Oh, don't worry, we're not on the same side." Vince smiled too, a sharp expression that lived more in his eyes than his mouth. "Only temporarily aligned."

"I'll drink to that." Commosky raised his coffee mug into the air and then took a sip. "But, in the meantime…" He shrugged. "I'll enjoy the win."

Bella cradled her mug of tea in both hands. "What will happen to the Ruby Gauntlet? I know they're shut down right now, but…"

"They'll stay shut down." That glint of triumphant pleasure returned to Commosky's eyes. "Court-ordered injunction, pending the results of our investigation and the trial."

That tracked with the news reports Vince had gathered, and the conversation he'd had with Brill. "Good. I'm glad to hear it."

"Do you think you'll be able to hold them responsible for all of the murders?" Bella asked.

"That's the plan." Commosky pursed his lips, his gaze focusing meditatively on a spot on the wall between Rychek and Bella on the couch. "I think we can do it. We have everything my team has compiled, and now we have a treasure trove of Letitia's information." His gaze snapped back to Bella. "They'll be held accountable. For the people they killed, as well as cutting the power and endangering the lives of everyone aboard this space station."

"I'm glad." Bella smiled, and then tilted her head in renewed curiosity. "Where *is* Letitia currently?"

Unexpectedly, Commosky smiled. "Officially, I'm not at liberty to say. But off the record, Ms. Escovedo, I can assure you that Letitia Theriot is someplace safe." His face took on a hard cast. "No one wants anything happening to her before the trial is over."

"Or afterward." This from Rychek.

Commosky acknowledged that with a nod. He started to rise from his chair, but stopped abruptly and sank back down. "By the way, Grable, I've been meaning to ask you. How did things turn out with that client of yours? Mrs. Kawana, was it?"

"She's delighted to have her statue back." Vince smiled. "Along with what was in it." He spread his hands. "She held up her end of our bargain with that girl, and I haven't heard a word from either of them since."

"Good." There was a definite note of finality in the detective's tone. This time, he did stand. Crossing the beige carpet, he set his empty coffee mug on the jade green credenza.

Vince glanced at Rychek to see if she intended to take this cue to leave as well, but the sergeant remained comfortably ensconced on the couch. She held her coffee mug cradled in both hands, as though warming her fingers, and seemed in no hurry to go anywhere.

Commosky turned around, addressing Vince again. "There's a good chance you might be called to testify. Both about your discovery of the other deaths of people who lost in the Ruby Gauntlet's Diamond Room as well as your part in helping Letitia turn Station's evidence."

"Understood." Vince couldn't say he was surprised. He'd expected something like this, in fact.

Bella raised a hand. "What about me?"

Her voice was even, but Vince could have sworn a hint of anxiety lurked in her dark eyes.

Commosky considered her for a moment. "There's a chance," he said at last, "but given that you're Grable's employee, it may just all fall on him."

Bella looked relieved. "Thank you, Detective."

"You're welcome."

Well, Vince thought, *that's good to know.* Rising to his feet, he extended a hand to Commosky. "Detective."

"Finder." The shorter man's grip was strong and firm. "I appreciate your help." His expression lightened, though he did not smile. "It's good to have people you can depend on."

Vince acknowledged this with a nod. "If you ever need help again, Detective, you know where to find me."

"Thanks." Commosky nodded to the ladies on the couch. "Ms. Escovedo. Sergeant Rychek."

"Detective," Bella and Rychek chorused together.

Commosky collected his hat and jacket from the hooks by the door and shrugged them on while Vince unlocked and opened the door for him. Just before he stepped outside, the detective looked at Vince, a crooked smile tugging at one corner of his mouth. "Don't take this the wrong way, Grable, but I hope I don't need your help again any time soon."

Vince just laughed. "You and me both. My cases aren't generally so high-stakes."

Commosky chuckled, and then he was gone, the door sliding shut behind him.

This time, Vince didn't bother with his security protocols. Instead, he shifted his stance to watch the detective through his office's one-way synthglass window. Commosky strode purposefully down the enclosed boulevard until he disappeared from view. No doubt he intended to walk a few blocks to put some distance between himself and Vince's office before he hailed a transport pod.

Vince couldn't fault him for that—he'd have done the exact same thing.

Turning away from the window, he found both Bella and Rychek watching him. Bella's expression was expectantly curious, but Rychek…Rychek looked thoughtful again.

He lifted his eyebrows at her. "What?"

"Nothing much." She shook her head slightly. "I just—" she hesitated, as though debating the wisdom of further speech, before apparently deciding to plow ahead. "I couldn't help but notice what Detective Commosky left out."

Vince couldn't say the observation surprised him—when it came to Station Authority, nothing did, really. Still…he found his curiosity piqued. Crossing the office to her, he held out a hand for her mug. "More coffee?"

Rychek glanced down into her mug and considered it for a split-second before declining with a small smile. "Better not."

She waited until Vince resumed his seat, and then her gaze flicked from him to Bella and back. "Commosky conveniently left out the fact that this entire debacle has caused a massive scandal."

Vince digested this statement in silence, turning all the words over and examining them in his head before he shot her a quizzical look. "That's not exactly a surprise. Newsfeeds are full of rampant—"

"Ah," Rychek held up a finger, "but the media hasn't got a hold of this part yet." She huffed slightly. "Between you and me, I'm astonished they *don't* already know."

What in the galaxy was she talking about? Vince looked askance at her, his confusion deepening. "What do you mean?"

"I mean," Rychek said grimly, her fingers tightening on her coffee mug, "that the Council voted tonight for Internal Affairs to launch a special investigation into this entire mess—starting with them and working their way down."

CHAPTER 59

Dead silence greeted this pronouncement. Startled, Vince blew out a deep breath and leaned back in his seat. A *special* Internal Affairs investigation? Wasn't that a contradiction in terms?

The implications of this unfolded in his head like an explosion blossoming with petals of orange, yellow and red. Beautiful—but potentially deadly, depending on how close you were to ground zero.

Bella broke the silence first. She canted her head to one side, frowning at Rychek and blinking a couple of times in confusion. "Does that mean what I *think* it means?"

"Yes." Rychek's dark eyes were full of concern—and wariness. "They're setting up for a shakedown the likes of which has never been seen in the history of Zyga Space Station." She paused. "At least as far as I know."

"No, no," Vince held up a hand, still feeling off-kilter. "You're probably right." He stopped, a thought occurring to him, and a bitter smile stretched his lips. "As long as these 'special investigators' actually do their job and don't get paid off."

The Finder ran a hand over his close-shorn hair, wondering if Brill knew about this—and if he did, why he hadn't mentioned it. A glance at Bella showed him the same question reflected in her eyes.

His assistant cast a considering, almost frightened glance at the office's front door. "And you're *sure* Detective Commosky knows about this?"

Rychek laughed. It was a rich, melodious sound, and Vince realized suddenly that he didn't hear it nearly enough. Real humor showed in the sergeant's lovely face, before sober reality dropped back over her like a veil. "Oh, yes. If even *I* know about this, somebody as high up and involved as he is has to know."

That was a good point. Vince blew out a breath. "Maybe he just doesn't care." He waved a hand. "His attention has been focused on bringing down Starlit and Lumen and the Ruby Gauntlet for months. It's consumed him."

"Well, he should care." Rychek straightened up on the couch, putting both booted feet flat on the beige carpet. "Like you said, if they actually do their job, an investigation this intense will affect all of us, eventually." She shook her head in wonder. "Stars, can you imagine the kind of dirt they're bound to find?"

Vince grimaced. "I can—and I don't want to." He shook his head. "Why now? Because this situation was severe enough that they can't just convict Starlit and Lumen and sweep everything under the proverbial rug?"

"Think about it, Vince." Rychek leaned forward and met his eyes. Her gaze was clear—and dead serious. "They actually managed to shut the power off to the entire Station. Unless somebody orders a closed trial, everything that comes out will be public record. Everything they did, everybody they influenced or paid off." She snorted. "It'll make Terrell Roda's trial seem like a minor traffic dustup in comparison."

"They were trying to set themselves up as another Family." Bella's voice sounded small. "That's enough to scare anybody."

"That's the problem." Vince continued to hold Rychek's gaze. "The Council has tolerated the Families all these years, and *now* they're going to raise a stink about corruption?" He grimaced again, another dire thought occurring to him. "You think Starlit and Lumen will make it to trial? Honestly?"

Rychek reared back against her seat like she'd encountered something poisonous, sucking a breath through her teeth. "I hadn't thought of that angle yet." She grimaced. "Stars, Grable, that's grim."

"But not outside the realm of possibility," Bella said quietly. Her almond-shaped eyes suddenly looked huge in her heart-shaped face. "Not where the Families are concerned."

"I don't think they know what to expect either." Vince shoved his hands into his pockets, frowning. "And that's a problem. Bok Chul and Amal Oswari aren't the kind of men who deal in uncertainty—unless they're the ones fostering it."

The three of them fell silent, contemplating this. Vince's airscrubber abruptly shut off, making Bella and Rychek both twitch.

"Well." Vince smiled, trying to lighten the dark mood that had fallen over his office. "With Commosky involved, it'll be hard for anybody to make a wrong move. He's probably the most invested person in this entire case, and there's no way anybody will be able to pay him off."

"That's true." Rychek allowed herself to relax, like a taut rope being allowed a hint of slack. "Still…" She pursed her lips together. "Prepare for upheaval and chaos."

"I'm surprised they're not starting with the Engineering Department," Vince said frankly. "That's where I'd start."

"Oh," Rychek waved a hand, "you know it's political. If the Council rules themselves out first, they can keep rebuilding public trust while they go on and investigate everybody else."

Bella wrinkled her nose. "That sounds about right."

"Regardless, things are going to get messy." Rychek pressed her lips into a thin line. "From what I hear, the Engineering Department is already on edge. This will only make it worse."

A wry smile touched Vince's lips. "So long as they don't go shutting the power off again…"

Both women laughed.

After a moment, reluctantly, Rychek rose from the couch. "I'd best head home." She held up her coffee mug while she made her way over to the jade green credenza to set it down. "Thanks for the coffee."

"My pleasure." Vince didn't mention that he'd made a note of which blend she preferred and had started making sure he kept it on hand.

He and Bella both rose to their feet and watched as Rychek shrugged on her jacket and put on her hat. It was late, but Vince knew that didn't bother Anita Rychek. Apart from the fact that she was a Station Authority officer (and probably armed), there was a confident air about her that warned she was not a woman to be trifled with.

"Take care, Bella." Rychek smiled at the other woman. "Make sure he—" she tipped her head toward Vince, "—doesn't work you too hard or do anything too crazy."

Bella just laughed. "He's a good boss. Can't make any promises on the crazy front, though." She shook her head, her glossy black hair swaying back and forth. "These cases just find us."

"You two are a special kind of magnet, apparently." The glance Rychek cast at Vince was fond.

"And I'm standing right here," he reminded her good-naturedly, coming to escort her to the door.

"I can see that." Somber mood temporarily lifted, Rychek grinned up at him. "Stay out of trouble, Grable." She reached out and took his hand, giving it a little squeeze. In a lower voice, she added, "Thanks for trusting me."

"Took the words right out of my mouth." Vince held her hand for a second, not squeezing back, but just holding it. Her light skin was smooth and warm against his dark fingers. He lowered his own voice to a quiet rumble. "You watch out for yourself, too, Anita. Zyga Station needs all the good Station Authority officers we can get."

Her answering smile made the corners of her eyes crinkle, but she didn't say anything further. Vince opened the door for her, and she was gone.

He wanted to watch her walk down the sidewalk until she either hailed a transport pod or else turned the corner, but instead he tapped the doorpanel to close the door. She was a grown woman—and a Station Authority officer—and she could take care of herself. She didn't need him.

The door sliding shut gave him a strange feeling of finality. Whether that was for this case, or some other reason, Vince didn't know.

Bella tactfully waited until he'd finished running through his security protocols and turned back around before she spoke. "Things are about to get interesting again, aren't they?"

Vince nodded slowly. "I'd say so." He glanced toward his desk and his computer terminal, the screen dark and blank. "It's mildly concerning that Brill hasn't said anything about this."

"Maybe he's just been busy." Bella turned gracefully back to her desk and bent to rummage through one of the drawers on the bottom.

"Maybe." It occurred to Vince then that he should have asked if Bella intended to go home before he set the night's security protocols. Ah, well. He waved a hand toward the door. "Are you—"

"Nope," she said cheerfully. "Camping out on the couch again." She produced a canvas bag with a pretty pink flowered design on it and waved it in the air. "I have a project I've been working on."

Vince blinked. "Since when?"

"Oh, three or four days." Bella shrugged. "Ordered it last week and had it delivered here." She went over to the couch and curled up in the corner again, turning on one of the lights mounted into the wall behind her. "I've been working on it while you're sleeping."

Vince ventured closer, craning his neck to see what was in the bag. "Do I get to see what it is?"

"Oh, eventually." She grinned up at him, one hand splayed possessively over the bag. "In the meantime, it's my little secret."

Before Vince could do much more than blink at her, his assistant made a shooing gesture with her free hand. "Go to bed, Boss. We finally got our closure and you need to sleep." Her beautiful face scrunched into a wry expression. "God only knows what'll happen tomorrow."

Given the events and revelations of the evening, Vince found he couldn't argue with her. He inclined his head. "Good night, then."

"Night, Boss."

As he turned away to the hidden door that concealed the staircase connecting his office and his apartment, Vince couldn't help but think of Brill again. The information broker's lack of communication niggled in the back of his mind, like a hangnail that wasn't bad enough to be really painful yet, but was just irritated enough to be annoying.

But, that was a job for another day.

The important thing was that, one way or another, all the people Starlit and Lumen had hurt in their brief reign of terror were going to finally get justice.

Vince smiled. He'd sleep well tonight.

ACKNOWLEDGEMENTS

Writing may be a solitary endeavor, but it doesn't happen in a vacuum. I am so blessed to have family and friends to cheer me on.

For my husband, Tim. Thanks so much for always encouraging me to keep pursuing the dreams and talents the Lord has given me. Thanks for putting up with a wife who regularly writes down what the voices in her head say. ::grin::

For my children—thanks for keeping things to a (mostly) dull roar.

For my mom and siblings—thanks for your encouragement and support.

A big thanks to Connie Trapp, for being a fantastic beta read¬er. Your insight over the years is much appreciated.

Thank you also to Kim Burns and Heather Stearns for being excited readers, great friends, and great listening ears when I need to talk about writing.

A very special thank you to all of the people who supported the Kickstarter I ran for Blowback. Thank you, James Palmer, David Bern, Susan Jones, Kimberly Burns, Wayne D. Kramer, Dean Wesley Smith, M A Sullivan, Jim Gotaas, Kate Sheeran Swed, Eva Holmquist, J.R. Murdock, Marcus M., Laura Rainbow Dragon, Cora Foerstner,

John Idlor, Matt P, Raphael Bressel, Joshua Hair, Pauline Baird Jones, A., and Anonymous Reader.

Y'all are amazing and I am so grateful.

Thanks also to Lori Christie, Sarah Reschar, Chelsea Stevens, Hannah Hatton, Sarah Gharib, Emily Bare, Kristie Sullivan, Felicia Bridge, Meta Clark, and many, many others for your encouragement and support.

NEWSLETTER SIGN-UP

I value honest feedback and would love to hear your opinion in a review, if you're so inclined, on your favorite retailer's site. Thank you!

Be the first to know!

Just sign up for the E.R. Paskey newsletter and keep up with the latest news, releases, and so much more, including the occasional giveaway.

Visit www.erpaskey.com and click on the 'Newsletter Signup' tab.

ABOUT THE AUTHOR

E.R. Paskey fell in love with mysteries and science fiction and all their possibilities at a young age. She is the author of fourteen novels, including the *Finder* series and a Christian space opera series, *The Guardians*, as well as a handful of short stories. She currently lives in Southern Indiana with her husband and their five children.

You can find her website at: erpaskey.com